I0597962

Praise for Lynn Cahoon and Her Irresistible Cozy Mysteries

AN AMATEUR SLEUTH'S GUIDE TO MURDER
"The prolific Lynn Cahoon starts another winning cozy series!"
—*Criminal Element*

"Cahoon launches a promising new series with endearing characters and a charming locale."
—*Kirkus Reviews*

"Plan a cozy day by the fire with a cup of tea, snuggle in, and enjoy. The day will be over before you know it. And there may even be time to make Lynn's Yummy Murderous Mac and Cheese for dinner."
—Nancy Coco, author of the Candy-Coated Mysteries

"If you love cozy mysteries, you will love *An Amateur Sleuth's Guide to Murder*—a delightful mixture of a practical guidebook and a clever fictional mystery."
—Valerie Burns, author of the Mystery Bookshop Mysteries

FIVE FURRY FAMILIARS
"A fun read for those who enjoy tales of witches and magic."
—*Kirkus Reviews*

THREE TAINTED TEAS
"A kitchen witch reluctantly takes over as planner for a cursed wedding… This witchy tale is a hoot."
—*Kirkus Reviews*

ONE POISON PIE
"*One Poison Pie* deliciously blends charm and magic with a dash of mystery and a sprinkle of romance. Mia Malone is a zesty protagonist who relies on her wits to solve the crime, and the enchanting cast of characters that populate Magic Springs are a delight."
—Daryl Wood Gerber, Agatha winner and nationally best-selling author of the Cookbook Nook Mysteries and Fairy Garden Mysteries

"A witchy cooking cozy for fans of the supernatural and good eating."
—*Kirkus Reviews*

A FIELD GUIDE TO HOMICIDE

"The best entry in this character-driven series mixes a well-plotted mystery with a romance that rings true to life."
—*Kirkus Reviews*

"Informative as well as entertaining, *A Field Guide to Homicide* is the perfect book for cozy mystery lovers who entertain thoughts of writing novels themselves… This is, without a doubt, one of the best Cat Latimer novels to date."
—*Criminal Element*

"Cat is a great heroine with a lot of spirit that readers will enjoy solving the mystery (with)."
—*Parkersburg News & Sentinel*

SCONED TO DEATH

"The most intriguing aspect of this story is the writers' retreat itself. Although the writers themselves are not suspect, they add freshness and new relationships to the series. Fans of Lucy Arlington's 'Novel Idea' mysteries may want to enter the writing world from another angle."
—*Library Journal*

OF MURDER AND MEN

"A Colorado widow discovers that everything she knew about her husband's death is wrong… Interesting plot and quirky characters."
—*Kirkus Reviews*

A STORY TO KILL

"Well-crafted… Cat and crew prove to be engaging characters and Cahoon does a stellar job of keeping them—and the reader—guessing."
—*Mystery Scene*

"Lynn Cahoon has hit the golden trifecta—Murder, intrigue, and a really hot handyman. Better get your flashlight handy, *A Story to Kill* will keep you reading all night."
—Laura Bradford, author of the Amish Mysteries

TOURIST TRAP MYSTERIES

"Lynn Cahoon's popular Tourist Trap series is set all around the charming coastal town of South Cove, California, but the heroine Jill Gardner owns a delightful bookstore/coffee shop so a lot of the scenes take place there. This is one of my go-to cozy mystery series, bookish or not, and I'm always eager to get my hands on the next book!"
—*Hope By the Book*

"Murder, dirty politics, pirate lore, and a hot police detective: *Guidebook to Murder* has it all! A cozy lover's dream come true."
—Susan McBride, author of the Debutante Dropout Mysteries

"This was a good read and I love the author's style, which was warm and friendly... I can't wait to read the next book in this wonderfully appealing series."
—*Dru's Book Musings*

"I am happy to admit that some of my expectations were met while other aspects of the story exceeded my own imagination... This mystery novel was light, fun, and kept me thoroughly engaged. I only wish it was longer."
—*The Young Folks*

"*If the Shoe Kills* is entertaining and I would be happy to visit Jill and the residents of South Cove again."
—*MysteryPlease.com*

"In *If the Shoe Kills,* author Lynn Cahoon gave me exactly what I wanted. She crafted a well told small town murder that kept me guessing who the murderer was until the end. I will definitely have to take a trip back to South Cove and maybe even visit tales of Jill Gardner's past in the previous two Tourist Trap Mystery books. I do love a holiday mystery! And with this book, so will you."
—*ArtBooksCoffee.com*

"I would recommend *If the Shoe Kills* if you are looking for a well written cozy mystery."
—*Mysteries, Etc.*

"This novella is short and easily read in an hour or two with interesting angst and dynamics between mothers and daughters and mothers and sons... I enjoyed the first-person narrative."
—*Kings River Life Magazine* on *Mother's Day Mayhem*

BOOKS BY LYNN CAHOON

The Bainbridge Island Mystery Series
An Amateur Sleuth's Guide to Murder

The Tourist Trap Mystery Series
Guidebook to Murder * Mission to Murder * If the Shoe Kills * Dressed to Kill * Killer Run * Murder on Wheels * Tea Cups and Carnage * Hospitality and Homicide * Killer Party * Memories and Murder * Murder in Waiting * Picture Perfect Frame * Wedding Bell Blues * A Vacation to Die For * Songs of Wine and Murder * Olive You to Death * Vows of Murder * Merry Murder Season

Novellas
Rockets' Dead Glare * A Deadly Brew * Santa Puppy * Corned Beef and Casualties * Mother's Day Mayhem * A Very Mummy Holiday * Murder in a Tourist Town

The Kitchen Witch Mystery Series
One Poison Pie * Two Wicked Desserts * Three Tainted Teas * Four Charming Spells * Five Furry Familiars * Six Stunning Sirens * Seven Secret Spellcasters

Novellas
Chili Cauldron Curse * Murder 101 * Have a Holly, Haunted Holiday * Two Christmas Mittens

The Cat Latimer Mystery Series
A Story to Kill * Fatality by Firelight * Of Murder and Men * Slay in Character * Sconed to Death * A Field Guide to Homicide * A Killer Christmas Wish * Caught Dead to Write * Murder on a Snowy Evening * Formal Fatality

Novellas
Body in the Book Drop

The Farm to Fork Mystery Series
Who Moved My Goat Cheese? * Killer Green Tomatoes * One Potato, Two Potato, Dead * Deep Fried Revenge * Killer Comfort Food * A Fatal Family Feast

SLEUTHING WITH THE STARS

Survivors' Book Club

Lynn Cahoon

LYRICAL PRESS
Kensington Publishing Corp.
kensingtonbooks.com

LYRICAL PRESS BOOKS are published by
Kensington Publishing Corp.
900 Third Avenue
New York, NY 10022

Copyright © 2026 Lynn Cahoon

All rights reserved. No part of this book may be reproduced in any form or by any means without the prior written consent of the Publisher, excepting brief quotes used in reviews.

Without limiting the author's and publisher's exclusive rights, any unauthorized use of this publication to train generative artificial intelligence (AI) technologies is expressly prohibited.

This book is a work of fiction. Names, characters, businesses, organizations, places, events, and incidents either are the product of the author's imagination or are used fictitiously. Any resemblance to actual persons, living or dead, events, or locales is entirely coincidental.

To the extent that the image or images on the cover of this book depict a person or persons, such person or persons are merely models, and are not intended to portray any character or characters featured in the book.

The L with book logo Reg. U.S. Pat. & TM Off

First Electronic Edition: March 2026
ISBN: 978-1-5161-1205-0 (ebook)

First Print Edition: March 2026
ISBN: 978-1-5161-1206-7

The authorized representative in the EU for product safety and compliance
Is eucomply OU, Parnu mnt 139b-14, Apt 123
Tallinn, Berlin 11317, hello@eucompliancepartner.com

155048300

To those who love a little life with their cozies...

CHAPTER 1

Lights surrounded the Next Chapter bookstore on the main drag in Sedona, Arizona, bringing in customers for tonight's special event. The store was bursting with people waiting for the start of the night's event. A local bike enthusiast had talked Rarity Cole into inviting an Olympic-winning racer who had just released his first memoir to come for a talk and to sign books. The annual Sedona Red Rock Race was on Saturday, so they'd scheduled the book event for the Wednesday night before. And the store was standing room only.

"I can't believe so many people came." Shirley Prescott stood next to Rarity Cole, owner of the store, as they both studied the crowd. "No one's touching the cookies or the coffee, but we've refilled the water pitchers three times. There are people in line outside, just waiting to buy a signed book. Katie's gone out with cups and water for the line. I'm not sure I ordered enough copies. And to make it worse, Friday's author sent his assistant to check on us. She's been badgering me with questions all night."

"Which one is that?" Rarity followed Shirley's directions and found the woman standing against a bookshelf, on her phone. She was furiously typing. "Are we doing something wrong?"

"According to Jane Carey? Everything. The light over the dais is too dark. The room too small. And the treats appear to be homemade." Shirley sighed as the woman looked up and frowned at her. Again.

"Well, Mason Pike's signing will be a totally different setup. Did you tell her about using the back alley for the talk, signing, and the movie following? No matter what, it's already planned. There's nothing we or she can do about it. Tell her to take a chill pill." Rarity watched as more people pulled books off the shelves and headed over to the purchase table.

"Seriously? I'd rather kick her out. She's giving me a headache." Shirley glanced at the treat table. "Maybe I should refill the water pitchers. One looks low."

"I'm sure we'll be fine," Rarity said, but as she checked her watch, she wasn't sure at all. Especially about the number of books they'd ordered. This was the biggest author signing they'd hosted since she opened the store. Maybe she needed to think about a new place to hold these events. Marc Billings was going to be happy with his signing. They'd set up a sales table near the door and had chairs filling the book club area as well as the ends of the book aisles. "I'm going to go get Darby and our guest and start this party a few minutes early."

Darby Doyle had been Rarity's first employee. She'd gone off to Scotland to finish out her undergraduate degree and was now back in town for at least the summer. Who knew where she'd land in the fall, but Rarity was glad to have her back for now. She'd volunteered to be the author wrangler for the upcoming events, and Rarity happily relinquished the role. Darby was outgoing, cute, and extroverted. She thrived in these situations. And from the way Marc kept looking at Darby, she was enchanting the author as well.

Rarity kept the moderating role mostly because she loved talking to authors about books. She'd just have to ignore the huge audience staring past her and at Marc.

Rarity would have rather been home, reading on the couch tonight. She was a true introvert and big events like this drained her energy stores, but since they also filled the store's coffers, it was a necessary evil of the job. Shirley loved the planning and coordination of the events. And her other employee, Katie Dickenson, just loved being around people and talking books. Rarity had already handled the sales of several Katie-suggested fiction books to the waiting throng.

Rarity walked into the break room where Marc Billings was just finishing telling Darby a story that had something to do with bike riding in Scotland. "I hate to interrupt, but I think we should start the talk. Darby, grab Marc a bottle of water to take up with him. Do you need anything else?"

Marc took a deep breath, nodding at the back door. "Maybe I should just sneak out the back."

"Oh, no, you don't. You have a store full of excited fans wanting to meet you and hear about your book." Rarity wanted to run away with him, but the show must go on. "Are you racing on Saturday?"

Marc smiled and Rarity's heart almost burst. He was adorable. "Since my accident, I leave the racing to the kids. I'll be on the sidelines, cheering and doing the commentating for the live feed. That's where they send the old guys out to pasture—as sports commentators. Although if I'd known what they got paid, I might not have worried about writing the memoir for a few years. Strike when the iron is hot and all that."

Rarity nodded as she waited for him to slip on his jacket over an expensive polo shirt and jeans. "I changed up my life a few years ago, due to a health issue. It takes a while to find out who you really are when you're not your job anymore."

He lifted his head and stared at her. "I've never had anyone say that so clearly. That's exactly how I've been feeling. Trying on new identities. Thank you."

Rarity shrugged as they stepped toward the door. "I'm not saying I have it all figured out, but I'm getting closer. I'll make a brief introduction, talk about our events over the next week, and then focus on your book. After that, we'll start with the list of questions I gave you last week. If there's something you don't want to answer, just tell me a different story. I'll move on and not press you. This is your time to shine, not a serious journalistic interview. At the end, we'll have about ten minutes for audience questions."

Rarity stepped out of the break room and, after making sure Marc was following her, headed to the fireplace where Archer Ender and Drew Anderson had built her a temporary riser that could be stored away between events. She let Marc get settled with a microphone and then did his introduction. After that, her memories of the event blurred together. And in what felt like a few seconds, the author talk portion of the night was over.

The signing line was almost out of people, and Rarity had left Katie with Marc to help with crowd control. She, Shirley, and Darby had handled the book sales. Darby pulled up the last box that they'd shoved under the table and stacked them so people could see the book. "I have one more box in the back that I had Marc sign earlier for stock. Maybe we should have bought a box or two less?"

Shirley shook her head. "We'll probably sell those this next week. We'll keep them out on a table during the weekend. Besides, Friday we have the filmmaker in for his book on the spider film that we're showing later that night. We're getting a nice set of signed books for the store, but the goal is always to sell out, so we have room for the next author. It's a rolling target."

"It sounds exhausting for the authors. You're only as good as your last book." Rarity stood and stretched since there were only a few more people in the shop. "Let's start putting away chairs. Shirley, you stay here, just in case we have some stragglers. I'd love to get home in the next hour or so to let Killer out for a walk and maybe sneak in a swim. My shoulders are killing me."

"I was supposed to tell you that Killer's with Terrance," Shirley said as Rarity and Darby walked around the table. "I'm sure he's gone for at least one walk tonight with his favorite neighborhood watch captain."

"I didn't know Terrance was going to be home." Rarity met her friend's gaze. "I didn't call and ask him to take Killer for the night."

"You know you don't have to ask." Shirley waved them away. "Go work. I'm going to try to figure out how many books we sold. Authors always want to know the numbers. For word people, they keep track of sales better than most accounting majors."

Rarity started stacking chairs and soon was joined by Archer and Drew. "Hey, guys. I didn't know you were coming by."

"Where else would we go?" Drew shrugged but then elbowed Archer. "Although, I remember a time when we were both single and we would meet up for a beer after work rather than stop by the bookstore or crystal shop to help you two move furniture or cabinets or boxes."

"Or chairs. Or build a stage," Archer added, but as he did, he leaned over to kiss Rarity. "And I wouldn't have it any other way."

"Good, because I was getting a little worried there." Rarity put the chairs she'd just folded up on the carrier. "Brown chairs are the rentals and need to go on these two brown carriers. We can store them in the break room. The silver ones are mine and go on the red carrier. Are either of you available to take these back to the rental shop Saturday morning? We'll need them for Friday's outdoor event. The carriers won't fit in my Mini Cooper."

"Excuses, excuses," Drew said, grinning. "As long as it's early. With the race starting at ten, I'll need to be here at eight. Archer, I think we'll need your truck too."

"I already told Jack he'd be opening the booth on Saturday. Katie just told me that you gave out all of my adventure tour flyers. We might be busy this week as well. Who knew a bike race would bring in so many hikers." Archer put the last silver chair on the rack and pushed it into the storage behind the fireplace.

Darby was behind him, waiting to put the lectern in the closet as well. "One more thing and we can lock this up."

"Teamwork, right? Good to have you back home, squirt. Except for the whole accent. You sound weird." Archer took the lectern from her and set it in the closet before closing the door.

"I don't have an accent. You should have heard some of my professors. I had to have my roommate translate lectures the first semester I was there. After that, I picked up the dialect." Darby glanced around the room. "Should we sweep and mop the floor before heading home?"

"You're kidding, right?" Archer rubbed his shoulders. "I'm heading to Rarity's to man the grill for tonight's dinner. Are you coming?"

"I'm walking Marc back to his hotel." Darby paused, blushing as she did. "Then I've got plans."

Rarity put her arm around Darby. "This girl already has a date for tonight."

Darby's blush deepened. "It's not really a date. Just someone I knew from before. I haven't dated since, well, it's been a while. I'm still getting used to the idea again."

"You move fast. You've only been home a month." Archer glanced around the almost empty bookstore. "I take it Katie's heading back to Flagstaff. What about the rest of your misfits? How many steaks do I need to grill?"

"Thanks for all your help tonight." Rarity squeezed Darby and let her go. "Six. You, me, Sam, Drew, Shirley, and Terrance."

"So the old folks," Archer clarified.

Darby watched Marc gather his things. She turned back to the group. "No, all the couples. The rest of us haven't found our soulmate."

Rarity glanced over to where Shirley was closing up the sales table. She was still claiming that her relationship with Rarity's neighbor, Terrance, was in the friend zone. Her husband, George, was getting worse and Rarity expected a call any day. But until that day, Shirley was committed to her marriage. Even though George didn't remember either her or their vows. "Let's not define the group that way."

"Old folks or couples?" Archer waved his hand up and down in a *so-so* gesture. Then he saw Rarity look at Shirley. "Darby, I think you should know, Shirley's a little touchy about what we call her spending time with Terrance."

Darby snuck a glance over to where Shirley was stacking the final books that Marc Billings had just finished signing. "Sorry. I should be more sensitive. Maybe you should have invited Marc too."

"I did invite him, but he says he wants to go back to the hotel and do room service. He says he's a bit overwhelmed with everything. Thanks for walking him back to the hotel." Rarity waved Shirley over when she saw her watching the small group. When she got there, she gave her a hug. "Best author event ever."

"So far," Shirley said, amending Rarity's statement. "I really enjoyed putting this together. I didn't realize doing this was an actual job. My professor said if I write up a paper on the process and the results, I can use it for my term paper in his class."

"Let me know if you need numbers. I wasn't kidding. This was the most successful event I've had here at the store. You're still coming tonight for dinner, right?" Rarity wanted to make sure Shirley celebrated her success.

"I'll be there. Terrance asked me to bring my Texas sheet cake, but I think with all the kids heading out to the street dance tonight, I might have to bring the leftovers to work tomorrow." Shirley waved as Darby, Katie, and Marc Billings left the shop. "I'm driving over to Rarity's if anyone wants to ride with me."

"We'll walk." Rarity met Archer's gaze, and he nodded.

"I've got to run and get Sam at her house. She's changing out of her book event dress and shoes into shorts. She's bringing our suits for a swim." Drew slapped Archer on the back and headed out the door.

"Okay, if you don't need me for anything else, I'm going to stop by the nursing home and check on George, then I'll be there." Shirley gave Rarity a hug and tucked her purse on her shoulder. "It was a good night."

As Rarity and Archer walked through the bookstore, turning off lights and checking doors, she paused, looking at the store before she locked the front door. "I never expected how much I'd love my life right now. I blew my life to bits when I quit my job and moved here to be closer to Sam. Now, I have a business, a home, a pool, friends, and you."

He leaned down and kissed her. "You forgot something."

She frowned as she tucked her keys into her tote. "Did I?"

"Killer. You have Killer. He's going to be sad when I tell him his mommy forgot about him." Archer pretended to be sad for the dog.

Rarity playfully poked Archer in the side. "Please don't. He's going to be mad enough at me that I made him stay home tonight."

When they got home, Terrance was on his porch and let Killer loose when they came up the driveway. The little Yorkie bounced all the way and up into Rarity's arms as she leaned down to get him when he reached her. "I missed you so much."

"Whatever. Terrance, are you ready to help me get that grill started? The gang should be here in a few," Archer called out to the older man standing on the porch, watching them.

"I'll be over as soon as I get my contribution for dinner out of the fridge. I might not cook a lot, but I make a mean macaroni salad for nights like this." He waved and disappeared into his house.

By the time they were all settling in the backyard, music was flowing and a large, galvanized water tub had been filled with ice and adult beverages. And a few bottles of water as well. Rarity sat on the side of the pool dangling her legs in the water while Archer, Drew, and Sam played in the water. Killer curled by her side, barking at the crazy humans. Shirley and Terrance were at the table, talking.

Rarity smiled as she looked around her deck. Her new tribe all liked each other. Her business was like working with family. Darby was home from Scotland. And the spring run of festivals, before it got too hot, had started out strong. She stood and walked over to where Shirley had a calendar and a notebook out making notes. "Please tell me you're not working. It's a party. A welcome spring party."

Shirley tapped her pen on the calendar. "I'm not working. Terrance and I are looking at going on a cruise this summer to Alaska. Separate cabins, of course. I'm just not sure about being on a boat that long."

"It's a ship, not a boat and it will be fine. You'll love it. Besides, I've never seen Alaska. We need to get up there before it all melts." Terrance took a sip of his beer. "You and Archer should come with us. It will be fun."

"Maybe," Rarity said as she turned to see Sam climb on a floating chair in the pool. "Maybe all six of us should go."

"Sam and Drew seem to be doing better lately," Shirley noted as she watched Drew get out and hand Sam her drink from the table where they'd left it earlier. Rarity got herself another wine cooler and opened it, watching as her friend took her drink, then laughed when Drew splashed her with water. "Maybe we should all get away."

"Let's get those steaks going and we can chat about it over a meal." Terrance stood and headed into the kitchen to get the steaks from the fridge.

Shirley watched him go inside, then met Rarity's gaze. "I know. He's a good man."

"He is, and I'm glad you know that. Look, I know you're in a hard place, but just know we're all here for you." Rarity followed Terrance into the kitchen.

They were just finishing dinner when Drew's phone rang. They fell silent and Rarity turned down the music.

"It might just be the station checking in." Drew stood and walked to the back of the yard, Killer following at his heels.

When he came back, he looked at Rarity. "Do you want to change before you go?"

Her heart sank as she heard his words. "Did the store get broken into?"

Drew shook his head. "Not the store. Someone broke into Darby's house. Nothing's gone or trashed, but I don't think she should stay there alone. Can you put her up in your guest room?"

Rarity nodded. "I'll go get changed."

As she left the group, she heard Shirley directing the cleanup from dinner. She would take care of things here so Rarity could go save one of their own.

It was what family did in a crisis. And this group was family.

CHAPTER 2

After picking up Darby at her house and checking in with the officer in charge, Drew drove them back to Rarity's. He pulled the truck into the driveway and climbed out.

Rarity looked over at him. "Are you hanging out for a while?"

"The guys have the investigation in hand. Mike hates it when I hang around, looking over his shoulder while he works. Ever since he got his last promotion, he's been trying to show off his leadership skills." He grabbed Darby's bag from the bed of the truck. "You okay, squirt? Not much of a welcome home for someone to break in like that."

"I've been gone for over a year but as soon as I come home, people are all trying to mess with my stuff. What kind of police department are you guys running here?" She reached for the bag, but Drew held it over her head. "Okay, sorry for the jab. Can I have my bag?"

"Once we're in the house, yes. My mama raised a gentleman." Drew nodded toward the house, and the three headed to the front door.

Archer must have been watching because he held the door open. "Everything okay?"

"Nothing missing. I'm not sure what the guy was looking for," Drew said as he handed Darby her bag. Rarity pointed out the guest room. After Darby left the living room, he dropped his voice. "Unless they were after her. Has she said anything about having trouble with someone? An old boyfriend or anything?"

Rarity shook her head. "She hasn't mentioned anything to me, but I'll ask Katie and Shirley. She might have told them."

"Well, let me know if she does." Drew looked around the room. "Is Sam outside?"

Archer nodded. "Shirley and Terrance came in right after you left and put everything away from dinner. Then everyone went back out to the pool. I heard you drive up."

"Go join them," Rarity said. "I'll check on Darby and see if she wants to come out for a while."

She walked over to the guest room, Killer at her heels. She heard the door open to the patio and then shut. She knocked on the open door. "There's an attached bathroom, and the dresser has two empty drawers. The bottom drawer has an extra blanket and pillow if I keep it too cool in here."

Darby sat on the bed, her bag next to her. She had been looking at her phone. "I'm not staying forever, Rarity. Just a night until the cops are out of my house."

"You can stay longer, if you want." Rarity leaned against the doorframe. "I want you to feel safe."

"I just invited Malia and Holly over for a weeklong sleepover. Of course, they're going to say yes. I've been meaning to have them to the house, and this incident just makes it more convenient. You can come too, and bring Killer, if you want." She leaned down to rub his head.

"Okay, then the guest room is yours for the night." Rarity laughed as Darby had Killer doing sit-ups and circles. "He listens to you."

"Because usually, I have a treat in my hand. Anyway, thanks for tonight. I'll sleep better." Darby's phone buzzed with a text. "And that's my girlies telling me yes."

Darby held up the phone, showing Rarity the message from Malia. Then she tossed the phone on the bed and grabbed a pile of envelopes. "Now I need to go through the mail. I swear, most of this is junk mail. Like this flyer."

Rarity watched as she opened the folded page. "That doesn't look like it came from the post office."

"No, I don't think it did. Rarity, look at this." Darby held out the page as Rarity watched the color drain from her houseguest's face.

In black block letters, someone had written, **Missed you tonight. The next time, you won't be so lucky.**

"We need to show this to Drew." Rarity urged Darby on her feet, but the girl paused before taking a step.

"I don't want to be a bother. You have company."

Rarity took in a breath. "You're not a bother, but stay here if you want. I'm going to get Drew. And before you say anything else, it's his job." She hurried to the back and waved Drew inside. Once he was in, she closed the door after him, but not before she saw Archer's questioning look. Ignoring it, she took Drew's arm and hurried him to the guest room. "Darby got a threatening message. Can you look at it?"

"Maybe," he said as he beat her to the guest room and swiped the paper from Darby's hands. "Where did you get this?"

"It was mixed in with my mail." She pointed to the pile of envelopes sitting by her.

"Anything else like this in that pile?" When she shook her head, he nodded. "Okay, I'll take this with me and have the guys look at it. Have you received any notes like this before?"

Darby didn't answer immediately, but the look on her face told the story.

"You have? Oh, Darby. What's going on?" Rarity stood in the doorway, listening.

Darby shrugged. "Not exactly like this, but I had a situation when I was in Scotland. I went out with a guy a few times, but then he was getting a little clingy, so I told him I wasn't looking for a boyfriend. After that, I never dated anyone more than twice and I was clear about boundaries. But after I broke it off, I started being followed. Or it felt that way. I talked to a detective, and he said there wasn't anything they could do."

"When did the messages start?" Drew asked, in police detective mode. He had already made several notes in his little book. "And what was this guy's name and what town did you report him in?"

Darby went through the timeline, then blew out a sigh. "Look, I'm beat. Can I just go to sleep?"

"Of course." Rarity looked at Drew, who appeared to have more questions, and shook her head at him. "Drew can chat with you tomorrow at the store."

Rarity grabbed Drew's arm and aimed him out of the guest room.

"If you need anything, check my bathroom or just ask. We'll be out on the deck for a while. I'll check on you when I come in, but if you need me, just come on out." Rarity called out to Killer, but he'd made his way onto the bed and was curled on Darby's lap. "Just kick him out if he bothers you."

Darby kissed the Yorkie on the top of his head. "How in the world would this guy bother anyone?"

"Oh, let me count the ways." Rarity laughed as she shut the door and followed Drew to the kitchen. "Do you think it was the guy from Scotland?"

"Maybe. I need to see what the police report said. But it's a good guess." Drew pulled open a drawer. "I'm stealing a baggie. I just texted April at the station. She's coming over to get this and get it to our guys. I don't want to just ignore this."

"You're the best. Do you want a beer while you wait? I can get one and bring it out."

He paused in the middle of the open doorway. "Just let Sam know I'll be right back out. And let's keep this between the three of us, okay?"

"Four—no—five, if you count April and the stalker," Rarity pointed out.

"Funny girl," Drew said as he closed the door.

Rarity paused a moment before she went back to the party. She saw Archer waiting for her. "I was just being accurate," she mumbled to no one as she opened the door to go outside.

* * *

The next morning, Darby went with her and Killer to the shop. She didn't talk much as they walked. Darby had been asleep when Rarity came inside after the crew left, but Darby looked better this morning. A little sleepy eyed, but she claimed she'd slept through the night. Killer had joined Rarity about one after sneaking out of Darby's room.

"I just hope this goes away soon. It's one reason I didn't want to tell Drew. He can overreact at times."

"He's worried about you. We're all worried. I just got you back at the shop. I don't want you to not be available for your shifts. Especially since Shirley's talking about going on a cruise with Terrance."

The distraction worked. Darby's eyes lit up as she talked. "Seriously? Those two would be so good together. I know, Shirley's husband was a good man, but she's been alone for so long and Terrance is just so alpha. He's going to totally take care of her."

"I'm not saying they're a couple; it's complicated, but I'd love to see her do more things now. She's been tied to just visiting the nursing home for so long." If Rarity was confused on the subject, Shirley's thoughts and emotions on the subject must be making her dizzy. "Anyway, don't bring it up, unless she says something first. She might have changed her mind last night about going."

They were almost at the store when Rarity's phone buzzed. "Speak of the devil. Hi Shirley. What's going on?"

"I can't come in today. George has been rushed to the hospital. They won't tell me what's going on, just that I need to be there. I'm heading to Flagstaff now." Shirley talked fast.

"Do you need someone to drive you? I can go back and get the car. Or just head over to your house and we can take yours."

"I'm already on the road. I was driving to work when the nursing home called. Just keep George in your thoughts. I've got to go, Kathy's calling me back."

And then Rarity heard the click of the call disconnecting. She put her phone away and took out her keys. They'd arrived at the shop. "So, Shirley's not working today. It's just you and me. And we have to get ready for tomorrow's book signing and screening. The dumpster has been moved down the block, and I've already talked to the other shops so we can set up the chairs and podium first thing tomorrow in the alley behind the store. We have permission to block the alley today so we can spray it down. Can you do that while I handle the store?"

"What's happening with Shirley? Is it George?" Darby asked as Rarity tucked her purse under the tote and let Killer off his leash. "You didn't tell me."

Rarity looked up from the notebook where she'd been writing a to-do list. "We don't know. The home sent George to the hospital, but they wouldn't tell Shirley why. That's all I know, so we'll just have to think good thoughts for our friends."

Darby nodded as she went to set her backpack in the break room. When she came back, Rarity could see she'd been crying.

"Are you okay?"

Darby wiped her face with her hands and took a tissue from the box that Rarity held out for her. "It's just bringing up when Grandma died. They just told me that I had to go to the house. No whys, so you think the worst. And it was for her. I guess with the break-in last night, and now this, it's messing with my head a little."

"I'd be surprised if it didn't," Rarity said. "Look, we don't know anything. He could have fallen. Shirley will call when she has news, and we'll deal with whatever happens. Until then, life goes on."

"So, I'm spraying down the alley?" A smile creeped onto Darby's face. "With a stalker threatening me?"

Rarity blinked. "Oh, no. You're right. You can't be out there on your own."

"Chill. I was just kidding. Besides,"—Darby pulled something out of her cargo pants—"I have pepper spray. Just in case."

"Put that stuff away before I can't pretend I didn't see it," Drew said as he and Archer came into the bookstore. "I hear you're down a minion. We're here to help, but can you call in Katie?"

"Who called you?" Rarity asked as Archer handed her a cup from Desert Coffee & Cream. "Thanks."

"My pleasure. Here, runt, a caramel mocha with whipped cream and enough sugar to run a suburban mall electric grid." Archer handed Darby a cup, ignoring her question. "And until Katie gets here, I'm your new minion. Where do you want me?"

"We're your new minions. I don't have to go in until five tonight. They wanted more people on nights this week, so I volunteered to work tonight. I told them I had to be at your movie thing tomorrow, so they let me get away with just one double shift." Drew corrected Archer as he sipped his coffee, watching Darby move around the shop.

Rarity thought Drew was here for more than just to help. She could see the concern in the look he gave Darby. She played along. "Shirley must have called you?"

"On her way out of town. I actually saw her leaving and I called her to tell her to slow down. Martin has a speed trap right out of the city limits set up this morning, and I didn't want her to have to talk her way out of the ticket." Drew smiled as he talked. "The woman has a lead foot."

"Okay, since I have you two, you can go spray down the alley. We need to clean it up before we set up chairs and the stage out there. The movie will be shown on the side of the building between my shop and Sam's. We'll have the projector over on the hill behind the alley. We'll have extra seating there, but people will have to bring their own lawn chairs." Rarity was thinking as she talked out the setup. "Too bad it's not grass out there. They could bring blankets."

"Grass wouldn't live there. Too dry. You could do Astroturf, but bugs might still get into it." Darby leaned against the table, sipping her coffee. When she saw the others watching her, she shrugged. "I called a landscaping company for the house. I wanted to do a grass backyard by the pool, but they laughed at me."

"Are you keeping the house?" Archer asked. "It's pretty big for one person."

Darby nodded. "I know. But I have plans. I'm going to open up a bed-and-breakfast for tourists. Not a fancy one with antiques and such… Well, except for what Grandma already had in the house. But one where people can come and relax after hiking or sightseeing all day."

"That sounds amazing." Rarity had wondered what Darby was going to do with the mini mansion her grandmother had left her, but she had assumed she'd sell it.

Darby grinned at Rarity's comment. "I know, right? Malia says she knows a chef looking for a side gig and she wants to be part of it. Holly's thinking about it too. We just need a cool name."

"And a business plan and a contract between the three of you, just in case something goes wrong with the friendship." Drew added to Darby's dreaming.

"And there's always someone to bring down the mood." Archer lightly punched Drew in the shoulder. "Let's get the alley cleaned up before you get called off to save the day, Superman."

"Dude, don't call me that." Drew and Archer headed into the back room to go out to the alley.

Darby went over and looked at Rarity's to-do list. "You think it's too much for us? Running a bed-and-breakfast? I know we're young."

Rarity laughed as she set her pen down. "Darby, I had a plan when I was your age. I did all the right things, and still, I had to adjust when I was diagnosed with cancer. When my upcoming wedding dream blew up during the treatment, I realized that it didn't matter what other people thought. This is your life. If you want to do this, why not?"

"Grandma used to tell me all the time to follow my dreams. That's why I went to Scotland to finish school. I'd always wanted to but thought it was too expensive. Especially after she got sick. I wanted to be here with her."

"And you were. I'm excited to see what happens next in your life. If this bed-and-breakfast is the next chapter for you, then I'm all for it." Rarity looked around the bookstore. "I have never regretted giving up everything I built in St. Louis and moving here. It's like I was meant to be here all along. You'll find your happy place too."

Rarity grabbed her cell phone. Time to call in the troops to help. It wouldn't be the same without Shirley, but they could pull together to get it all done.

CHAPTER 3

Later that afternoon, Rarity sent Archer and Drew to the park to set up the bookstore's booth there for the festival. She'd been planning on setting it all up tomorrow, but with the guys' help and with Katie arriving midmorning, she was ahead of schedule. They'd completely set up the alley stage, movie theater, and book sales stand. She was working on the staffing plan for this weekend in case Shirley wasn't able to work. She'd be okay, but it would be tight. She might have to close the store on Saturday just to have enough people for the festival booth.

Overtime was going to kill her budget this weekend. But sales at the Wednesday signing had been strong and today had been busy. Marc Billings had come by and asked Darby if she'd join him for lunch. Rarity had sent them away with a grin.

Katie had waited until they were out of the bookstore before she said, "Wow, he's like a bee to a wildflower with her. Can you see it in his eyes?"

"He does seem smitten. And from what I can see, he's a good guy. Besides, Darby needs a distraction from last night's mess." Rarity sighed as she handed Katie a piece of paper. "Go get everyone's order for lunch at Carole's. My salad is already on the list. And an iced tea, please."

"We need more waters too. I'll stop by the store so we can get stocked up for tomorrow." She reached for the credit card that Rarity kept in the drawer. "I love spending your money."

"Just remember, I need money for payroll too," Rarity teased. "Oh, get additional water and some sodas for the booth this weekend. So buy twice as much as you were planning."

"I'll get our lunch order in and then head out to the store." Katie glanced around the bookstore. There were several customers browsing. Foot traffic had been strong all morning. "Unless you think I need to stay. I can go to the store after we close."

Rarity shook her head. "No, you're going to be working too many hours this weekend as it is. Take tonight to do something fun."

"Actually, Darby's having a bunch of the girls over tonight for a sleepover. She invited me to come along as well. I really like having her here. She's not what I expected, but I'm dying to see the inside of her house. And her pool." Katie took off to help a customer in the romance aisle.

As she did, the bell over the door rang, and Rarity called out, "Welcome to the Next Chapter."

"Thank you. I know I'm early for Tuesday's book club, but I am having a bad case of writer's block and Drew thought I might be useful here." Jonathon Anderson, Drew's father, and a full-fledged member of the sleuthing club, walked into the store.

"Jonathon. You're just on time. Give Katie your lunch order, then come over and tell me all about what's going on with Edith and Savannah, of course." Rarity knew that Drew had asked his dad to come up from Tucson where they lived probably sometime last night. Jonathon was a retired detective and a really nice guy. He was also an aspiring author.

"I didn't come for a free lunch," he grumbled as he set his laptop bag on the counter.

"Perks of the day. Never turn down food when it's offered. You don't know how long it will be until the next meal. Especially with as busy as this weekend is going to be. Besides, I'm down a set of hands. This way I don't feel bad about asking you to help." She waved Katie over. "Now give her your order and then I'll tell you what's going on unless Drew updated you this morning."

"No, I talked with him late last night." After he'd given his order to Katie, he sat down at one of the stools. "Where's Darby?"

"She went to lunch with Marc Billings. He's a retired bike racer and we hosted a book signing for his first book last night. He's also enamored with our Darby. She should be back any minute." Rarity took a book from a customer who'd come up to the register and processed her checkout. Once she was finished and the customer had left, she turned back to Jonathon to finish the update. "Shirley is at the hospital with George."

Concern filled Jonathon's face. "Do we know what's going on? Should I ask Edith to join me this weekend?"

"I don't know anything more than what I said." Rarity thought for a minute. "Can you ask Edith to call Shirley? It might be a welcome distraction from the waiting."

"I just texted her." He held up his phone and then tucked it back into his jacket pocket. "So if you're feeding me, I want to work for my supper. Where do you want me?"

Rarity glanced at her list. "As soon as Katie's back with the food, can you take Drew's and Archer's food over to the park? Then you can help them finish the setup. We'll be open there and here all weekend, so we need a mini store ready for tomorrow morning. I was going to have Shirley run the store and I was going to run the booth, then come back at five for the signing and the movie. But now, I don't know."

"What hole do you want me to fill?"

"I can't believe I went from a one-person show to this. Now, I count on everyone so much." Rubbing her eyebrow, she glanced at the list. "Archer has his own store and booth to run."

"Rarity." Jonathon took her hand. "Breathe. It will be fine. I'll either be here helping one of the girls, or you can have both girls here, and I can help you at the booth."

Rarity took in several deep breaths. "I'm just worried. About the shop, the next signing, Darby, Shirley, I guess all of it. You're right. Everything will work out. With what's going on, the best place for you is with Darby. I'll take Katie to the booth tomorrow and you and Darby can run the shop. Just don't let her leave alone."

"I'll watch her with my good eye." Jonathon pointed at his left eye, then at the right. "Hmm, I seem to have forgotten which one is my good eye."

"You're a nut. And thank you." Rarity made notes on her list. At least one thing, okay, maybe two concerns were off her list. Now to finish boxing up the books that would go to the booth tomorrow. As she worked on her list, Darby came back into the shop from lunch. "Darby? Watch the register as I get Jonathon set up to gather books for the festival."

Darby came around the register counter and put her bag underneath again. "Thanks for letting me out for lunch. Marc is really a nice guy. Oh, and don't forget to bring twice as many kids' books as you think you need. We always run out."

* * *

Friday morning, Rarity felt calmer than she'd expected. Darby had left Rarity's house last night to go back to her house for the girls' night she'd planned. When they met up at the bookstore, everyone seemed rested and a little less on edge. Rarity handed out the coffee she'd bought as well as the scones from the little bakery. "Okay, here's today's plans. I'm heading up the booth from nine to five. Then we'll close and move back here to get ready for the night's events. Katie, you're with me, and Darby, Jonathon will help you out here."

"Oh, I get to be his boss?" Darby snuck a peek at Jonathon.

"No evil smiles. We need to get through this day. Saturday and Sunday will be busy, but this is the killer day." Rarity glanced at the list she'd made last night. "Malia will be dropping off lunches from the Garnet for both groups, so you need to get your order to her no later than ten. Then she's bringing over a taco bar at five for us and the next author—Mason Pike—who will speak from six to seven. The signing will happen then and the movie—his first film, *Attack of the Venus Spiders*—will start right at seven thirty. The movie is a little over an hour and a half—so we should be done and cleaned up right at ten. Then we're back at our stations at nine Saturday morning. Don't forget, the race starts at ten so parking and traffic will be a nightmare. Anyone who wants to can park at my house and walk into town with me."

"So, you're talking to me, since the rest of them are in walking distance too," Katie deadpanned as she looked at everyone at the table.

"Okay, so yes, fine, I was talking to you. I was thinking about Shirley as well, but I don't think she's going to be here. George might have had a stroke so they're doing testing today and maybe surgery." Rarity paused for a minute, remembering how stressed her friend had sounded when she'd called last night. She hadn't even left the hospital yet. "So keep her in your thoughts. I'll keep you all informed, and if she's still in Flagstaff, I'm going over to see her Sunday afternoon as soon as we shut down the festival."

"I asked Edith to come up and sit with her until Kathy can get someone to watch the kids while she's gone." Jonathon added to Rarity's statement. "So this guy really named a movie *Attack of the Venus Spiders*? What did he call his book? *Aliens and Me*?"

Rarity snorted. "No, it's *Making the American Horror Movie*."

Katie giggled. "Stop it. Mr. Pike presented at our drama class in April and he was really interesting. He started doing movies when he was fifteen. The spider movie was the first one picked up by a studio and shot. He made a lot of money off the licensing."

"Let me guess, you had to read his book for the class." Jonathon sighed. "I'm never going to get a book published if all the slots are taken by Hollywood celebrities and those in the legal profession. At least it's not election season. Then there's even fewer slots."

"That's a scarcity mindset." Darby shook her finger at him. "You need to think abundantly. There are plenty of slots open, and my book will get one and bring in tons of money due to its popularity."

Jonathon nodded. "I get it, but when did you start writing a book?"

"I'm not writing…" Darby paused. "Okay, fine, I see what you did there. Rarity, are you sure I can't have Katie at the store?"

Rarity tried to hide her smile. "Okay, kids, stop teasing each other. If I have to turn this car around, I will."

Jonathon poked Darby. "See what you did. Mom's mad."

"I didn't make her mad, you did." Darby stuck her tongue out.

"Did so," Jonathon said as he leaned closer, staring at Darby.

"And on that note, we're going to leave so we can open the festival booth. Open the store at nine, and please, don't kill each other. Bloodstains are so hard to get out of hardwood." Rarity stood and snapped her fingers, calling Killer to her side. She clicked his leash on. "Sometime tonight, Terrance is coming to get Killer and take him home before the movie. So if you see him and you have Killer, you have my permission for Terrance to leave with him. You don't have to find me. Just tell me when you see me. I think it's going to be a madhouse here tonight. Here's to a colossal day of sales."

"Okay team, break," Darby called out as she stood. "We'll see you at five. Bet we outsell you."

"You won't even be close," Katie challenged back.

"How much do you want to bet?" Darby pushed.

Rarity pulled Katie toward the door in front of her. "No betting allowed. I'm not running a back parlor casino here."

At the park when she opened the festival tent door, Rarity had to admit, the guys had done a great job of setting up the off-site bookstore. She set Killer up under the sales table and then went to adjust the piles. They had young adult over with the thrillers and not with the kids' books. They were only open a few minutes before the first wave of customers hit.

Marc Billings wandered in when the customers started to slow near lunchtime. He raised his hand and looked around the tent. Then he came up to the sales table where Rarity had just finished with a customer. He picked up a signed copy of his book on the front table. "Hey, you guys take festivals seriously around here. I heard you were featuring the book here, but I thought they meant the actual bookstore."

"No, we brought a little over half our signed stock of your book since there are probably a lot of people taking in the festival who are also here for the race. And then there's the film festival that starts tomorrow too." Rarity waved at Malia, who had just come into the tent with their lunches. "I used to close the shop on festival days, but I get people at both locations now. You should come to the book signing tonight. We're hosting an outdoor showing of a horror flick."

"Darby mentioned that. You guys are too busy for me. When I raced, I trained all the time. Early to bed, early to rise. I kept the same schedule when I was writing the book. I tend to be a homebody, just getting out for signings and the races. It's a lot slower of a pace." He nodded to Malia as she set the lunches on the back table. "But it looks like you need to take a break. I'm going to wander over to the bookstore and say hi."

"Honestly, it's either feast or famine here too. You just arrived in our busy festival season." Rarity handed him a flyer for the signing and showing that night. "Seriously, come to the event tonight. Darby will be there."

He blushed, and Rarity knew that he liked the bookseller for more than her friendship as he'd navigated his author signing that week.

As he walked out of the tent, Malia stood next to Rarity. "Darby wasn't wrong. He's gorgeous and nice. Now I feel bad that I missed his signing. Is the book good?"

"From what I read, yes. And now that I've met him, the voice matches his personality. Laid back, but thoughtful. Is Darby interested?" Rarity went over and pulled her sandwich out of the bag as Killer watched from under the table.

Malia shrugged. "You know Darby. She flits from one thing to the next. I think she's still a little worried about that guy from Scotland."

"Does she think he was the one who broke into her house? That he followed her here?" Rarity didn't like the sound of that at all. Darby had been frightened by the message left in her mail. "Was everything all right last night at the house?"

"We had a blast. Katie swam for hours, so we hung out at the pool until we could drag her away." Malia poked Katie's arm.

"That's not true," Katie complained. "You all were drinking. I wanted to enjoy that pool as long as possible. It's beautiful."

Rarity smiled at the younger version of herself. "I know the value of a good pool. It's my happy place, especially swimming in the morning. And at night after a stressful day."

"So basically, anytime. No wonder the two of you get along so well," Malia teased as she checked her watch. "I've got to drop off food at the bookstore, then get back to work. I'll be there tonight right at six, though."

"I'll save you a seat. I hear the next author is handsome as well," Rarity called after her.

The rest of the day went by quickly. The one thing about having so much going on was that Rarity was never bored. This new life she'd built had enough going on to keep her busy as well as a group of friends who were close enough to feel like family. She looked around the mini bookstore and quickly found Katie, who was rearranging books and making notes on what they needed to restock.

The weekend was only just beginning, and there was going to be a lot of work from now until Sunday night. She noticed a man walking through the book tables; he'd stopped at the children's section. He was younger than most dads who were looking for a book to take home to their kids, but maybe he had a niece or nephew whom he wanted to share his love of reading with. Customers came in all sizes and ages. Another reason that Rarity loved the bookselling business. As he was the last one in the tent, she went over to let him know that they were closing up.

"I loved that book as a kid," Rarity said as she saw him pick up a middle grade mystery. "I always wanted to be the one to solve the mystery or find the missing relic. How old are your kids? Or is it for a relative?"

"What?" The young man dropped the book. He took a look at her, then ran out of the tent.

Rarity watched after him. She walked back to Katie. "My hair isn't bad, is it? Or do I smell?"

"No more than the rest of us." Katie reached out and pushed a wayward curl from Rarity's face. "I think your makeup melted off. Why?"

"Just asking why I would have scared off a customer." When Katie looked confused, she shook her head. "Never mind. Let's start shutting down."

After Rarity and Katie finished closing the festival booth and returned to the store, Darby was in the break room, listening to Mason Pike tell stories about his life. He was older than Rarity had assumed—maybe in his mid-sixties—but that didn't diminish his charm. And he was focused on Darby. What was it about the ginger-haired young woman that intrigued men so quickly? Maybe her makeup hadn't melted off like Rarity's.

Rarity quickly ate then went out to the alley to make sure everything was ready. She was soon joined by everyone but Darby and Mason Pike. He'd come out just before the talk was supposed to start.

The seats filled up fast. Rarity sold a lot of Pike's books while they got ready for the show. Archer and Jonathon were setting up the audio as well as making sure the projector was ready. And right on time, Mason walked out of the back door and greeted Rarity, who was going to introduce him and his talk. Darby fell in behind, her face red. When Rarity met her gaze, she shook her head. Whatever was going on, she didn't want to talk about it.

Rarity took Mr. Pike up onto the stage, and the festivities of the night began. When he started talking, she moved back to the side where Darby and Katie were waiting. "Okay, as soon as he finishes, we'll move him to the signing table, and hopefully, he'll be done before seven thirty when we start the movie. If not, we'll have him continue to sign books during the movie in the break room. Darby, do you want to handle that?"

"I'd rather not," Darby said, her face turning a red that matched her hair.

"Okay. Katie?" Rarity looked over at her.

"Maybe Jonathon should handle Mr. Pike for the rest of the night," Darby said before Katie could agree.

Rarity didn't know what had happened, but if Darby felt that strongly, she'd support her decision. "Sure. Would you run up and get him off the hill? He can be the author wrangler for the rest of the event."

The talk finished right on time, and Mason Pike was led by a smiling Jonathon to the signing table. Rarity watched as Mason looked around for Darby, but when he didn't find her, he focused on the first reader holding the book out.

Darby came back from hanging with Archer when the signing line had ended and Mason Pike was inside, signing stock for the store. Jonathon came out and glanced at his watch. "He's got about twenty more books to sign and then he'll be out. Are we starting the movie now? Or waiting for him?"

"Start it now," Rarity said. "I'll make the introduction from the script he gave me."

Once the movie was going and the lights had dimmed, Rarity realized that Mason Pike hadn't rejoined them. She left her seat and went into the bookstore through the back door.

Mason was sitting at the table, his eyes shut.

Rarity shut the door behind her. "Did you want to watch the movie or just relax until the ending? I'm sure we'll have some questions."

Mason didn't move.

"Mr. Pike?" Rarity went up and shook his shoulder. He fell over, and a large black spider fell off his chest.

CHAPTER 4

The scream coming from Rarity's lips was echoed by the one from the movie outside the bookstore. The spider inside didn't seem to notice. Rarity got a magazine from the counter and tried to squish it. It still didn't move. Or squish. She reached out with a shaky hand. The spider was plastic. Dropping the magazine, she hurried over to the slumped-over man and checked for a pulse. "Mason? Mason Pike?"

Nothing. No response. She grabbed her cell phone from her purse on the counter and called 911, asking for an ambulance. "Come to the front of the shop. I don't want to freak out everyone watching the movie."

"Stay on the line with me. Can you tell if he's breathing?" the dispatcher asked.

Rarity leaned closer to Mason and tried to hear his heart or any breathing. "No, nothing. I'm going to go unlock the front door so they can get in. I hear the sirens."

She hung up on the dispatcher, then called Drew. As soon as he answered, she said, "I need you at the bookstore."

He responded quickly. "Is Sam okay?"

"She's fine," Rarity answered, truthfully. She'd seen her friend during the signing but then had lost sight of her until she sat down next to her when the movie started. "It's Mason Pike. I think he's dead."

"You should call 911. Who is Mason Pike?"

"I already called them," Rarity said as she heard Drew's truck start up in the background. "He's our author guest. He wrote this movie. But Drew, there was a fake spider on his chest when I found him. The movie is about alien spiders. Isn't that weird?"

"Weird? For normal people, yes. But for you? I don't know. Kind of par for the course, isn't it?" He paused for a minute, then asked, "Any chance this is a natural death?"

"Maybe. He's in his sixties. He'd just finished talking and signing. It's hot today. Maybe he had a heart attack?" Rarity waved the EMTs over to the open door. "The ambulance is here."

"I know, I'm right behind them. I'll talk to you as soon as I know what's going on. Go back to the movie and keep people out of the store," Drew said, then hung up on her.

Rarity directed the EMTs to the break room, letting them know that Drew was following, and left out the back door to keep people away. Jonathon stood there, watching as she came out.

"I can't let you inside," she said, shutting the door behind her.

"I know. Drew texted me. I'm standing guard. So the author?" He looked at her and sighed when she nodded her head. "Darn. I wanted to have a few words with the guy about how to handle being around a young girl. I don't think he realized that no meant no."

"Is Darby okay?" Rarity scanned the chairs, trying to see where she was sitting.

"She's fine. He was handsy with her, though, and insisted that she come back to his room for a drink. Apparently, he's used to getting his way with women. At least he was."

"Thank goodness Darby was with you for the night. With that incident, Drew might see it as motivation."

Jonathon didn't answer her.

When she looked up at him, she groaned. "Darby left for a while, right after the signing, didn't she?"

Jonathon nodded. "She said she needed to go to the bathroom. I offered to go with her, but then you called me over to wrangle Mason. Remember?"

"And Archer was still working on the movie setup."

"Let's hope Mason died of natural causes, or both Darby and I have motive and opportunity in the murder." Jonathon watched the movie. "This really is horrible. The spiders all look fake."

* * *

Somehow, they got out of the Q and A session after the movie. Rarity went up to the microphone and thanked everyone for coming out. She didn't mention Mason or any excuse. No one apparently had questions, but she did hear a few people mutter about how bad the movie had been. But others left talking about the differences in special effects in the last twenty years. Everyone left happy. Well, except Mason.

Rarity started folding up chairs as the audience left the alley. As she did, she noticed the same man from the festival booth standing and watching the signing table where Darby and Katie were packing up the leftover books as well as the event materials.

Archer brought the cart with the projector on it to the door, pausing to ask, "Is this yours? Into the closet?"

She turned to answer the question, and when she turned back, the man was gone. Probably a tourist who liked books. She shouldn't read as much into people and their actions. Especially tonight. She would see everyone in the audience as a potential murderer. Except she'd been at the back door, and after Jonathon came out, no one had gone back inside.

She wondered about that, then realized something she hadn't noticed earlier. The front door hadn't been locked. She'd opened it using the doorknob when she went to find the EMTs. The deadbolt hadn't been thrown. Who had locked the door when they'd all gone out into the alley for the event?

And who had known that Mason had been in the bookstore, alone? These were questions she needed to ask Drew. And stay out of the fray. But she knew she wouldn't. Come Tuesday night, the part of the book club that saw themselves as sleuths would be demanding to know what she knew.

She didn't have to tell them. Maybe Mason had gone quietly into the night all on his own. At least that was her hope.

The teardown of the event site took way less time than the setup. Probably because the older group wanted to head home and chill and the younger staff wanted to head to the street dance that was going to start in a few minutes.

Either way, she had all the chairs back in the store and the alley clean and ready for its usual purposes by nine forty-five. The group was all in the bookstore when she gathered everyone together.

"Look, something happened tonight." Rarity paused, wondering how to say it.

"Mason Pike is a loser," Darby said. "He has ten sets of hands. Don't get near him unless you want to be felt up."

"I'm sorry that happened. Maybe we should rethink our author wrangling assignments." Rarity focused on Darby. "But that's not what I wanted to say."

"I know, but I didn't want Katie to have to deal with him. Just don't be in a room alone with him. He sees you as someone he wants to impress, so you're probably safe, Rarity." Darby shook out her shoulders. "It was just gross."

"Like I said, I'm sorry that happened. And we'll consider it next time we have a signing. But you all need to know that…" Rarity paused again, wondering how to break the news.

"What Rarity is trying to delicately tell you is that Mason Pike died in the break room. The body will have an autopsy, but for now, type of death is undetermined. I'll need to talk to all of you, but we'll do it tomorrow morning. I assume all of the same staff will be working tomorrow?"

"Unless Shirley shows up, then, yes, this is tomorrow's crew." Rarity needed to hire more staff just so she had more backup. Then she chided herself from thinking about work when she needed to be mourning a dead man.

A man she didn't know and one who had mistreated her friend. Right now, she didn't feel all that sorry for Mason's death.

Archer walked home with her after locking up the bookstore. An action they did almost every night, but tonight, Mason's death had made the walk tense. She let out a long breath. "I don't think Mason Pike was a very nice man. You heard what Darby said. She was clearly upset at the way he treated her. I know I should be sad that he passed, but I'm still mad at him for what he did to Darby. He was a guest in my store."

"Sometimes people don't act the way we expect them to or even with social grace. I'm sorry you had to find him. Are you okay?" Archer squeezed her hand.

"I'm fine. I guess. I was scared about the stupid fake spider on his chest. It fell off when I touched his shoulder. I thought it was real for a minute. I even swatted it with a magazine. What if Mason had still been alive and I delayed calling 911 because I was killing a fake spider?"

"According to Drew, he'd been dead a while before the paramedics got there. I think the heat of the day and the excitement might have done him in. You know some people don't acclimate to our climate very well." He dropped her hand, then pulled her into a hug, stopping in the middle of the sidewalk. "It's not your fault."

"Then I feel guilty about what he did to Darby and I'm mad about that. I need a swim before I head to bed tonight." She let her head sink into his shoulder for just a second. Archer was the best hugger ever.

"What if I make us some tea? You swim and I'll hang out with Killer until you calm down a little. I hate to see you worked up."

She nodded, hoping he could see her in the dark. "I'd love that."

As she got into the pool, she heard voices on the other side of her fence. Terrance must be entertaining. He'd brought Killer home earlier, and now her dog was inside watching Archer make tea. She focused on her laps, letting the stress of the day float away from her and into the water. Or she tried to. As much as she enjoyed the feel of the water and stretching her body as she swam, random thoughts kept interrupting her meditation time. Finally, she gave up, hoping she'd worn her body out enough to sleep later.

While she'd been in the pool, Archer had invited Terrance over for a nightcap. And his guest. She was surprised to see Shirley sitting at her patio table with the men. "Hey, how's everything? Are you okay?" Rarity tried not to bring up George when Terrance was around. It wasn't like Shirley was cheating, but sometimes it felt odd.

"George is stable. They're sending him back to the home tomorrow so if it's okay, I'd like to come to work tomorrow. Kathy is here and will make sure he's set up in his room with everything he needs." Shirley picked up her wineglass. Rarity hadn't noticed it before.

"If you want to, I'd love for you to handle the shop with Jonathon. Then Darby can work with me at the booth. And it will get her away from the whole Pike thing." Rarity took the glass of wine that Archer had poured for her and took a sip, setting it down while she used the towel she had wrapped around her to dry off some more. She had the tea next to the wine glass. One of the two should work.

"The Pike thing? Oh, don't tell me there was an issue. I've heard rumors about him, but I was never able to verify anything. I meant to handle him myself. No one would dare mess with me, and I had my lecture ready, but then I forgot when I rushed to the hospital. Who did you have on him?" Shirley rolled her head back and forth to stretch her neck. "I swear I'm going to start writing down everything so I don't forget. But then I'd forget to read my planner."

Rarity met Archer's eyes. Apparently Terrance and Shirley didn't know about Pike's unfortunate situation. "Shirley, Pike died during the movie. Drew hasn't told us what happened, but he was in the break room between his signing and the movie when I found him. And yes, Darby had an issue with him being handsy too. Darby told us later, but we had Jonathon handle him just before the signing. I wish she'd told me earlier. I guess I need to do a talk on what boundaries we need to set for visiting authors."

Shirley finished her wine before speaking. "I can't believe how much has happened here and I was only gone two days. I'm so sorry about Darby. Is she okay?"

"She says she's fine. She just rolled it off, but now that Pike's dead, I probably need to chat with her again." Rarity yawned after she spoke. "I'm beat. Archer, can you continue to host?"

"No need, I was just about to drive Shirley home." Terrance stood and held out his hand to Shirley.

Shirley looked over at Rarity. "Kathy has my car in Flagstaff, so Terrance came and got me from the hospital. I just couldn't stay there, but I didn't want Kathy to have to drive me home and go back."

"How's she doing with all this?" Rarity asked as Shirley stood to leave with Terrance.

Shirley shrugged before she spoke. "As good as expected. She knows she's saying goodbye. Maybe not today, or next week, but soon. The doctor told me that much. He'll be on hospice when he returns to the home."

"That stage can last months," Terrance said, obviously trying to reassure her.

Her eyes were sad as she met Rarity's gaze. "That's what I worry about. If he's going, I don't want him to be in pain."

After Shirley and Terrance left, Rarity and Archer went inside. "I'll go change and be right out."

"Go to bed. You're dead on your feet. I'll clean up around here and then head home. Tomorrow's going to be a busy day at the festival. My bookings are reaching capacity, so I need to see if I can carve out more time. You may not see me for a while."

"This is the moneymaking season, right? Go make money." She kissed him and headed to the bedroom. She didn't even hear the front door close when he left.

Early the next morning, Rarity sat at her breakfast table, looking at her planner and drinking coffee. Mason Pike's signing and the movie had made the paper, but not his death. She wondered if Drew was holding the news off until there was a cause of death. Announcing that someone had died during a festival weekend was sad, but saying the death was a murder, well, that affected a lot more things. Like tourists leaving or not feeling safe to wander through their town.

Rarity had only met the mayor once, at one of those commerce chapter meetings, but he was very concerned about Sedona's image. Including making sure stores, especially on Main Street, kept the front of their shops clean of trash and looking pristine. Rarity had set up pots with fake flowers that she rinsed off once a week to keep the dust down.

And since they were near the door, they attracted tourists as they tried to see if the plants were real.

She pulled over her phone and texted Drew.

What happened to Mason Pike? Do you know yet?

The response came quickly.

You know it's five in the morning, right? I'll be attending the autopsy at ten. Do you want to come along?

Rarity blinked, took a sip of coffee, then read it again. Was Drew really inviting her to attend an autopsy? Could she deal with it? Or, more likely, he was joking with her.

Seriously?

This response took a little longer. Rarity was just about to ask again when Drew answered.

Not on your life. I'm messing with you. Were you really considering going? It's not as discreet as the ones you see on television. Not sure you could handle the process.

His teasing should have made her feel better, but instead, she felt more on edge than before.

Not funny. Call me if you find out it's anything but natural. I'll need to tell my staff and prepare them for questions from the public and the media.

Then she put her phone away and went swimming. If she had to be up, she might as well get one thing off her list. Exercise.

Getting some solid dopamine hits would ease her into her morning, especially since she didn't know how the day would unfold. She had to be prepared for anything. Especially if Mason Pike had been murdered.

Somehow, she knew the coroner would rule against natural causes.

It was just her luck.

CHAPTER 5

With the bike race getting ready to start near downtown, Rarity chose to walk to the bookstore first, then head over to the park to open the booth. She needed to open the shop so Drew and Archer could take the rental chairs back. When she arrived, someone was already inside the store, leaving the front door open for early shoppers. Rarity looked around as she let Killer off his leash, but she didn't see any of her staff. She headed to the break room and almost ran into Shirley coming out of the room, a mop and bucket in her hands.

"Oh, I hope you don't want coffee yet. I just scrubbed those floors. I can't believe all the trash emergency responders leave on-site after they do the transport. I get it. They're in a hurry to get to the hospital, but that wasn't the case here. They couldn't have picked up after themselves?" Shirley rolled her eyes and set her cleaning tools down. "I was just about to clean the bathrooms. Might as well while the water's hot. Besides, we should get a lot of walk-in traffic here today."

"Thanks for stepping in, but you should have locked the door. I hate thinking of you here alone." She glanced at her watch. "I need to grab a couple of boxes of books to take with me. Jonathon brought over some yesterday afternoon, but I don't think it will hold us and I don't want him to have to leave you here alone."

"You worry too much. What could happen in Sedona? Okay, don't answer that question. Besides, the boys just left with the rental chairs.

Did you forget they were coming to help this morning?" Shirley grabbed the mop bucket. "I better get the bathrooms cleaned. Is the crew meeting you here this morning?"

"I think so," Rarity wondered aloud. She hadn't mentioned a meeting on Saturday morning, but they'd had one on Friday morning. She guessed she'd see who could read her mind.

As the minutes passed, it seemed all the staff had read Rarity's mind about a staff meeting. Now, with the floor clean and dry, Katie made coffee and brought out the plate of cookies that Shirley had baked last night. Or probably this morning, knowing her friend.

Rarity made the updates and the new assignments, and afterward, she pulled Darby aside. "I hope you're okay with working the booth with me. I think Shirley and Jonathon should stay inside today. I worry about them."

Darby met her gaze. "Me too. I'm glad you're trying to keep them safe. My grandmother never ever thought about what might happen. She was too busy talking about all the good things coming her way. Definitively a positive force. Now that I'm home, I think I miss her even more."

"You okay to work today?" Rarity noticed the dark lines under Darby's eyes. She knew she had another set on her own face.

"I'm fine. Are we ready to go?" Darby clearly didn't want to talk about what had happened.

"Sure. Grab those boxes and put them on the wagon. We need to resupply the tent." Rarity got her tote and Killer's leash. She wondered if he would ride on top of the boxes in the wagon if the pavement was too hot for his feet. Maybe on the way back. "Oh, and Marc Billings came by the tent yesterday to see you. Did he find you at the store?"

"I didn't see him," Darby said as she adjusted the boxes on the wagon. "But then again, Mason was hanging around most of the afternoon, so I had to keep watching for him. Thank goodness Jonathon was here. Whenever he came near, Jonathon would distract him."

Jonathon smiled from where he sat at a table, working on his laptop. "All in a day's work. Oh, and Shirley, Edith said to thank you for the call yesterday. She needed some girl time."

"Actually, I think you put her up to calling. If I hadn't stopped it, she would have been here waiting on me hand and foot at the hospital." She stared at Jonathon. "I'll tell you when I need hand-holding."

"Yes, ma'am. No wonder you and Edith get along so well. You're both strong-willed women." He stood and walked with Rarity, Katie, and Darby. When they'd wrangled the wagon outside, he leaned next to Rarity. "Edith was already in the car when Shirley told her to not come. Don't tell Shirley that, though."

"I won't. Although if things had gone a different way, having Edith here would have been a godsend. Especially this weekend. So thank her for me." Rarity reached down and laid her hand on the part of the sidewalk that was in the sun. "I think you can walk, Killer. Just let me know if you need to be picked up."

Jonathon laughed as she started after the other women and the wagon. "Does he tell you everything he needs?"

"Of course he does. You just have to pay attention." Rarity waved and hurried to catch up. They'd need to open right after they got these books out. Several town residents had asked about books that Rarity hadn't had on hand yesterday, or had run out of, so she hoped they either had gone into the store or would come back today. This weekend might just refill her emergency fund and leave money over for Rarity to be able to send some to her personal emergency fund too.

When she caught up, Darby was telling Katie about her run-ins with Mason Pike. She looked up at Rarity as she talked. "Look, I know I should have said something sooner. Next time I will. I thought I could handle it. I don't understand why Marc keeps showing up, though. He sent me flowers, thanking me for handling him during the book signing. He's too nice for his own good. Some girls would take advantage of that goodwill."

Katie snorted and met Rarity's gaze. "You need to tell her because she's not getting it."

"I'm just the boss. I probably shouldn't even know about this." Rarity smiled back at Katie. "Okay, if you're too chicken, I'll say it."

She stopped walking and put her hands on Darby's shoulders. "Dear, innocent Darby. Marc Billings sent you flowers, not only to thank you, but because he's interested in dating you. Like for real."

Rarity had to use that phrasing on the end since Darby loved saying it. Besides, it might get the point across.

"He likes me. Like, likes me?" Darby looked between Rarity and Katie. They stood at the corner, waiting for the light to change. People were piling up behind them and the chatter was loud.

When the other two nodded, Darby sighed. "Great, one more guy who I can't be with wants my attention. Can I just tell the universe enough all ready? She keeps throwing all these guys at me, even though I want to find the one all on my own."

"The answer will come, grasshopper, when you least expect it," Rarity said in her best mystical voice. "Ohhh, maybe we should have Madame Zelda do a reading for you. Then you can pick logically between all the suitors."

"Let's not." Darby nodded to the light since it had changed. As she stepped out onto the street, a black truck flew through the intersection and the red light.

Rarity saw the truck coming and grabbed Darby's shirt, stopping her forward movement. Her heart pounded as she watched the truck go through the space where Darby would have been. She kept holding on and tried to slow her breathing.

People crowded past them, and Rarity unfroze enough to reach down to pick up Killer so he didn't get mixed up in the crowd. When they were gone, she turned back to Darby, who looked like she was still in shock. "You all right?"

Darby shook her head. "Because you saved me. What is up with people today? And look, now we missed the walk light."

"We can wait for another light. I just want to make sure you're okay." Rarity looked up and saw the red-light camera on the light pole. She was going to call Drew and make sure the driver of the black truck had a really bad day. Someone needed to besides her and her staff.

At the tent, she let Katie and Darby set up the new books and used Killer as an excuse to leave the tent. As soon as she was outside of earshot, she called Drew.

"I told you ten. Not eight fifteen," he said.

"I'm not calling about that." She heard a dog barking in the background and knew he must be at home. Jonathon and Edith had recently adopted the dog from the humane society where Jonathon had just started volunteering. "I didn't know Jonathon brought Romeo. He can bring him to the bookstore while he's there, I must have told him that."

"My father has been a little distracted. Besides, he thought Mom was coming, but then Shirley shut her down. Why are you calling me then?"

Rarity told him about the speeding black truck that ran the red light. "I know your crew is running thin this weekend, but that guy's going to kill someone. He would've killed Darby if I hadn't stopped her from stepping off the curb. He was way too close to the sidewalk too, now that I think about it."

Drew was silent for a moment, and she assumed he was writing what she'd told him down. "Rarity, you don't think he was actually trying to hit her, do you?"

After the call, Rarity was still thinking about Drew's last question when she ran into Marc Billings heading toward the start of the race. She waved at him. "I won't keep you since they need you to start the race, but thanks for sending Darby flowers. It really made her feel appreciated."

A frown came over his face. "I didn't send her flowers, but I should have, right? She's been so great helping me with this signing, I should have thought about that. Sorry, I need to run, but I'll fix my error as soon as this race is done."

Rarity watched him run off and then sighed. Killer looked up at her. "Let's get back to the tent. I think there's something going wonky around your friend, Darby. Now I'm freaking out."

The tent was busy with customers when she got back, and Rarity fell into place after tying Killer up to the leg of the table next to his bed. She didn't have a chance to pull Darby aside to ask about the flowers until a few hours later. The race had started to have winners announced as they came back from the trail ride. The local radio station was live streaming the race, and she watched Darby smile as she listened to Marc talk about the different leaders.

When the tent emptied out, she pulled Darby aside. "What made you think Marc sent the flowers? Did he sign the card?"

Darby had just restocked the kids' section and looked up at her from where she was kneeling on the ground, tucking the box back under the table. "No, it was from what he said. He thanked me for watching out for him. It's what he said when he first arrived and you told him I'd be helping. Remember? He said that he needed someone to watch over him."

Rarity did remember now, but instead of it sounding romantic like it had on Wednesday, now it had an ominous tone. "You need to tell Drew. Marc didn't send the flowers."

Rarity called Drew.

"Seriously, you need to give me some time," he groused as he answered the phone. "The autopsy ran late and I don't have the report yet."

"It's not that. It's about Darby. We think she got flowers from the stalker guy." Rarity turned away from the front as a few customers walked inside. She walked over to the back table, pretending to move around books.

"You think?" Drew asked. "Isn't it a yes or no question? Did she get flowers or not?"

"She got flowers with an unsigned card. She thought they were from Marc, but he just told me he didn't send flowers. Is there any way you can come over and talk with her? She's freaking out a bit."

"I'll be there in ten. I'm over at the winner's circle watching the racers come in. Your new friend Marc is a very entertaining moderator." He hung up the call and Rarity turned to the sales table, just as someone came up with several racing books, including Marc's.

"I never thought I'd like watching bike racing, but this was a blast. We're here for the film festival this week. We were over at your bookstore last night. What a creative way to get people to a signing. Mason is a legend in the indie horror community. I'm glad my new film isn't in his category. He can be vicious when he wants to win." The woman, dressed in linen shorts and a silk tank, handed Rarity her credit card. Her blond hair was cut in a straight bob and made her face even narrower. "You should come to my showing tonight. It's over at the Sedona Pix at six. I'm telling everyone since I probably won't get a lot of buzz from the festival organizers. It's all about the OGs like Mason at this festival, but I still wanted to come and see how the film's received. Here's a card about it. It's a love story."

Rarity handed her the credit card receipt and looked at the card. It listed the movie and the producer's name matched the one on the credit card. Miranda Vail. "*Mountain Valley Meet-Cute*? It sounds fun, Miranda. Thanks for the invite. I'll try to get over there."

"I know, everyone's busy. But you and your staff really should come. Especially after seeing Mason's movie. Mine's so much better than that one ever dreamed of being."

Katie came up to the table with a pile of books for the next customer. She picked up the card that Miranda had left and read the blurb as Rarity handled the purchase. After the customer left, she held out the business card. "I saw this woman at the movie last night. She put one of these on every seat before the movie started. She's very smart with her marketing."

"She's definitely focused on marketing. I thought the racers would be our competitive group this weekend, but it seems like the movie producers are that way too." Rarity looked at the flyer. "Maybe we should go to a few of the movies this week. It's been a little crazy around here. A movie might be fun. I'll bring it up at book club. This one will already be done, but I bet we could get some tickets for Wednesday or Thursday."

Katie was already on her phone. "There are three in the evening on Wednesday. We'd probably want the early slot, right? Should I just get ten tickets? That's the max for one order."

Rarity counted up the numbers of regulars plus Archer and Drew. Then she had to add Terrance, if Shirley went. She wondered how long Jonathon and Kathy would be in town. "Right now, I have eleven on my mental list. But if Kathy goes, Terrance probably won't, so ten should be enough. If we have more, we'll try for additional seats on Tuesday. Thanks for doing that."

"No problem. I'm going to at least two movies a day from now until next Saturday night when they announce the winners. Jared's studying movie production." Katie's face turned red.

"Jared? Who's that?" Rarity hadn't heard Katie talk about a guy, ever.

"Jared's her boyfriend," Darby said as she came up to the table. "I saw them kissing last night before the movie started."

"We might need more tickets, then." Rarity asked Katie to send her the link where she could order tickets. "I'm going to get another ten. If we decide we're not going, I'll give them away at the register Wednesday morning."

"Jared and I will definitely go. He was so excited to meet Mason Pike last night. You would have thought he was a real celebrity."

"Maybe in that world, he is." Rarity watched as Drew and Malia came into the tent. Darby needed to talk to Drew, and Rarity was starving. At least they were at a good stopping point for lunch. Customers had dwindled off after Miranda left the tent. Probably heading somewhere for lunch.

And with a break, Rarity had time to think about what Miranda had said about Mason. Were the movie festival attendees as competitive as it appeared they were? She really needed Drew to tell her if Mason's death was from natural causes.

CHAPTER 6

Drew followed her out of the tent as she took Killer for a short walk, letting Katie and Darby man the store as they finished their lunches. She didn't say much until they were near the carnival rides. "So what do you think about Darby? Is someone stalking her?"

"I hate to say yes, but it seems that way. Too many things are happening for me to overlook them. Why is it happening? I have no clue. Maybe the perpetrator feels like they have a connection with Darby. And the other men are getting in the way. She said Marc used that same phrase when they met. Were there people around?"

"Just a few hundred or so for Marc's talk about racing. I don't remember thinking one person was too close to her or Marc. Now you have me worried about her." Rarity looked back in the direction of the tent. "Maybe we should go back."

"She's fine for right now. People walk into these festival booths all the time. If someone's after her, he's going to make his move in the dark when she's alone. We need to limit that time. Make sure someone walks her home after a shift. No working a shift by herself. And can one of her friends stay with her at the house? I know she had a few over the last two nights. We need to keep that up, or she needs to stay with you if they need to go back to their lives."

"I think Malia and Holly will take care of that. Katie needs to go back to class next week. Maybe. She said her boyfriend is taking her to a bunch of these festival movies. I'll talk to Darby and Katie when we get back." She stopped to let Killer sniff a patch of grass. "So what about Mason Pike?"

"It's looking like he didn't die naturally. The tox screens aren't back, but the coroner found a needle mark on the back of his neck. If I were to guess, someone came up behind him and shot something into him. Something that worked really fast. He wasn't alone that long, was he?"

Rarity shook her head. "No, but I think the front door was open. I was sure I locked it but the deadlock wasn't thrown when I went out to meet the paramedics. Someone could have left through that door."

"Maybe he opened it. He might have been waiting for someone. I'll stop by the store this afternoon and check the security tapes. I'm glad we have Dad hanging out there. At least I know no one is messing with my evidence. And they probably didn't know you even had cameras." He grinned at her. "I'll probably have this one in the bag before your book club can even meet to talk about the murder."

"I hope that's true." As they walked back to the tent, Killer pulled on the leash again. This time, he ran to the side and came back with a leather work glove. Rarity took it from him, looking at Drew as she did. "Where did you find this?"

Drew went over and looked at the tent. "You have an opening right here. I think it was an expander for the tent booth, but someone has loosened the Velcro that kept it together." He leaned down and picked up a candy bar wrapper. He took a plastic bag out of his shirt pocket and put the wrapper inside. Then he held it out for the leather glove.

Rarity dropped it inside, and Killer barked his displeasure at losing his toy.

"Sorry, dude. It's probably nothing, but I'll get them dusted for prints. Maybe we've actually found a clue."

Rarity took a breath, inhaling the smell of the corn dogs that were being cooked a row over. "You think someone was here, watching us?"

He glanced around the site, and Rarity noticed they were out of sight for both rows of booths, at least for the people walking by. "I think someone might have been standing here, watching Darby. What has that girl gotten herself into?"

* * *

At the end of the day, Rarity went back to the bookstore with Katie and Darby. Killer rode in the wagon with some empty boxes that they'd planned to use to restock the tent for tomorrow's last festival day. As they walked, Rarity told them about what Drew had said and what they'd found. Darby was quiet.

Finally, she spoke. "You don't think that truck almost hitting me was an accident, do you?"

"Honestly, no. Is there any way this guy from Scotland is still around? Did you tell him where you were from?" Rarity hated seeing the fear in her eyes. Darby was bold and brash and not afraid of anything. Except now.

"Maybe, probably. He was American, and that's one of the reasons we hit it off. Strangers in a strange land kind of thing. I probably mentioned my grandma's passing and how I was doing this as an homage to her." She shrugged as she walked next to Katie. "You talk about yourself and your dreams on first dates. That's how you know if you click."

"Drew said they were looking into the incident there. Maybe that will give him something to go on." Rarity smiled at Darby. "You just need to keep yourself safe. No hiking by yourself, and if you see the guy, scream. If you're wrong, you'll just embarrass yourself. But you'll be alive."

"You give the worst advice, Rarity Cole," Katie said as she handed Darby a small cylinder. "Here's something that will keep you safe. Don't worry, I've got two more in my car. My folks wanted me to have protection when I moved away from home to college."

"They sent you to college with pepper spray?" Darby held it up, trying to figure out how to work it. "This is better quality than the one I have."

Katie nodded. "It was either that or a small handgun. I didn't want to be caught with one at school since they are a gun-free campus. Besides, I didn't like the idea of having one and having someone steal it. I can shoot, no problem, but what if my roommate can't? She'd just make the guy mad if she tried to shoot him."

Rarity stared at her bookseller. "I didn't realize you even knew how to shoot."

"Back home in Kentucky, we learn early. Mostly for hunting and protection from bears. I never shot at anything but targets, but I was better than my older brother. His hand shakes when he shoots," she said as they arrived at the bookstore. "Don't get me wrong, my folks are caring people. They just wanted me and my sisters to be able to protect ourselves. It's a mean world out there."

As Katie went into the bookstore with the wagon and Killer, Darby and Rarity shared a shocked look, then smiled. "You learn something new every day," Rarity said as she held the door for Darby.

"I know who I want to invite to my police-mandated sleepovers now," Darby joked as they entered the bookstore and saw the group watching them.

"Now what," Rarity said as she shut the door behind them.

"So Drew was here," Jonathon started. "But there was a problem."

"Someone shut off the security cameras about noon on Friday. So there was no way to know who came in." Shirley finished his sentence. He stared at her. "What? You don't even work here. This is something I should tell her, not you."

Jonathon nodded then added, "Fair enough, but I can tell you that he's going to check out all the surrounding shops to see if he can see who might have walked out of the bookstore after attacking Mason."

"And it also means that my date for tonight has been canceled," Sam added to Jonathon's report. "So who wants to go to a screening or two with me tonight?"

Rarity raised her hand. "I'll go. Archer is busy with Jack getting ready for tours starting Sunday afternoon when the festival ends."

Darby glanced at Katie. "Are you staying over?"

"Sure, but Jared wants to go to all three screenings tonight. You can come too," Katie offered.

"No thanks. I hate being the third wheel." Darby took out her phone and nodded. "Besides, it looks like I have plans. Malia's coming over now and we're ordering in pizza and having a pool party. Holly will be there until she has to go to work, but the rest of you are invited. I'll set up a schedule for my babysitting while they're at the house. If there are any gaps, I'll let Rarity know."

"You're taking this well," Rarity observed as Darby texted Malia back.

"I'm just glad that Drew believes me. I didn't feel that way when I reported Roger, the guy I dated briefly in Scotland." She looked around the group. "Who's walking me home and staying there until Malia arrives? Katie has to go meet up with her movie man."

Jonathon stood. "If we're done here, I can walk you home. Rarity? Do you need to be walked home too?"

"Sam can walk with me to drop off Killer and then we'll walk to the theater. No one's after me, so don't worry."

Jonathon pulled her into a hug. "I worry about all of you. Especially when I'm home with Edith. You all need to move to Tucson so I can keep better track of you."

"Okay, Dad. Stop hovering," Shirley teased. "I'll walk with the girls since I'm heading to Terrance's. He's making me dinner."

With the night's plans made, they talked about the morning and who would be where. Jonathon and Shirley would be in the store. And Katie, Darby, and Rarity would return to the booth with a few more books. Then at eleven, Shirley would close the store and she and Jonathon would arrive at the booth to help tear it down and move the unsold books back to the store.

"I'm thinking about closing the store on Monday. You all deserve a day off." Rarity leaned her head back. "I know I need one."

"If you don't mind, I'd like to open for a few hours. Kathy will be leaving to go back home, and I hate saying goodbye to that girl. She acts like she'll never see me again." Shirley held up her hand. "I don't need a second."

"But I need to write, so if you don't mind, I'll meet you here." Jonathon stood. "Are you ready, Darby? I have a dog to feed."

"You know you can bring him here," Rarity mentioned as they were walking out the door.

"Romeo likes Drew's couch too much. All he wants to do is watch movies and take walks with me. Drew walks too fast for him. I swear, I adopted a couch potato, not a dog. He doesn't even play fetch."

Rarity walked around the store, checking the back door, rechecking the security system, and even walking through the bathrooms. When she came out, Sam and Shirley were waiting at the door.

"Everything okay?" Sam asked as she held Killer's leash.

"I hate the fact that someone was in the store and knew enough about it to find the security system and know how to turn it off," Rarity admitted. "It makes me feel vulnerable. Even though I wasn't the one working the store the last three days. I worry."

"Worry seems to be the word of the day. Kathy's worried about her dad and me. Drew's worried about Darby. Jonathon's worried about everyone." Shirley stepped outside and waited for Rarity to lock the door. And then smiled when Rarity double-checked the lock before dropping her keys in her pocket. "And you're worried about your staff and the bookstore. Matthew 6:34 says, 'Therefore do not worry about tomorrow, for tomorrow will worry about itself. Each day has enough trouble of its own.'"

"Thank you, Pastor Shirley," Sam teased.

"But it's true. It's been one of my favorite verses since I was a young mother. I worried so much about the kids and George. Now, years later, I could still be worrying, but what good would it do? All I can do is trust that everything will work out the way it's supposed to." Shirley stepped between Sam and Rarity, linking arms. "Now, let's talk about when those men of yours are going to pop the question. Have you been leaving hints?"

There was only one thing that Rarity wanted to talk about less than the current upheaval in Sedona, and that was if or when she and Archer were getting married. Shirley must have brought it up at least once a month. "You have to have a note on your planner reminding you to ask that every so often."

"Not really. It's just on my mind a lot. Especially when I see you all together. You're both such cute couples. I need replacement grandchildren nearby so I can get my fix without flying out to Kathy's."

Sam changed the subject without even mentioning Drew and her relationship, and the three were laughing by the time they reached Terrance's house. They said good night to Shirley and headed to Rarity's house next door. Inside the house, Sam fell on the couch. She started to giggle. "I've met Romeo, and Jonathon's exactly right on his description. The dog is lazy."

"We use the term 'energy challenged' in this house." Rarity rubbed Killer's head. "I bet you're going to go right to sleep. You won't miss me at all."

The look Killer gave her told her she was way off the mark. But he walked over and lay down on his bed anyway.

"Do you need to change?" Sam asked, looking at her watch. "The first movie starts at six."

"I'm going to change my shirt and shoes and grab a jacket. It might be cold walking home or in the theater. They turn the air up too high. Do you want to borrow one?" Rarity headed to the bedroom. "I hate that Darby's having issues here in Sedona. I don't want her to sell the house and move."

"You just don't want to lose a bookseller," Sam called back from the living room.

Rarity grabbed a nicer shirt from her closet and changed, slipping into some boots that she wore out a lot. They were comfortable and looked nice. "Not totally true. Did you hear her talking about opening a bed-and-breakfast with Malia and Holly?"

"I give it three years, maybe five before one of them gets serious and moves in with some guy. Or Darby moves a guy in." Sam stood as Rarity came out of the bedroom. "They're all at that age where they're probably going to be getting married soon."

Rarity shook her head. "You've been hanging around Shirley too much. We're ten years older than those three and we're not married."

"Life happens." Sam caught the jacket Rarity threw her way. "Hey, I've been looking for this."

"You left it here last month." Rarity grabbed her keys and tote. "Ready to go see a movie?"

"I think we're all going to be tired of movies by the time this festival is over," Sam said as she put on the jacket. "And going back to the marriage thing, you and I are both in relationships. Maybe we should just be thankful for that and not label it."

"I'm sure Jonathon and Edith would love to hear you say that." Rarity checked Killer's dry food and water dishes. "I'll be home soon."

"After three hours of bad movies. You're lucky you get to stay home, Killer." Sam glanced over at the sleeping dog. "Should we turn on the television?"

"Probably." Rarity found a channel that had light movies and turned down the volume. "Let's go have some fun."

After two really bad movies including the one the woman, Miranda, had talked about at the booth, Rarity and Sam were at the bar in the lobby, getting a drink. "Do we want to try number three or give up?"

"In for a penny," Sam said. "Besides, they gave me a voting ticket for tonight. I just hope I can give this one a higher rating than the other two. There's Darby. I thought she was heading home?"

"I did too." Rarity paid for the drinks, then looked around the crowded lobby. "Where did she go? I want to make sure she has someone to walk her home."

"You're hovering and she's not even your kid," Sam pointed out. "Just text her and ask if she wants to walk home with us."

"Good idea." Rarity sent Darby a text.

Instead of a returned text, Darby called her. "What are you talking about?"

"I just saw you at the movie theater. I thought you were staying home, but since you're out, do you want Sam and me to walk you home after this last movie? Just because of all that's going on."

"Rarity, I still don't know what you're talking about. I am home. Malia and Holly are here too. Maybe you saw Katie?"

Rarity told her she must have been mistaken, then hung up. She looked at Sam. "That was Darby, right?"

"I thought so, why?"

"She's at her house with Malia and Holly. Did we just see a look-alike?"

CHAPTER 7

The next morning, they were at the bookstore, when Rarity told everyone about the look-alike. "I swear, Darby, she looked just like you but more dressed up."

"So my doppelganger has better fashion sense? Nice." Darby took a bite of the scone in front of her. "She probably runs every morning and only eats green leafy vegetables too."

Rarity chuckled as the box of scones made its way around the table. "I don't know about that, but she did look like you."

"They say that there are exact replicas of each person in the world. The reason you never see them is they live so far away from each other. But with modern travel, finding your nongenetic twin is more likely to happen. It's like how there are only nine story plots in the world. We just keep putting our own spin on the old plots," Jonathon said as he reached for a second scone.

"Maybe your stalker is going after that girl and not you?" Katie had finished boxing up the new books to bring over to the booth. "Do we want these in the wagon again?"

"Sure." Rarity leaned back into her chair. "We've only got until noon today, and then everyone will be off the clock until Tuesday."

"Except me," Shirley added.

Rarity sipped her coffee. "Right, except Shirley who begged me for permission to open the store for a few hours tomorrow."

"What time are you opening?" Jonathon opened his notebook, pen in hand.

"You don't have to come," Shirley protested. "I think I told you that before."

"I need writing time. I've been busy with bookstore stuff since I got here. Don't send me away. I never get anything done with Romeo around. All he wants from me is cuddles and treats." Jonathon pleaded with Shirley, holding his hands together in a symbolic prayer gesture.

"Fine, you can come, but no stocking books. I want to see your word count when we're done," Shirley warned, a smile on her face.

"I brought my laptop today, just in case we're slow." He turned to Rarity. "I take it that the sleuthing club is taking over on Tuesday night?"

"That's the plan. I've already called the other two members and told them we'd be cutting the book discussion time short. And that we might do the same the next week."

"I really enjoyed this week's book," Katie said then slapped her hand over her mouth. "I know, keep it for book club."

"And with that, let's get our day going. Darby number one? You and Katie are with me." Rarity stood and went to get Killer from his daybed by the fireplace.

"Not funny." Darby finished her scone before she stood.

Katie grinned and hugged her friend. "You'll always be Darby number one in my book."

"Still not funny, guys," Darby said as she followed Rarity out the door.

* * *

Drew came into the booth around ten. Rarity had asked Sam to fill him in on the woman they'd seen the night before. Rarity used the excuse to walk Killer, and they took the conversation outside, again.

When they were far enough from the tent, Drew paused in a narrow area between the rows of tents. "I showed a picture of Darby to the organizers of the bike race and the film festival. The bike race people identified her as working at the bookstore."

"So Darby number one." Rarity told him what they'd been calling their Darby.

"I bet she loves that, not." He chuckled as he scanned the crowd over Rarity's head as they talked. "Anyway, so no duplicate. But the film festival people all identified her as Talia Brooks. She has a movie in contention for best short film under two hours. She's from Riverside, California, near Los Angeles. So yes, our Darby has a double. And you're wondering if these attacks on Darby could be misplaced?"

"But how would he know number one's address and phone number? If you're stalking someone, wouldn't he know she lives in California?" Rarity thought knowing this explained the Darby sighting last night, but not the attacks. "I still think it's the Scotland ex-boyfriend."

"She only dated him a few times. I don't think she'd like hearing him called her ex," Drew said, reaching down to pull Killer out of the way of the passing crowd. "The plate on the black truck is from California. We're running it now."

"Aren't you sensitive?" Rarity shortened Killer's leash. "So the truck could have just been a bad driver? Part of the film festival group?"

"That's the theory. Besides, hanging around Sam will do that to a person." He smiled at her. "Anyway, that's my news. There is a Darby doppelganger in town."

Rarity and Drew walked back to the tent, and then he left. Rarity was glad the weekend festival in the park was almost over. Keeping Darby in her line of sight all the time was harder here than at the store. She needed to make sure that Darby wasn't going to be alone next week. If they got through the film festival, maybe the stalker would realize he had the wrong person and head back to California with the rest of the festivalgoers.

Unless he truly was after Darby number one.

Tuesday night, she'd introduce a Keep Darby Safe campaign at the book club meeting. Then they could get down and dirty in the who killed Mason Pike investigation. Having two projects might strain their resources, but they had Jonathon in town until the murder was solved. Jonathon and Romeo.

And Jonathon still hadn't brought his dog to the bookstore. She needed to talk to him about that.

Archer came into the tent at the end of the festival. "Do you want to load the books in my bus? It's just outside the park in the vendors' parking lot. Jack's coming over as soon as he takes the last load for our booth over."

Killer came out from under the table and pulled on his leash, trying to get to Archer. Laughing, Rarity unclipped his leash, letting him run to one of his favorite humans. "Of course I do. Even if we sold out, there are still the tables to get back. Maybe I need to get a bookstore van just in case I lose my boyfriend."

He shrugged. "As long as there isn't an active search going for a new one, I'm fine with this being a permanent gig. Picking up your booth remains, that is."

"Almost a nice save, dude." Katie stood from packing up the picture books. "I thought you were going down on one knee."

"Believe me, I've got more swagger than to do it at the end of a festival in an empty booth in front of you all. Especially when we're all tired and hungry. She might say no." Archer grabbed the box and put it on the dolly he'd brought in. He winked at Rarity. Then he stacked three more and headed out the door. "Just wait until you see the fireworks."

Darby and Katie looked at each other, then at Rarity. "He's kidding, right? Or do you have something to tell us?"

"He's messing with you. No plans have been made." She put Killer into the wagon along with the register and stuff from the table they'd used as the point of sale. "Now let's get these tables cleared off before Jack shows up."

"Too late," he called as he came into the tent. "Wow, Archer wasn't kidding. You guys are slow at packing."

"We had a lot more stuff in our tent than you did," Darby countered.

With Jack's help, it didn't take them long to finish shutting the booth down. Rarity's bookshop was the first stop, and they got the boxes and tables unloaded and into the store in record time.

Shirley glanced around at the book boxes. "And this is why you need me here tomorrow. I'll get the books all returned to their shelves before I go home on Monday. We had quite a bit of walk-in traffic this morning. We sold out of the Pike book. They're doing a memorial screening of his new film tomorrow night. It was supposed to be a dark night where people could regroup, but now they have this fundraiser for his charity at the theater. I bought tickets for the group."

"Put an invoice in and I'll reimburse you." Rarity met Archer's gaze. "We'll have to change our date night plans."

"It's still dinner and a movie, just not the movie I'd planned." Archer put his arm around her and kissed her neck. "I've got to go. Jack has a date."

When Archer was out the door, Jonathon came over, his laptop bag packed. "I'm ready to go when you are."

It didn't matter how many times she'd explained to the men in her life that she didn't need a chaperone to find her way home, when something happened, like Pike's murder, she apparently became unable to walk alone. Now, she just accepted it. They weren't going to change anyway. "Give me a couple of minutes to tie everything up. Darby? You have people with you tonight?"

"Me, it's me." Katie raised her hand. "I'm staying over one more night. Then Malia and Holly are taking over Operation Darby Number One."

"To be clear, I hate that name," Darby added.

Katie giggled. "We know. That's why we called it that."

"Be careful, I'll banish you from the pool if you don't be nice." Darby grabbed her backpack. "Anyway, I'm staying home today. We're doing fajitas for dinner if you want to come by."

"Kathy's taking me for dinner since she's leaving tomorrow. She wants to talk about her father and the future. She's worried I'm going to be broke and will have to live with her." Shirley smiled as she picked up her purse. "She thinks that's why I work."

"It's not, right? I could increase your pay rate and hours, if you need them." Rarity hoped she hadn't been underpaying Shirley. Especially since she did so many book clubs and now author visits. She was essential.

"I'm going broke too," Katie said as she and Darby raised their hands. "If Shirley doesn't want the pay raise, split it between us."

"You two are fine," Rarity said with a laugh as Shirley shook her head.

"I'm fine as well, dear. The reason I work and why I'm going to school now is to keep my mind busy and to be around people who aren't all my age. Being here keeps me young. We're doing a race car book at the Mommy and Me class on Wednesday. I couldn't find a bike race picture book. They need to fix that."

"I'll put in a request with the publishers," Rarity teased. "Okay, so everyone has plans this afternoon. I don't want anyone to be alone. Archer and I are going to take full advantage of the film festival. I hear there might be some big actors in town for the screenings today."

"Take pictures if it's anyone I might know," Katie said, clearly feeling like she was missing out on the festival. "I just don't think I could deal with another movie that was as bad as the ones yesterday. Even Friday's spider picture was a dud. I don't know how this guy got to be so famous."

As Rarity and Jonathon walked home, she wondered about Katie's last question. "Has Drew done any research into Mason Pike?"

"No warrants, no prior convictions. He and his ex-wife had a rather public and contentious divorce a few years ago. She accused him of cheating; he accused her. They both were siphoning money from the joint account. I think he was better at hiding it. Still, she got a few million over the prenup she'd signed, but not as much as she wanted." Jonathon rattled off Mason's history from memory. "He'd been rumored to be in a couple of relationships lately. But no one has come forward, claiming to be next of kin or a new wife. He has a brother who's probably going to inherit."

"So there is money? In bad films?" Rarity paused for Killer to relieve himself on a tree.

Jonathon chuckled. "Bad is in the eye of the beholder, I guess. Just like beauty. Do you have a theory?"

"Honestly, no. I've been so worried about Darby that I haven't even thought of what happened to Mason." Rarity glanced over at Jonathon. "Sam thinks I baby the staff too much."

"You're a good boss who makes friends out of her staff. Don't listen to Sam. She likes a smaller group of people around her. You're more of a Pied Piper kind of person. You take in everyone." Jonathon nodded at Terrance as they passed his porch. He was sitting outside, reading. "You've never met a stranger."

After she got inside, she decided to take advantage of the free time she had until Archer came to pick her up to swim. She needed to work out some of the kinks in her body as well as her mind. Had Jonathon been trying to tell her that she was too trusting? She'd done that with Kevin. Never questioning his call when he said he had to work late. She didn't know if he'd cheated on her, but he'd been quick to dump her when she didn't meet his definition of what a fiancée should look and act like.

She trusted Archer. And Sam. And Drew. And the people who worked for her. And Jonathon, who might as well work for her, as much time as he spent in her bookstore. And Edith. The list went on from there. Drew's sister. Terrance. She did have a large group of friends and acquaintances. She liked it that way. And Jonathon was right. Sam took longer for a person to become part of her inner circle. A place that Rarity had held since college. Thinking about her friends got her thinking about Mason and who had been in his circle. She got out of the pool after finishing her laps and took her computer as well as a pen and notebook from the counter. Sitting out on the deck with a bottle of water, she let herself drip dry as she did some research on Mason Pike.

His memorial fundraiser was one of the first things she found online. The event was actually being held on Wednesday, not Monday. Shirley had been wrong. As she read about the event, she found that the proceeds were going to an orphanage in Los Angeles that worked with kids who had been in the foster care system for over three years. Had Mason been a foster care kid himself? Or known one? A close friend?

She kept looking. Scrolling through his Facebook page, it appeared it was handled by a team, not Mason. It didn't feel personal. The last post was an announcement of his book signing and the movie at the Next Chapter.

She scrolled through the comments on the page.

"Wonderful talk. Great movie, but a little cheesy. And finally, did anyone hear what happened to Mason? He missed the next event where he was supposed to talk."

No mention of his death, just comments about how they hoped everything was fine, and looking forward to the screening of the new movie. Was Drew holding off on announcing the fact he'd been murdered for some reason?

She was about to text him when she heard Archer's Jeep pull into the driveway. She hurried inside, then opened the door for him, leaving her laptop on the table. "Hey, I got behind. Come on in and I'll be ready in a minute."

"No hurry." Archer followed her inside, then swept Killer up into his arms. "I've been missing me some Killer time. Does he need to be fed?"

"Yes, if you wouldn't mind. I wish we could take him, but he's probably going to sleep until Tuesday. Festivals do him in," Rarity said as she headed to the bedroom to change.

When she came out in a sundress, tennis shoes, and a sweater around her shoulders, Archer whistled. "Date night here we come."

"I'm enjoying this film festival. All the others I have to have a booth in the park to help sales and bring in customers. This one, except for the Friday night event that Shirley brought to our door, is more of a slow burn. We have books about all the film topics, history, memoirs, and the making of…but mostly this week, all I have to do is run the store. In one location."

"Oh, so the Tuesday night group isn't doing its regular sleuthing around Mason Pike's death? I thought for sure you'd at least be looking into Darby's stalker." Archer set Killer down on the floor.

"Don't get crazy on me, of course, there's that. I just don't have to have a booth at the park this week." She walked over and opened the slider. "Do you need to go potty?"

"I'm good." Archer grinned. "But Killer might need to. He ate all the food I gave him."

"You think you're funny, don't you?" Rarity knew she was smiling as Killer hurried out the door. "So do you know why Drew hasn't made an announcement about Mason's death? Don't you think it's odd?"

"Maybe he's waiting to contact next of kin. Besides, the film festival people know since they are doing the memorial." Archer pointed to the door. "Killer wants back inside."

"Of course he does. He's not much of an outdoor dog, especially when it's hot." She opened the door, then shut it again, locking the door as she shut the blinds. "I guess that could be it. Mason's Facebook page hasn't even updated yet."

"Wouldn't he be the one to update it, and, well, he's unable?" Archer waited for her at the front door, his keys in his hand. He watched as she walked around the kitchen island. "I already filled his water."

"It looks like he has people who do that. Anway, I was going to give Killer a treat." She nodded to the television. "You can just turn that on. It should be at the right channel and volume since he watched it last."

Archer rolled his eyes but followed her directions. "You realize that dog is spoiled rotten."

"He had a bad childhood, losing Martha like that. I just want him to be happy." She stepped outside, locking the door behind her.

"Puppyhood, not childhood. He's a dog."

Rarity shook her finger at Archer, then whispered, "Don't let him hear you say that."

CHAPTER 8

Several people at the film screenings greeted her and Archer. The community was out in force, except she didn't see Drew and Sam. Jonathon was missing from the event as well. She hoped Shirley hadn't bought too many tickets for the Wednesday event. She rolled her shoulders. It was a business expense and the proceeds went to charity, so why was she worrying?

As they settled into their seats, Archer took Rarity's hand. "You okay?"

"Just thinking. Pike's death and Darby's stalker have me a little rattled. I've been able to not think about either much since this weekend was so crazy busy. But now we've slowed down, and…"

"You're letting the implications in. Look, Pike wasn't a nice guy. His one interaction with your staff taught us that. And, it tells us something about the guy. He was a taker. And if that's true, there's probably a line of suspects for Drew to look at. None of them are your staff members. As far as Darby is concerned, the girl's smart. She's dealt with this before. She's not going to put herself in harm's way."

"Why is it happening again? She deals with this jerk in Scotland and now she has to deal with one here? What is it about our Darby that she collects these types?"

"She's kind and doesn't like to hurt other people's feelings. She also sees the good in everyone, even though some people don't deserve that kind of allowance." Archer kissed her on the cheek. "I could go on, but the movie's starting."

Archer was right, of course. It felt like the people who were kind and considerate and didn't deserve to be treated badly tended to get the bad end of the stick. Darby was one other thing. She was resourceful. She'd be fine. And the sleuthing club would find out who was messing with her along with who killed Mason. They were just that skilled in investigations, even though it wasn't their job. Well, except for Jonathon. And it wasn't his job anymore. The club was insightful and curious, which made them perfect for finding out why some things happened.

She settled into her seat and started watching the movie. This one looked like it might be really good.

* * *

Monday flew by with a long list of errands and chores. She stopped by the bookstore to see if Shirley was okay and was surprised to find Kathy there with her. As Rarity left, Kathy pulled her aside.

"I just wanted you to know that they've put my dad on hospice. I'm going home to get some things in order, and then I'll be back for the duration. Mom, well, she's dealing with it like she deals with any problem. She works. And bakes. And ignores it. But there's going to be a time when she falls apart. If I'm not here when it happens, will you look after her and call me?" Kathy pressed a business card into Rarity's hand. "I've asked her to think about selling the house and moving closer to me, but I doubt that's going to happen. She has a life here. A life that you're a big part of, so I just wanted you to have my number. Just in case."

"I'm so sorry about this. Shirley mentioned it to me this weekend." Rarity was surprised when tears started falling and Kathy hugged her. When Kathy pulled herself together, Rarity dug into her purse and took out a small package of tissues and her own business card. "This one has the shop's number and my personal number. Call if you need something or you think someone should check on Shirley. She has a lot of friends here. Not just me."

"Thanks." Kathy took the card. "I thought people who complained about being sandwiched between their folks and the kids were just whining. Now I know their pain. Mom's going to hate having me here, but I'm going to try to stay out of her way and ignore Terrance as much as possible."

"He's a good man." Rarity squeezed Kathy's arm. "And they're just friends."

Kathy snorted. "Believe me, I've seen the way he looks at her like a lost puppy. They are not just friends. He's in love with her. I've made my peace with that. Dad doesn't even know me or Mom. He thinks I'm some nice volunteer. Or he did before this week. Now, he's pretty much out of it. I can just sit with my dad, and I'll do the work of remembering what a great father he was and how lucky I was to have an amazing family. My brother, on the other hand, is ignoring the whole thing."

Rarity didn't know what to say. This was the most Kathy had ever talked to her. Especially about her family.

"Sorry to dump on you." Kathy tucked Rarity's card into her pocket. "I just wanted you to know everything, just in case Mom needs you. Thanks for being her friend."

"I'm the lucky one," Rarity said, but then Kathy ducked into the bookstore. Rarity headed back to her car. She needed to get home and put away the groceries. But as she did, she thought about Shirley.

Tuesday morning, Rarity was at the store by nine. She'd swum, ate breakfast, and packed a bag for Killer to come to work with her. She didn't like leaving him alone for so many hours. And even though she'd given away to employees the running of the other book clubs, this one was special. She'd probably always be part of the club.

She was deep into making sure the new book order was started since they'd almost cleaned themselves out of kids' books at the festival when the door opened and Katie and Darby came in together. Darby was on the schedule, but Katie wasn't. "What are you doing here?"

"I came to drop off my charge." Katie lifted Darby's hand and dropped it onto Rarity's arm. "Mission completed. Now, I'm heading back to school. I won't be at the Tuesday night book club this week. I will see you on Wednesday for the memorial, but I'm not on the schedule until Saturday. It's Middle Grade Book Club weekend. So I'm making up some sort of chemistry experiment to go with the discussion. Don't worry, we won't blow the shop up."

"I told her to do a lava volcano. Those are cool." Darby removed her hand from Rarity's arm. "When do you think Drew will let me off house arrest? I'm getting a little tired of being treated like a football, passed from one friend to another."

Katie paused on her way out the door. "Not before next weekend. You said I could stay with you and use that pool from Friday to Tuesday morning when I have to go back to my studio apartment in town."

"I don't have to be in danger for you to stay with me," Darby groused. "You can stay any weekend."

"Yeah, but this way, I don't feel guilty." Katie waved as she left.

"Where do you want me? And I was serious about the Drew question. Any clue?" Darby came out of the back room with a cup filled with coffee.

"Maybe having a cruiser by your house for the last few days has scared him off? No random flower deliveries or break-ins?" Rarity looked up from the computer and focused on the young woman in front of her.

Darby stared back, defiantly. She was the first one to blink and held up her left hand. "Okay, fine, I guess you don't know either. As far as the house is concerned, I swear, it's been quiet. Well, besides having people all over the house. Who knew that three women could make such a ruckus. And we've got a solid plan for the bed-and-breakfast."

Darby told her about the plans as she restocked the bookstore from books in the back. She finished the last box as the door opened and Jonathon came inside, with a dog on a leash. "Hey, we have another shop dog."

Killer barked once to greet the newcomer, did three circles on his bed, then crashed again.

"See that, Romeo, that's what you're supposed to do. At least recognize that there's a new person in the room." Jonathon dropped his laptop case on the table, then tied Romeo's leash to a chair. "Tell me you have coffee."

"Of course, what are we, pagans?" Rarity waited for him to come back and then asked, "So what's going on with you?"

"Nothing. Edith called late last night to talk about Savannah. I guess she's keeping her mom up at nights because she's teething. Edith's staying over there for a few days to help out. Another reason I'm glad I'm here. I love that little squirt, but her howl can break eardrums." He sipped his coffee. "Then I have Drew up and pacing all night. Doesn't anyone sleep a full night anymore?"

"What's got Drew pacing?" Rarity asked. Darby was over on the other side of the bookstore, so maybe she wouldn't overhear.

"He's worried about that one." Jonathon nodded toward where Darby was working. "As well as trying to figure out if Mason dying here was just an easy place to kill him. He's been going over camera film from your neighbors to see who might have turned off your system. But it's a lot."

"Maybe the group will come up with some ideas tonight." Rarity glanced at her watch. "You're just in time for lunch. You and Darby figure out what you want and I'll go get it. Now that there's someone here to be with her."

"You seriously don't think I can't be alone for the time it would take you to walk to the Garnet?" Darby asked from behind Rarity.

"You weren't supposed to hear that," Rarity admitted. "Besides, if Jonathon hadn't come, I would have just had lunch delivered."

Shirley showed up at five with a casserole and brownies for the club meeting later. "I figured you all might be hungry before we started the meeting. You can't live on restaurant food forever."

"I beg to differ. I lived on restaurant food for three months before Edith moved to New York with me. The ladies at the diner started thinking I was making up the little woman and just wore a wedding ring to keep people from bothering me." Jonathon closed his laptop. "But now, I appreciate a home-cooked meal when I'm away from Edith. My wife is an amazing cook. I would have married her just for that skill, except I fell in love with her."

"Good save." Rarity smiled as she watched Romeo stand, stretch, and then sniff toward the casserole dish. "We probably better get that into the back room before he jumps."

"I'm taking him out for a stroll. Do you want me to take Killer too?" Jonathon unwrapped the leash and took the one Rarity handed him. "Don't eat all the casserole without me."

"I don't think that's possible," Rarity said, knowing Shirley's propensity for baking more than she could eat on her own.

As she finished up the order that they'd been adding to all day, she heard the door open. "That was fast. I guess it's hot out there."

"It's really hot out there, but I don't think I'm the one you thought came inside," a woman's voice answered. "I'm Talia Brooks and I'm looking for a Darby Doyle?"

Rarity looked up, and it was Darby's double. The one they'd seen the other night. "Hold on a second. She's in the back. Darby? Can you come out?"

Darby hurried out, a brownie in her mouth. She asked around it, "Do you need help?"

She froze as she saw the woman in front of her. She took the brownie out of her mouth and wiped the back of her hand over her mouth. "I knew they said you looked like me, but wow. Besides the clothes, you look just like me."

"Or what you might look like in a few years. I believe I'm a little older than you are." Talia walked up and pushed Darby's red hair away from her eyes. "Just as I suspected, no crow's-feet. So, you do exist. Friends saw you the other night with Mason here at the signing. They all thought it was me. Especially since he and I, well, we were an item years ago."

"He said I reminded him of someone, but he didn't say much more about that." Darby looked shocked. "They told me that you're in the movie business and live in California?"

"Yes, guilty on both counts. I've lost touch with most of my family, but I haven't heard of anyone living out here in Arizona. Most of my distant family lives in Boston, if they aren't in the old country. What about you? Do you have a lot of family here?"

Darby shook her head. "Just my grandmother, but she's gone."

Talia's phone rang. "Sorry, I need to get this."

She turned away, taking a few steps toward the door.

"So, this is weird," Rarity said, smiling at Darby.

"You're telling me. I know you guys said she looked like me, but this is like looking in the mirror. Except the clothes. She has upscale threads. Maybe she'll send me some of her castoffs. Movie people don't wear the same thing twice, isn't that what they say?" Darby looked hopeful.

"I think that's actresses, but we don't know what she does yet." Rarity nodded toward the approaching Talia to let Darby know she was coming back.

"Sorry, things are going bad around the memorial. The other producers don't want to use the new movie for his send-off. They want to use the spider one again. I guess they think they can make more money off the other one in an LA release." Talia rolled her eyes. "You're never hot until you're dead. Mason should have faked his death years ago. They would have loved his last picture."

Rarity swallowed. For the second time in as many days, she was left without a response.

Obviously seeing her discomfort, Talia laughed. "Sorry, I'm just upset. I'll be more appropriate the next time we chat. Darby? It was so nice to meet you. Maybe we can have dinner on Thursday or before I leave town? I'd like to explore our roots. Maybe we're related distantly. Wouldn't that be a surprise."

Darby made arrangements to meet Talia at the Garnet on Thursday night, and then the woman left the store.

Jonathon came in a few minutes later. "Did you let Darby leave without a second? Or did she sneak out? I wouldn't put it past her."

"Hey, I'm right here, okay?" Darby came out of the back room. "Shirley says the casserole's ready. Do you want me to put a 'Closed' sign up?"

"You go eat and I'll get a plate and come out here." Rarity nodded toward Jonathon. "And I can tell him about our visitor."

"Sounds good." Darby disappeared back into the room.

Rarity looked at Jonathon. "Darby's doppelganger was just here." She explained Talia's stop and how she'd heard about Darby. "So she decided to stop in and meet her."

"Weird. They could be twins. Or mother and daughter," Jonathon muttered as he unclicked Killer's leash and tied Romeo up to the chair again.

"You can leave him untied," Rarity said. "He should be okay."

"There's no way I'm letting him go today. Maybe tomorrow when I bring him back. He gets spooked in new places. He almost ran off at Drew's. Edith would have killed me. She loves the mutt."

CHAPTER 9

The book club started right at seven. They spent thirty minutes talking about *What Happened to the Bennetts?*, chose the books for next month, and then took a break. The other two members, Deb and Ginny, bought next month's books, grabbed a brownie, then took off, wishing the rest of the group good hunting.

At first, Rarity worried that the sleuthing part of the book club would drive away the readers who just wanted to talk about books. But they'd hit a nice flow between talking about the books they'd read and then switching into investigative mode.

Jonathon was already standing by the whiteboard, setting up the discussion points. Rarity noticed he'd divided the board into two sections. One for Darby's stalker and the other for Mason's murder. She trusted the process, but every time they set up the process to look into the most recent crime in town, she wondered if they were overstepping. Maybe Drew and his peers were tired of them coming up with off-the-wall solutions. Maybe this time, they wouldn't see the killer until he struck again.

"Stop thinking so loud," Jonathon said as he set the pen down. "You're screaming over here."

"I was just…" She paused, wondering what to say. Especially to Jonathon, who was a prior member of law enforcement.

"You wonder if we're in over our heads. It's not like the idea hasn't crossed my mind. And Drew's, for that matter. But the group has brought in some good leads in the past. All I'm here for is to make sure you all don't go over the rails, chasing suspects." He studied the board. "But I have to admit, even with the amazing work we did on the last investigation, I'm worried about this one. It hits too close to home."

Rarity saw he was tapping Darby's side of the whiteboard. "I think even if it's a case of mistaken identity—and after meeting Talia, that's a logical answer—I feel like Darby's still in danger."

Rarity felt a hand on her shoulder. Darby was standing there, watching them. "Look, I know the risk. I'm not being stupid, even if Holly and Malia are tired of living with me."

"Am not," Malia chimed in. She'd come from saying good night to Deb and rejoined the group. "It's just practice for when we start up the new venture. Besides, you'd do it for me."

"True." Darby pulled Malia into a side hug. "It's weird. When I was talking to Talia about not having family, I was thinking about all of you. I feel like you guys are my family."

"Found family is the best. You don't have to love us all the time, and you choose to be part of the group," Holly said as she returned to the group as well.

Shirley followed her into the circle and sat down with her knitting. "I told Kathy the same thing yesterday when she left. If George leaves, well, I guess when he goes on, I still have family here. Not just friends, although I do have those too. You all are my family and there's nothing any of you can do about it."

A smile curved Rarity's mouth. "Well, Sam, if you can pull yourself from the treat table, I guess it's time for the second part of tonight's meeting. We've all been so scattered, maybe we need to do a round-robin and see what everyone knows."

"Your new paper inserts for the investigations are on your chair," Shirley added. Shirley always made new notebook papers for each case they worked on. "Along with a new divider so you can keep the two investigations straight. If you need more notepaper or a new pen, there's some on the register table over there."

Shirley was a big part of why they were family. She kept everyone going.

Jonathon started the discussion. "Okay, then. I like Rarity's idea, but let's do the two cases separately. First up, what do you know or what have you heard about Darby's stalker? Darby, since you probably have the most information, you can start. Drew said it was okay to talk about your conversation with him."

Darby walked them through the problems she'd had in Sedona since she'd arrived. Then she talked about the Scotland stalker.

Rarity raised her hand. "Do you think the two men are the same guy?"

Darby shrugged. "No, it feels different. Roger, the Scotland guy, he was from Detroit. He and I talked about things we missed from home. Then after I realized he was getting too close and broke it off, he was upset. He would call and cry on the phone while he left a message. The guy was a mess. I wouldn't have called the cops except he'd tried to break into the dorms one night. The RA called for me that time."

"Your house was broken into. That feels the same," Rarity pointed out.

"Without any buildup. Unless Roger has turned his pain to over-the-top, calculated anger, it's not him. And last I heard, he was dating a girl from New Jersey and still in Scotland."

Jonathon shook his head. "You haven't said anything that would make me reconsider taking him off, except you have a feeling. He stays on until we, or Drew, find out where he is. What's his full name?"

Darby gave those details, then worked on adding them to the pages in her binder. "It's weird talking about a stalker like he's doing it to someone else."

"Been there, done that." Shirley smiled at her. "You should have another brownie."

As they went around the room, Malia brought up Talia Brooks. "The woman is an older version of Darby. What if the stalker just got confused?"

"You're saying he's either brilliant or stupid. This is really nailing down the possible suspects," Holly teased. "But seriously, that woman looks just like you, Darby. Are you sure you don't have other relatives?"

"That's a good question," Rarity pointed out. "Maybe your grandmother had some genealogy done. Is there anything like that in the house?"

"If there is, it would be in the den. I can look there tonight, after the meeting."

Holly nodded. "I'll help. I've got to stay awake for work anyway. I'll try to get into your grandmother's computer." Holly worked for the City of Sedona in the IT department. Mostly it meant that she updated software and replaced hardware when necessary and worked the graveyard shift.

"Okay, so we have that side going." Rarity wrote down a note. "I'll see what I can find out about Talia Brooks online. And I'll try to talk with her tomorrow at the memorial before the film starts."

They finished the round-robin on Darby, then Jonathon changed the subject to Mason Pike. "Shirley, what did you know about him? You set up the event, right?"

She nodded, setting her knitting down. "When I found out about the film festival, I noticed that Mason had a book he'd just released. I figured it would mesh well with the festival, and he'd be here anyway so it wouldn't be a financial bother. Even though he lived in Southern California."

Rarity continued writing as Shirley talked. She wondered how close Talia and Mason lived to each other. Southern California was a large, densely populated area, but Talia had mentioned that they'd been close, once. Was that why he'd been inappropriate with Darby? He'd fallen back into time and thought she was Talia? Or had he been that way with all the pretty young things? She might not ever find out. People tended to forgive a dead man his errors. Especially if they were famous.

As they broke for the night, Jonathon hung around after the others left. "Is Archer coming by or may I have the pleasure?"

"He's driving back from a tour, so he won't be walking me home. You're welcome to join Killer and me if you think Romeo can make it that far." Rarity smiled at the dog that was sprawled on the couch near the fireplace and loudly snoring now that most of the humans had left.

"It would be my pleasure. Anything I can help with?" he asked as he picked up his laptop bag and put the leash back on Romeo. The dog didn't budge.

"I'm checking the back and turning off lights. Put Killer on his leash and I'll be ready to go." Rarity double-checked the lock on the back door and made sure the security system was turned on, then grabbed her tote to meet Jonathon at the front door. After she locked it and armed the security system, she took Killer's leash. "You did a great job leading the discussion tonight."

"Thank you. Drew keeps harping on me to make sure you all don't go rogue on him." Jonathon fell into an easy pace with her and the dogs. Killer had to hurry to keep up, even at this slow pace, but Romeo didn't seem to be in a hurry at all. The two dogs walked together, stopping at smells as they went down the street to Rarity's house. "You were quiet tonight. Are you worn out or something got you worried?"

Rarity snickered. "I'm always worried about something. The bookstore, my employees, my friends, Archer, Killer, you name it, I can give you a reason I'm worried. But this thing with Darby has me concerned. I was going to say she can't have someone staying with her forever, but if their mini hotel project gets up and going, I guess she can."

"The girls will take care of her. And we'll figure out who's been stalking her. I hear she went out to lunch with the bike racer. What do you think about him?"

"Marc? He's super nice. Laid back. And he's obviously taken by Darby. Could he be trying to break into her house and threatening her with flowers and phone calls? I don't think so. One, they only met on Wednesday. They went out to lunch once, maybe twice now. But he's leaving town sometime this week. I'm sure with his new job, he'll be following the circuit again." Rarity stopped, waiting for Killer to get his fill of a new smell with Romeo next to him.

"Too bad, he was my best suspect." Jonathon gently tugged on Romeo's leash, and they started moving again.

"On the other hand, with what I've heard about Mason, he seems more the type." Rarity shrugged. "But of course, he's dead."

"One less suspect to consider." Jonathon started to say something, then paused.

"What are you thinking?" Rarity paused at the edge of her driveway.

"I'm just wondering if these two cases are tied by more than just Darby being Mason's author wrangler the night of his death." Jonathon held his hand up to stop Rarity from responding. "Look, I'm not saying that Darby's a killer. Just that she's involved in both situations. It's just odd."

"It's bad luck, that's what it is. Anyway, will I see you tomorrow? Are you going to the memorial tomorrow night?"

"I'll be writing with Romeo at the bookstore during the day if it's still okay I bring him. Then I'll take him home and come back with Drew for the memorial. I suspect black suits will not be the dress code since we're having it at the theater before his movie reveal?" Romeo lay down as Jonathon was talking.

"I'm really not sure. Maybe at least muted colors?" Rarity would text Shirley regarding the dress code. She'd know. "I'll let you know if I hear anything."

At that, Jonathon coaxed Romeo to stand and walk the few additional blocks home. Rarity watched them leave from her porch. From the dark, she heard a rocking chair move. "Terrance, is that you?"

"Guilty as charged. I was staying up to see if Shirley might come by, but she texted me that she's worn out from today. That woman is going to run herself into an early grave if she doesn't watch herself."

Rarity unlocked the door and let Killer inside. He was beat. "I know. I worry about her too."

Then she went inside. Worry did no one any good. Not the person worrying or the one they worried about. That's what Rarity's mom had always said. So she hadn't worried about anyone. But Rarity had taken the other side of the coin and had worried more.

She headed straight to bed. Maybe she'd even fall asleep. Miracles did happen.

* * *

Wednesday morning, Rarity dressed in a darker blue dress and flats. Over it, she had a light floral sweater jacket. She looked at herself in the mirror and felt she'd hit the mix between being ready for a memorial or a movie premiere. It was a hard line to balance.

Today, she left Killer at the house. Terrance would check on him before he left for the premiere and then she'd be home early to snuggle with him. The joys of having a dog. You always had to include them in your plans or figure out someone to help out. Thank goodness Terrance loved Killer almost as much as she did.

At the store, she finished her chores and relaxed a little after she'd marked tasks off the list. Shirley had the Mommy and Me class today so who knew what kind of uproar and disaster the store would be after that club. It wasn't the babies from the class that were the problem. It was their older siblings who ran wild in the bookstore. But the mamas bought books, so Rarity didn't quite mind. Killer, on the other hand, hated Wednesdays. Another reason she'd left him home. He usually spent most of the day hiding under the cash register cabinet where no one could see him. And yet, the kids still knew he was there and did what they could to get him to come out.

While the store was quiet, she opened her laptop and started looking for anything on Talia Brooks. The good news was that she was easy to pick out from the line of Talia Brookses on the search engine since she looked like Darby. She was an actor. Or had been. It didn't look like she'd had many parts in the last few years. Was that due to the relationship with Mason? Had she not wanted to go on set and away from him? Or was it just the ebb and flow of her career?

Rarity didn't know, but she kept making notes. The last movie she'd had a role in had filmed in Scotland. Now that couldn't be a coincidence, could it? Now the dots between her and Darby were coming together. And as she thought about Jonathon's question last night, she wondered if he was onto something.

She set it away to consider later and dug deeper into the material available to her. She wrote down the names of Talia's parents and looked them up with little luck. As she was about to give up, she saw a mention of a boyfriend or at least someone Talia had been connected to as she made her way through the premieres and social events. Bret Black was handsome, charming, and an up-and-coming actor. He'd also played Talia's love interest in the last movie she'd been hired to play a part in. Was the studio trying to make some news to bring attention to the movie? Maybe.

And maybe he'd be here at the memorial tonight. He might talk about their relationship, especially if he thought it would help his career. Oh, the things she did in the name of snooping.

Jonathon and Romeo came into the bookstore, followed closely by Shirley with a plastic bowl filled with cookies. Either she'd gotten up early to bake, or she'd stayed awake late and had lied to Terrance about being tired. Maybe she was just worried. Like Rarity.

There were a whole lot of maybes floating around the bookstore and in Rarity's head this morning.

And the Mommy and Me crew would be arriving any second. Rarity mentioned the fact to Jonathon, and he immediately moved from his regular table to a place in the back room with Romeo. "At least there I can shoo wandering children away. Romeo likes Savannah, but I'm not sure how he would react to a horde."

Shirley laughed as she heard him. "Those children are angels. Well, except for that Thompson boy and the Cartwright girl. Those two could scare off a crossroads demon in less than ten minutes. But the rest, they're good kids. A little loud at times, but good."

"Shirley, I think you have a different definition of good kids. I just hope that between Drew and his sister, they keep the grandkids under ten. Edith, of course, is hoping for double digits. It makes me feel ill." Jonathon refilled his coffee. "Anyway, I'll be in here until the club is over. I need to get words on the page. I'm falling behind."

"I think that's an excuse, but you've been very helpful this last weekend, so I'll forgive you this one white lie." Shirley grabbed a bottle of water and headed out front. "Rarity, I need you at the register as soon as class is over. You know most of them need to get to lunch before their babysitters have to leave."

Rarity stood in the doorway and told Jonathon what she'd found about Talia. "At least we have another person to check into. Maybe this Bret Black wasn't acting in his relationship to Talia and was jealous of Mason?"

"It's a theory," Jonathon said as he continued to type.

Rarity turned as the front door opened and kids ran into the shop. Time to play hostess and keep the books from being destroyed in the process.

CHAPTER 10

Archer showed up at the bookstore just as she was closing up. She smiled as he walked in. "Just in time. And you look so handsome."

"I had no idea what to wear. Why on earth would you do a memorial fundraiser?" He brushed off his cotton pants and adjusted the light blazer he wore over what Rarity knew was a short-sleeved button-down. "Casual yet respectful. At least that's what I went for. I would have worn the Hawaiian shirt if it wasn't Pike's memorial too."

"You look great. Besides, we're country townies and we're not supposed to have any style." Rarity slipped on the sweater she'd taken off during the day. She checked the locks then grabbed her purse. "I'm ready."

"Did you do any sleuthing today? Or have you just been busy working?" Archer followed her out, waiting until she locked the door.

"Honestly, I'm not sure how to go about this. Pike was almost invisible on social media. The stuff that's there feels like it's through an assistant. But I did poke around Talia's social media presence. She still has pictures of her and Pike together at some industry party. She reposted one of them on his birthday a few months ago. They were at least friends."

"Well, maybe we'll hear something this evening about Pike that makes sense. I talked to Drew last night and he's frustrated with the whole group. He said that the film guys are stonewalling him. Everyone loved Mason Pike. He was close to being a saint. A genius filmmaker who was ahead of his time. Blah, blah, blah."

"I don't think we'll hear anything different tonight." Rarity linked her arm with Archer's. "It is a memorial."

"Yeah, Drew thought the same thing. But he and Sam are meeting us there. Terrance is picking up Shirley. And the girls are walking in together. So we shouldn't have to worry about Darby."

"And yet…" Rarity smiled as she tucked her head on his shoulder as they waited for a light.

"You need to learn to contain this worrying. You'll be a mess when we have kids." Archer kissed the top of her head. "Let's go find out what this new movie is about."

At the theater, pictures of Mason Pike were all over the lobby area. An open bar was set up at the end of the room, and it looked like the Garnet was doing passed trays. Malia waved to them from a couch they'd taken over.

"I'll go get us wine and you snag us a spot on those chairs." Archer went to the left, leaving her to meet up with the crew. As soon as Rarity got close, Malia pulled her down on the couch.

"Talia's over there with Bret Black. He's the actor who starred in this film. And they're looking pretty chummy." Darby pointed out the couple. "Do you think Mason's already been replaced?"

"Talia said they broke up a while ago. I don't think seeing someone now is too soon." Rarity took the wineglass from Archer as he walked up. "Although I haven't seen a mention of Bret on her social media page lately. She went to the last one of these events solo according to the reporter."

"So maybe it is new." Darby was watching the couple. "But I don't think so, the way they are together. His body language is very strong. He's claimed her with his hand on the small of her back. They're standing too close to be just friends. And he leans into her when she talks. He's definitely into Talia."

"Maybe we should look at his social media. Maybe he's the one who wants a relationship. And with Mason out of the picture, Talia has no reason to say no." Holly looked thoughtful. "Darby? Can you get me a napkin from the bar?"

"Sure." Darby stood and walked across the room. Right in front of Talia and Bret. As she did, Bret's eyes widened, and he looked from Talia to Darby.

"There. That's what I wondered. Bret didn't know Talia had a look-alike. She must not have mentioned meeting Darby to him." Holly leaned back in her seat. "I think we need to know more about Bret Black."

"You think he's Darby's stalker? He thought he was following Talia?" Rarity studied the man who now was focused again on his date.

"It's a question for Drew." Holly smiled at the approaching couple. "And speak of the devil, hi guys."

Drew shook hands with Archer as he pulled a chair over for Sam. "Uh-oh, what did I do now?"

"With you, who knows," Jonathon said as he came up behind him. The lights flickered behind them. "Shirley and Terrance just came in the door after us. Time for us to find our seats, I guess."

Rarity stood, putting her hand on Drew's arm. "We'll chat more later, but do you know the man with Talia Brooks?"

"Can't say I do. Should I?" Drew turned back from studying Bret Black as he and Talia headed out of the lobby.

"Like I said, I'll catch you up after this. Late dinner at the house?" Rarity asked Sam.

"As long as I don't have to cook, I'll be there." Sam nodded as they all made their way to their seats.

* * *

Later that night, out on the deck, Rarity filled Drew in on what happened just before they arrived.

"His jaw about hit the floor," Holly added as she stood at the griddle, sautéing veggies and shrimp for tacos. Archer had taken on chopping toppings in the kitchen, and Rarity had been banned from both tasks.

"It doesn't mean anything, but if he didn't know that Talia had a younger double in town, maybe someone else didn't either. Or he could be the freak following me," Darby added from the pool.

"There are still a lot of maybes in that theory, but I'll check out Bret. I know that Talia came into town on Thursday. She said she wanted to spend some time relaxing before any events and she'd planned on going to Mason's signing as support. Did anyone see her there?"

Rarity shook her head from the table where she had a second glass of wine in front of her. "No, and I would have noticed a second Darby."

"See, that's the thing. I think we all would have. So why did she lie about being at the signing and the movie?" Drew asked, looking around.

Archer came out with a tray. "I don't know what you're talking about, but I'm starving, so let's eat. Shrimp fajitas and there's Spanish rice in one slow cooker and black beans in the other."

Rarity waited as her guests filled their plates. But now, she had one more question to write down in her notebook. Where had Talia been on Friday night? And why didn't she want Drew to know about it?

The one thing she did know how to do was make a timeline. And after everyone left that night, she pulled out a pad of sketch paper and started a timeline. Two timelines, actually. One for Darby's stalker and one for Mason's death. They'd had different start times, but she'd kept the real time the same on both lines, so she could see any similarities.

Then she ran out of points to add. Frustrated, she decided to bring the timeline to the next sleuthers' meeting and see if anyone else could add points. This investigation was stalled, and Mason had already died. Hopefully, Darby wouldn't be the next one just because they couldn't see a pattern.

She headed to bed and hoped she'd be in a better mood tomorrow. Because today had sucked.

Thursday morning, Rarity headed into the store early. She didn't have much to do, but staying home seemed like she was giving up. As she arrived on the street, she saw Madame Zelda on her porch. "Good morning, you're here early."

"The spirits are hindering my sleep these days, so I gave in and came into the shop." She waved her up. "You're early too, so come up and have a cup of coffee with me. And bring that little mutt with you."

Rarity smiled and headed left to the next storefront. She had to pull on Killer's leash to get him to understand they weren't going into the shop. She sat on a chair, and Killer went to drink out of the water bowl Madame Zelda kept on the porch for the dogs of sightseeing tourists.

"How is everything going? Did you have a lot of business last weekend?" Rarity took the cup of coffee her neighbor had poured from her carafe. "Thanks."

"No problem. I felt like I was going to have a visitor this morning, so I set up the coffee service for two. And filled up that water dish. I'm glad you were able to stop and chat." Madame Zelda leaned back in her chair. "Last weekend was busy. Lots of visitors, but I kept seeing the same man. Dark hair, tanned, and I think his eyes were blue. Drew Anderson took his description, but I think he's forgotten about him. I feel like this guy might solve at least one of your questions."

"My questions?" Rarity wondered if she'd seen Bret Black. Or maybe the guy from the tent late Friday afternoon. He met that description.

Madame Zelda started shuffling her tarot cards. Back and forth. She smiled as Rarity watched her. "Sorry, it's habit. It calms me and helps me think. I know he was watching your store, but I'm not sure why. But this was before that poor man was killed, so what could he have been watching for? Can I offer you a reading? At no cost, of course."

The change of subject threw Rarity a bit, but she nodded. "That would be nice."

The fortune-teller held out the cards she'd been shuffling. "Maybe this will calm us both down. Cut the deck, please."

Rarity did as she was told, then Madame Zelda mixed the cards a few more times. She pulled her first card.

"The Fool. Start of a new journey. This is in the past position, so it might relate to your life reinvention when you moved here a few years ago. You started over, changing your career, your home, and your family. I'm so glad you chose Sedona, as are the spirits."

Rarity nodded. "I am too. I did start completely over and it has paid off. I didn't know anything about running a bookstore. I've got a cute house with a pool and room for my new dog. And a bunch of friends who feel like family. The cards are one hundred percent right, so far."

"That's right, you're a skeptic. Anyway, here's the second card, for the present, the Star. The card of hope and healing. It's very positive. Your relationships are healing as well as your body. Your love life is moving from one of pain to a new beginning, especially next to the Fool. Success is yours if you just believe in yourself. Is that ringing any bells?"

"Maybe." Rarity didn't want to go into the fact that Kevin had dumped her and now Archer seemed to be the perfect boyfriend. The perfect fit. If she'd believe in herself, and them. She gathered her things. "I should go open the bookstore."

"Hold on a few minutes. There's one more card in the reading. I know you don't want to talk about your personal life, and I get that. So we'll just say that the Star is a wonderful card to have come up in any situation."

She turned the next card. The Death card grinned up at her. "Oh, my. Not what I was expecting."

"That looks bad." Now Rarity wished she'd never sat down. This is what happened when you let woo-woo into your life. It took a life of its own and tried to scare you.

"Not necessarily. It may or may not mean a physical death. Or it may be talking about the body that they took out of your shop. But if that was true, it should have come earlier in the reading. Maybe the death of a situation. Something is going to change with you and a friendship. I can study the cards more. I wouldn't worry, though, the other two cards are too hopeful for this one to mean an actual death."

Rarity thought about Madame Zelda's reading most of the morning. Had the cards been warning her of a change or of an actual death? Feeling silly, she sighed a breath of relief when Shirley and Darby arrived for their shifts.

"I went over and picked this one up for work. She was going to walk from her house. Can you believe it? What part of dangerous stalker do you not get, Darby?" Shirley rattled on about the morning and what Katie had decided to do with the kids who would overrun the shop on Saturday morning.

"Oh, guess who called and bailed on dinner tonight? I guess I'm happy I wasn't sitting there waiting for her," Darby said as she headed to the back room. "Is there coffee?"

"I can't believe she didn't do something with the movies. We probably could have asked someone from the film festival to come and talk about how movies are made. We should think about monthly themes around the book clubs based on the events we're hosting or the festivals in town that month." Shirley snapped her fingers in front of Rarity's face. "Are you awake?"

"Sorry, I couldn't sleep last night," Rarity said. It wasn't quite a lie, even though she'd been thinking about Madame Zelda's reading, not zoning out. "Shirley? Do you believe in the other side? The spirits and the crystals and the vortex stories?"

"You mean the magic surrounding Sedona?" Shirley settled on a chair at Jonathon's usual table, even though he hadn't shown up yet. "Well, you're going to be surprised by my answer, but yes. I do believe the veil is thinner here. I believe in God and the stories from the Bible. If he could perform miracles back then, why would I expect anything different in my day-to-day life? Or question powers I don't understand? If God sends me a rowboat, I'm going to assume that it's going to flood sooner or later, and I'm going to get in."

Rarity smiled at her mention of Rarity's favorite joke where a man drowned after refusing to be saved off his roof by a rowboat, a bigger boat, and finally a helicopter. When the man complained to God at the pearly gates, God told him that he sent all those things to save him, and he rejected them.

So what was the meaning behind Madame Zelda's third card? And what could she do to make sure a real death didn't happen? Especially to Darby.

Symbols and signs were easy to pick out. Assigning meaning to them was a lot harder. Especially when they were swirled up in a pretty picture.

"What do we need to do to get ready for tomorrow's swarm of preteens?" Rarity asked, ready to get out of her head and be busy.

The next few hours were spent getting the club area ready for the group as well as checking out the young readers shelves to make sure they either had the popular books on the latest list or that they'd ordered them.

When Jonathon came in with Romeo and a bag from Carole's with lunch, they were all ready for a break. Rarity took the sandwich from him and then went back to grab drinks from the fridge. When she came back, everyone was sitting at tables, talking.

She sat next to Jonathon after dropping off bottles of soda and water. "Did you sleep in this morning?"

"I wish. Edith called, and so Romeo and I went walking while we talked. Edith walks and talks too. That way we both get some exercise first thing in the morning, and we're touching base. Couple stuff, you know."

Rarity smiled at the idea. "I'm glad you and Edith find a way to still be together after so many years and trips to Sedona."

"She likes having me out of the house, to be honest." He waved away her arguments. "Just wait until you've been married for thirty years. It changes with every decade. Anyway, after that, Drew threw out some possible theories around Mason Pike's death. One interesting thing, though, was his house in California was broken into on Friday night."

"After he died?"

"About the same time. Which, okay, he announced he'd be out of town on his media so it was a good time to rob him, but they don't think anything was taken. From his housekeeper's notes, everything was right where it was supposed to be. Whatever they were looking for, Mason didn't have it stored at the house." He ate a chip from the bag he'd gotten with his sandwich. "So what did Mason have that someone would want bad enough to break into his house?"

"Maybe a screenplay?" Rarity didn't know how these things worked. "Or do they copyright those?"

"Good questions that neither Drew nor I have answers to. I did hear last night in the men's room that a producer was taking over the development of Mason's film we saw last night. There are some changes they're going to make before releasing it. I don't know if that changes what Mason would have gotten from the movie or not." He picked up his sandwich then set it down again. "However, I would have thought that if the movie needed changes, with Mason dead or alive, it wouldn't have changed his participation in the funding and rewards."

"Okay, so we're still at the same place with Mason Pike. Nowhere." Rarity set half of her sandwich down on the plate. "What about Darby?"

"She hasn't had an issue since the flowers. Maybe her stalker was following the wrong person?"

"Can Drew ask Talia if she had any unwelcome attention in the last few months? If she has, maybe Darby was just in the wrong place, wrong time?" This was Rarity's favorite theory because it meant that since Talia was here in Sedona and would leave soon, Darby was safe.

"It's a good theory." Jonathon said. "And we just got into the stalker idea because of the guy from Scotland who's already moved on."

"I'd love to not be babysat twenty-four seven," Darby added, obviously overhearing the conversation. "I feel less stressed right now. Maybe that's because no one is watching me with bad intentions?"

CHAPTER 11

After their talk, Darby agreed to keep her houseguests around for a few more days while Drew researched Talia and her current boyfriend, Bret. If Bret was upset that Talia was hanging around Mason again, it could explain the problems that Darby was having. Especially if Bret thought Talia had rented Darby's house for a getaway with her old boyfriend. Rarity thought that he'd looked confused when he saw Darby on Wednesday night.

On Friday, Rarity still thought she was missing something. She decided to let it marinate a bit. Maybe when the sleuthing group talked on Tuesday night it would come to her. Katie showed up at three that afternoon.

Rarity greeted her as she came in the door. "Hey, you're not scheduled until tomorrow morning."

Katie looked around. "I told Darby I'd stay at her house tonight through Sunday. So I thought I'd come in and set up, but you guys have already taken care of that."

"We had a slow day and I was angsty. Shirley asked why you weren't doing a movie-themed activity." Rarity smiled at the look now on Katie's face. "And, there's the answer, you didn't think about it."

"It would have been so easy. Especially since all the kids will want to talk about tomorrow is either the bike race or the film festival. I have the perfect activity. Do we still have Mason's film?" Katie grabbed a piece of paper as she wrote down her thoughts.

"Yes. His assistant, Jane Carey, was supposed to pick it up on Sunday, but she hasn't come by. I reminded her of it Wednesday night at the memorial." Rarity thought about their short conversation. "Maybe she thought it was this Sunday. Anyway, if she comes in, I'll tell her we need it for tomorrow morning. Then she can come get it or I'll send it over to her hotel."

"Thanks. I need to do some work to make this mesh with the book, but it will be fun." Katie nodded to the back. "Coffee in there?"

"Of course." Rarity felt Killer by her foot. He was looking up at her, a sign that he needed something. "Shirley, can you watch the front? I need to take Killer out. It won't be long. I think it's still hot out there."

"It is hot," Katie called out from the back room.

Rarity clicked Killer's leash on and headed to the front door. The sun would have crossed the point where Killer's little fake yard of grass would be in the shade. She always kept water out for the local dogs that walked by the bookstore. She even had a sign on the window telling people that the store was a pet-friendly environment. She didn't want dogs to be overcome in the heat. Especially if their owners weren't smart enough to keep them inside during the worst of the day.

She dumped the warm water and refilled the bowl with cold water from the bottle she'd brought out with them. Darby came out and stood by her as they waited for Killer.

"This is going to go away someday, right?" Darby asked as she scanned the street and the area around the buildings.

Rarity pulled her into a side hug. "We hover because we care. Yes, you will have your life back. And, according to Drew, it should be sooner than later. As long as the stalker doesn't find a new way to torture you."

"Rarity, that's almost comforting." Darby hugged her back, then went to the door. "Sorry, it's too hot for me. Scotland is a lot cooler."

As she waited for Killer to finish so she could clean up his mess using a pet bag, Rarity saw Jane Carey standing across the street. She waved at her and prepared to tell her that she couldn't have the movie. At least not until tomorrow afternoon. She knew that someone would come by to pick up the film, but she hoped they'd allow her to honor her promise to Katie.

To her surprise, Jane didn't acknowledge the wave and instead got back into the car she'd just parked. Rarity watched her drive away until she heard Killer barking. Telling her to hurry since it was hot out there.

She cleaned up his mess then headed inside. After taking the bag out to the alley where the dumpsters had been returned after Friday's outdoor movie theater had been broken down, she went back and sat near Jonathon.

He looked up from his writing. "Yes?"

"Maybe nothing, but definitely in the weird category." Rarity told him about seeing Jane.

He glanced toward the door then shrugged. "Maybe she got a phone call. All those film people are wearing the earpieces for their phones. I thought I was having a conversation with someone at the memorial when they stood up and walked away. My discussion was one sided and I didn't even realize it. He probably thought I was a crazy old man."

"That could be true." Rarity hadn't seen Jane closely. She could have had a call and realized she needed to be somewhere else. She might not have even seen Rarity wave.

But she thought she'd seen recognition on the woman's face.

"Anyway, I wanted to let you know I'll be heading into Flagstaff tonight to meet up with my writers' group. They moved the meeting from Wednesday so I could read from my chapter this week." He glanced at the computer. "Can I use your copier? I'll pay you for the copies."

"Consider it a part of your benefit package for being here. I know you only write here to please Drew. It's not like we're going out to scan the streets for drug dealers to ask them questions about local murders." She held up her hand when he started to say something. "Wait, let me rephrase that. I'm sounding a little grumpy. Thank you for being part of the Next Chapter's unofficial staffing. The copies are on me."

He chuckled, then said, "You're welcome and all I was going to say before is I like being here. I know you don't need me, but I need all of you. It's been tougher than I thought changing my life where my job had life-and-death choices. Now, I write and, sometimes, get to think about why a murderer would kill. Although my years of law enforcement experience doesn't seem to be helping with this murder. I feel like I'm missing something important."

Rarity's eyes widened. "I feel exactly the same way. There's something I should be seeing but I'm not. Anyway, make as many copies as you want. And thank you again. I will be fine walking home alone. I have Killer."

Jonathon snorted. "And with that image, I'm back to work. Romeo would probably think less of me if I pointed out Killer's size and threat level."

She glanced at her watch. "Another hour and I'm kicking you out of here. I've got a pool waiting for me at home. As well as leftover shrimp fajitas."

At the house, after she'd closed the bookstore and seen off Darby and Katie as well as Jonathon, Romeo, and Shirley, she checked her fridge to make sure she did have enough leftovers for dinner, then hit the pool. Tomorrow night there would be the mid-festival ceremonies, and she'd already told Archer she'd go with him. Still, she was beginning to feel grateful that this festival was only once a year. For their small town, the festival committee had made the event feel like they were living in Hollywood and seeing premieres on a nightly basis. Darby and Katie were dressing up for tonight's showing and had offered to lend Rarity one of their theater dresses for tomorrow's event.

She had another little black dress that should be fine. And since they were walking into town, she'd throw on some flats rather than the heels. She'd pull her hair into a fancy updo, which had two benefits. One, it looked great. And two, getting the hair off her neck would be cooler. She'd have a shawl to cover her from the sun on the walk over and from the chill on the walk home. She had Arizona clothing down to a science now after a few years.

As she swam, she let the lists and worries of the day seep out of her head and into the pool water. Killer was on the deck, lying where he could be in the path of the cooling fan as well as still be able to see her in the pool. Rarity blamed his needy nature on losing his first mommy to a violent crime.

Even though Killer hadn't been at the scene of her death.

Maybe she spent too much time alone with her dog? She pushed the idea out of her head and concentrated on the next stroke. One after another. Until she'd reached her lap count and her shoulders were no longer tense. They'd be screaming at her tomorrow, but today, she was loose. She climbed out of the pool and heard raised voices. Then a door slammed.

She looked out the fence gate and saw Shirley getting into her car that was parked at Terrance's house. The gate from his backyard opened and he saw her standing there.

"Sorry about that. I didn't know anyone was home or we would have taken our disagreement into the house before we started yelling." He watched Shirley's car back out. "I'm a fool."

"Same argument?"

Terrance nodded. "I need to stop pushing. She gives me what she can. I just love her."

"Shirley's in a hard spot right now. You need to be patient."

He sighed. "I'm trying. I've got to get dressed. I'm meeting some friends at the movie thing tonight. Which is why she was mad at me. She doesn't want anyone to misconstrue our friendship as anything but just friends. Which is why I told her that we needed to be out in public now. People notice secrets. If you're just open as friends, people let it be."

"I think people decide what they want to think, no matter what you do. All you can do is what you feel comfortable with. I think with Shirley, she's doing the best she can." Rarity met his gaze, trying to help her friend. Both her friends.

He took off his hat and ran his fingers through his gray hair. "You're right, of course. I'll give her some time to calm down, and then I'll apologize. I just pray that I can keep my mouth shut the next time she brings up the future. I know she's feeling pressure. I don't want any of it to come from me."

Rarity went back inside her backyard, and as she did, she heard the click of Terrance's gate right after her own. Sometimes relationships were hard. Sometimes they were impossible. Terrance and Shirley were right on the borderline of impossible.

She went back inside with Killer to start her evening. She had plenty to think about to keep herself busy.

* * *

Saturday morning, kids were running around the bookstore. Cars still lined up on the street, waiting for a spot they could pull in and drop off their kid. In three hours, the kids would be sitting on their phones, waiting for a text message telling them their mom or dad was right outside.

Romeo and Jonathon were in the back room along with Killer. He'd started shaking in his bed under the counter, so Rarity had moved him to the back and shut the door. Hopefully, the closed door and "No Admittance" sign were enough to keep the kids out.

She knocked on the door, then stepped inside to refill her coffee. "So did Drew find anything?"

"Not a drop of controversy on either one of them. Talia had been heartbroken when Mason broke it off, but she was a businessperson and she understood the game. If you worked in the same field, you had to keep it professional. Especially when you found out he'd been cheating. Talia was the wounded party, but she took the high road. And she got a little money in an account from Mason."

"So he'd done something that warranted a payout."

Jonathon shrugged. "Or he just wanted to be a nice guy."

"Odd question, but who's in Mason's will? Who will inherit whatever totals the guy had?" Rarity had been thinking about Mason's life all morning.

Jonathon shrugged. "No clue, but I know Drew's trying to find this out as we speak. I didn't see him last night since I got back late. He was already tucked in bed. For someone who's a bachelor, he's acting like an old married couple."

"And what about Bret? Any charges of stalking anyone?"

"One could only hope, but no. He has a squeaky-clean record. Drew's trying to pull on any loose strings there today. Are you going to the mid-festival ceremonies?"

"Wouldn't miss it." Rarity sighed, then headed to the door. "I guess I better get out there. Thanks for keeping an eye out for Killer."

"He and Romeo are protecting me." Jonathon looked back at his screen. "Come get me when it's over."

As the movie started, Rarity assumed the kids would quiet down. Instead, Katie kept stopping the movie and asking questions, a flashlight tucked under her face making her look spooky. Rarity kept listening and realized that Katie was teaching story structure with each question, using the beats from the classic Joseph Campbell book *The Power of Myth*, and *The Writer's Journey* by Chris Vogler. Katie had been taking a class comparing the two books this last semester. Something Rarity never thought would be useful outside the ivy halls of academia or a writers' workshop. She had turned an alien spider movie into a teaching moment.

And the Sedona English teachers were getting kids who were way ahead in their knowledge of how literature worked.

As Katie continued the book club, Rarity looked for a book that taught these concepts in a younger text just in case a kid asked for a book to study the concepts. But she didn't find anything.

By the time the last kid and their parent had left, she'd sold eight copies of *The Writer's Journey*—with seven of those on back order since she only carried one. Ten copies of *The Power of Myth*—all of them having to be ordered. And three of *The Heroine's Journey*, a little different take on the hero's journey material. Rarity had to believe that the kids' parents would be helping out with some of the reading. Most of the kids bought the book for the next meeting. Rarity kept track of the kids who didn't. She had a fund for keeping these kids in the club and paying for their books. She handed five books to Katie with a list. "Here's the winners list for this month."

A young girl looked at Katie walking away. "I never win a book." Then she watched Katie stop by the first boy and hand off the book. The girl turned back and handed her the money for her purchase. "Never mind. I get it."

Rarity smiled at the young girl's wisdom and nodded. "You're already lucky."

After everyone had left, Jonathon and Killer came out of the back room. He nodded to Katie. "That was well done. I learned a lot from your presentation."

"Did it go okay? I worried that the kids would get tired of me stopping the movie. I gave them a list of the beats before we started." Katie flopped down onto a chair. "I'm worn out."

"You need to write a book about that." Rarity pointed to her computer. "I went looking, thinking the kids would ask, and they did. So I had to sell adult books to the group. I let the parents who ordered the books know that if it was too hard, I'd let them return it in a week."

"I can probably list off everyone who ordered additional material. And they're all highly advanced readers. I think they'll be fine." Katie leaned up with her elbows on her knees. "Are you serious about me writing a book? I've been looking for my thesis subject. I would have to get it approved, since it's not science based, but it would be good, right?"

"It would be amazing," Rarity clarified. Darby and Malia came into the shop.

"If the kids are all gone, lunch has arrived." Darby peeked around the corner. "Malia was nice enough to come to my house and get me before bringing the food here."

"You are relieved of your charge, Malia." Jonathon held out his hand. "Now give me my salad. I'm starving."

Gathering around the counter where Malia had dropped the bags, they all found their lunches. Rarity could hear Katie, Malia, and Darby making plans for tonight.

"Are you all going to the first week closing ceremonies?" Rarity unwrapped her turkey and ham sub.

"Of course. Malia met this guy last night and he said he's bringing his friends tonight. Maybe we'll be invited to an after-party." Darby grinned, unwrapping her salad. "No carbs for me today if I have a snowball's chance of getting into that dress tonight."

"Crisco, or butter. My mom swore on it. But then you're all slippery," Katie pointed out.

Rarity didn't want to be the one to tell them that an after-party maybe wasn't a good idea. She met Jonathon's gaze and he nodded.

Then he broke all their dreams of the night.

CHAPTER 12

The parking lot in front of the theater had been cordoned off, and tables were scattered all around. Lights were draped from pole to pole, lighting up the entire area without being a harsh spotlight. Waiters in black pants and white shirts had already started passing trays. Rarity and Archer made their way through the crowd.

"Maybe we're the first ones here?" Rarity asked Archer as they paused at the left edge of the parking lot without finding anyone.

"You give up too easily." He laughed and moved her so she could see the south side of the lot. There, around three tables, were their friends. "And here we go."

"I've been waiting for you for hours. What happened?" Sam walked toward Rarity, handing her a glass. "You're at least one round behind. Better get chugging."

Rarity took the glass. "My chugging days are behind me. Today, it's all about the sipping."

"Smart girl," Archer whispered in her ear. "But if you want, I can be the DW."

She turned to him, confused. "What's a DW?"

"Designated walker." He grinned at her. "I promise to get you home safely."

"Always the jokester." Rarity sat at the table with Sam. "So what did we miss?"

"A woman whose film didn't make the cut has been coming around to all the tables asking us to put in a protest. She said that it's a patriarchal decision for the awards." Sam pointed the woman out as she lobbied another table for others to help her protest.

"I thought these awards are based on audience voting. I turned my card in on Wednesday." Rarity glanced at the list of finalists on a sheet that had been left on each table. "And several of my favorites are on here. Which film was she part of?"

Sam turned away from the rest of the group and lowered her voice. "That really bad one about a meat market. Not a singles club, a real meat market and how we're killing the planet by eating meat."

"The one where they rushed the back room, which was spotless, and then complained that someone tipped the place off because there should have been baby lambs in there or something?" Rarity had seen the movie with Archer.

"Yeah, I thought it was a comedy and just in the wrong category, but I guess she feels she's an investigative reporter trying to blow the lid off the meat producers." Sam shrugged. "This next week, they're doing a second screening of all the movies that got the most votes so they can do awards next Saturday. There are a few here I'd see again, and there are a few I missed. Are you and Archer going to tomorrow's showings? Can I play third wheel? Drew's working."

"Of course you can." Rarity glanced at Archer. "Are we going tomorrow?"

"I've got hikes scheduled so I'm off the hook. You two can do whatever you want. The store's closed, right?" Archer sipped the wine they'd passed out. "No wonder this is free. It's really bad."

"You just have to drink more and then it will taste fine." Sam stood and grabbed several glasses off the waiter's tray. She sat down after distributing the new glasses. "So it's girls' day at the movies?"

"Sounds like it." Rarity saw Jane Carey standing by the side of the building. "I'll be right back."

She made her way over to Jane. "You look like you hate these things."

"Guilty as charged. I'd rather be home in my pj's, watching a movie. But it's all part of the gig. Besides, I need to find a new assistant job, so I'm here meeting a few of the up-and-coming guys and giving them my résumé. It's all about the connections, right?" Jane sipped her wine. "And this is horrible. I guess it keeps people from getting drunk since you can't drink much of it."

Rarity smiled, thinking about Sam's completely opposite observation of the quality of the wine. "I don't drink a lot anyway. So, do you still want to pick up Mason's movie? We used it for an elementary-age-level discussion on story structure, but it's ready for someone to pick up. I don't know who's handling his affairs now."

"It's me. I'm on salary with the estate until it all gets settled. Mason's attorney called to let me know I'd have a job for the next couple of months, at least. I'm sure he didn't leave me anything in the will." She nodded to a man who'd just walked into the party. "Sorry, I need to go introduce myself. It might take a few months for me to find a new placement."

As Rarity went back to the table, she realized Jane hadn't answered her question. She guessed she'd just keep the movie in an envelope for her at the bookstore to pick up at her leisure.

As they talked, Darby walked in with Marc Billings. They made their way over to the group of tables.

Rarity waved the couple over to their table. "You look amazing, as do you, Marc. I thought you were heading out of town for the next race."

"I'm not needed for a couple of weeks, so I thought I'd hang around here. Darby says she's been having some problems with an ex?" Marc had his arm protectively around Darby's waist.

Rarity shook her head. "We don't know if it's an ex or someone we don't even know about yet. Darby, you need to make sure you're not alone."

"I haven't been alone since that Wednesday night," Darby confirmed. "Marc called and asked if he could come over yesterday, so we've been talking."

Rarity hoped that Darby hadn't been alone with the ex-racer. She liked him, but until Drew found out who was doing this, strangers were a problem. "Isn't that nice?"

Marc chuckled. "Which is mom-speak for just wait until I get you alone, kid. Rarity, I promise, I've been a complete gentleman, and other than a little romantic interest in this woman, I'm not a stalker."

"Says every stalker, ever," Rarity joked. "Just remember, Marc Billings, I have your address, your Social Security number, and your shoe size. If Darby goes missing, it's on you."

"Why would you have my shoe size?" Marc asked, then waved the question away. "I promise, I belong to the good guys' cartel. Not a dishonest bone in my body."

"Dude," Sam called out, her words slurring. "You're male, so all your bones are dishonest."

"She might be drunk, but she's not wrong." Rarity smiled at Marc. "Anyway, I'm going to stop grilling you so you and Darby can have a nice evening. It was nice to see you again."

They went over and joined the table where Sam and Drew were sitting. Archer put his arm around her. "What's going on in your head?"

"I'm just hoping that the fox hasn't snuck into the chicken coop dressed like Big Bird."

Archer broke out into laughter. "Now that's an image. I can even see Marc's face in the middle of the yellow feathers. He's a good guy, Rarity. I took him out on a hike a few days ago and he's solid. At least that's my opinion."

"Well, Darby must feel that way as well, so there are two people I trust who trust him." Rarity sat back down and sipped her wine. "Sam's right about one thing."

"What's that?"

"Drinking more of this dulls your senses." She smiled at him. "Want to dance?"

* * *

At home, Archer made them coffee that he brought to Rarity as he came to sit next to her on the couch. A movie played in the background and Killer snored on her lap. "Unless you want something else?"

"No, this is good. It should cut the alcohol from tonight. I hope they will increase the quality of their wine for the closing ceremony next week. Otherwise, I'm going to have to figure out a way to sneak in quality liquor so I don't have a headache the next morning." She snuggled onto the couch. "What do you really think about Marc Billings?"

"He seems nice. He's quite taken with Darby." Archer frowned as he sat up and looked at her. "We already had this conversation. Is there something that's bothering you about the man?"

Rarity shook her head. "No. And that worries me. This whole thing has been weird. Darby's house gets broken into. She gets a threatening message. Mason dies, after being handsy with Darby. Then she gets flowers from a mystery sender. Except Darby only met Mason the night he died. She thought he was creepy. So why would someone focus on Darby if they were going to kill Mason?"

"Or why would someone kill Mason if they're really focused on Darby? That's why you're still worried about Marc. You can't rule him out for doing all of this." Archer rubbed his face. "This is too heavy of a conversation for late on Saturday night. Can I come over Monday and make waffles?"

"You don't have to." Rarity sat up as well. "We could go get brunch."

"I like making waffles." He rubbed his face again. "You and Sam are going to the movies tomorrow. Hey, make sure you keep your eyes open to see if anyone freaks out when Mason's name is mentioned. I've got an early morning hike. I'll call if I get in early so I can come play too. I work, you play. I'm starting to sense a pattern here."

"Shut up," she said as she tossed a pillow at him.

He kissed her and then stood. "Until Monday, then. Stop worrying about Darby. Drew still has a police car watching the house, and Katie was staying with her tonight. She's probably already in bed for the night."

After Archer left, Rarity tried to focus on the house flipping show that Killer liked to watch. Instead, she went to get her laptop. She could multitask. She'd looked up Talia and Mason, but not Marc Billings. She'd thought he'd already been out of town, but seeing him tonight with Darby got her spider senses tingling.

She rolled her eyes at her own pun. "Okay, so making fun of spiders isn't appropriate."

Killer ignored her. The people in the show were driving through the countryside. Killer loved going for rides.

Marc Billings had a much more personable social media presence. More like him. Rarity would bet that he did his own posting, not a company or assistant.

He'd posted pictures from the signing last week. One he'd taken from the stage after asking the audience to smile. One photo that he must have asked Darby to take of him signing. And the last one of Darby, moving his books. The book was the star of the snap, but Darby was clearly in frame and grinning. A comment hung under that: *"Wow, she's a knockout."*

Marc had put a thumbs-up on all the comments.

Looking between the different social medias, Marc posted the same thing. He might have a service that did that. Darby had mentioned it to Rarity when she'd complained about having to repost on every social site the bookstore was on.

So she focused on the posts just before and just after Marc's signing. He'd made several posts inviting people to come to the signing. Good author. Then he'd made more posts about the race, adding a short note that he'd be signing his book at the store and when. Somehow, he'd been social and fun on all the posts, yet still had reminded people about the book signing. It wasn't a skill everyone had.

So Marc, if he did his own marketing, was skilled in making himself look good.

She was about to give up when she found a comment on an older post. *"Stop stalking my sister, loser."* Marc hadn't liked the comment. Maybe he hadn't even seen it. The post was a few months old and the comment was from a couple of weeks ago. She wrote down the commenter's name, then went back up to the post.

The post was about a race. The photo showed several women as they fought for the last few feet of the race. The winner had her hands up in victory as she crossed just a few inches before the others.

The caption didn't look stalkerish. Just a comment on how Tyra McAdams had won the women's division. The name sounded familiar, so Rarity wrote it down, then went to look up the race winners here in Sedona. Tyra had won the women's division in last weekend's race too. And according to her post, she was still here in Sedona and was hiking with a local guide tomorrow. Rarity thought she knew which one.

She set her alarm for six then headed off to bed. She needed to talk to Tyra McAdams and see how she knew Marc. And why her brother would ask Marc to stop stalking her.

Maybe Rarity had just solved one of the mysteries.

As she lay in bed, trying to wind down, she used her phone to look the brother up on Facebook. Rufus also raced bikes. He wasn't as good as his sister or what Marc had been, but he placed okay. It looked like he had sponsors too. She zoomed in on the picture of him and gasped.

He was the guy who Rarity had thought was a young dad at the booth. The one she'd scared away by asking how old his kids or the kids in his life were. She stared at the photo. So why had Rufus been in her shop, and why had talking to him made him react like that?

Rarity's first thought was that he had a guilty conscience. He didn't want anyone to know he'd been in the bookstore's booth. Had he been checking out Marc's book? Trying to see how it sold? Or had he been checking out Rarity or one of her staff?

Like Darby?

CHAPTER 13

The next morning, she texted Archer as soon as she got up.

Where are you meeting your customer and is her name Tyra McAdams?

She watched the little bubbles for a long time. Then the response came back.

How do you know that? I'm at the shop. She's supposed to be here at seven. She's not a killer, right?

Rarity smiled and then told him she'd be right there and not to leave before she got there. She didn't answer the killer question. One, because she didn't know the answer and it would make Archer a little nervous while he waited. It wasn't bad to keep a man guessing. At least on some things.

When she pulled her Mini Cooper into one of the parking spots for the building, Tyra had just arrived. She smiled brightly when she saw Rarity get out of her car. "Oh, good, another hiker. My mom always worries when I go out alone with a guide. I guess she thinks I can't defend myself."

Rarity hurried over. "Sorry, Tyra, I'm not hiking with you."

"I would hope not. Not in those shoes. You'd be dying in ten minutes, fifteen tops. So you know me; why do you look familiar?" Tyra leaned against her Jeep, watching Rarity.

"I'm Rarity Cole; I run the local bookstore. The Next Chapter? Maybe you came in for Marc's signing?"

Tyra shook her head. "No, I tend to stay away from ex-husbands. Especially when they write books. I hate to think of the way I'm portrayed in the book. Do you know?"

"I haven't read it, no. So you and Marc were married? Is that why your brother thinks he's stalking you?"

Tyra started laughing. When she stopped, she wiped her eyes. "That's a good one. But I can see you're serious. Rufus and Marc never got along. We were only married for five years. Most of them, we were out on the road, racing. When we spent time together, we talked about racing. So then when he was hurt and decided to retire, we had nothing to talk about. Racing was the thing that brought us together and, in the end, the thing that drove us apart. We weren't in love. We were convenient."

A marriage of convenience in a nonliterary way. "So, Marc's a good guy?"

"Marc's the best. He's devoted to his mother. He remembers birthdays and sends flowers on all the right occasions. He just wasn't in love with me. We're great friends, though." Tyra waved as Archer came out of the building, keys in hand. "I thought you scared up another hiker."

Archer walked over and kissed Rarity. "No, just my girlfriend. She's trying to solve mysteries before she goes and watches movies all day. Besides, she's in the wrong shoes."

"I told her the same thing." Tyra laughed and held her hand up for a high five, which Archer gave her. "Anyway, anything else I can tell you about Marc? Are you friends with that new girl he's courting here?"

"I am, I mean, we're all friends. And I'm her boss." Now Rarity was stumbling over her words. She'd made assumptions about Marc and his ex-wife. Now she wasn't sure what else she wanted to know. "Anyway, thanks for clearing up the thing about your brother and Marc."

"No problem. Are we ready to slay this hike?" Tyra turned back to Archer, ready to start their adventure.

"Hey, one more thing. Does your brother have kids or know someone with kids that he'd be buying books for?" Rarity turned back from walking over to get into her car.

"Weird question, but no on both counts. He's not even dating." Tyra said as she locked her Jeep. "Let's get this show on the road."

Back at the house, Rarity got ready for her day. Killer sat by the door, watching her. She'd already left him home alone once, and somehow the dog knew a second time was coming. She scooped him up into a hug then sat down on the couch. "Look, Aunt Sam and I have to go watch movies and they won't let you in the theater. I know, it's a crime."

Rarity heard Sam's knock on the door. "Come on in, I'm ready."

Sam opened the door and saw Rarity holding Killer. "I take it he knows and he's not happy?"

"Worse, I took off this morning for a few minutes and left him alone. Now he's really mad." Rarity kissed him on the top of his head then set him on the couch, turning the television on to a movie channel. "I'm ready. I'll fill you in on my sleuthing fiasco this morning on our way to the theater. Do you need water for the walk?"

Sam took a bottle, then listened as they walked into town. "So you thought Marc might be Darby's stalker? I have to admit, the idea occurred to me too. Did I say something rude to him last night? I think I overdid it on the cheap wine."

"The wine was free." Rarity told Sam what Sam had said about Marc being a liar because he was male.

"Foot in mouth, check. I really need to slow down when it's hot outside. I forget how wine affects me." Sam sipped more from her bottle. "No wonder I'm parched today. This is my third bottle of water."

"You weren't horrible, just a little sloppy." Rarity rubbed her friend's back. "Anyway, Marc has an ex-wife who said their divorce was amicable. The brother-in-law doesn't like him, but she's very clear that they were just about the racing. When he wasn't racing anymore, they didn't have anything in common. Sometimes when circumstances change, people change with them."

"So now you have no suspects in Darby's stalking pool." They stopped at the red light where Darby had almost gotten hit by the truck. "Did Drew get anything off the cameras? Maybe that might lead you in the right direction."

"Not that I know of, but I'll text him. Good question."

Sam beamed at the compliment. "Just because I'm not as involved in the sleuthing as the rest of you doesn't mean I'm not interested. You all get a little crazy when you've got a case going on. You're all Sherlocks and Watsons. Jonathon's an actual ex-detective. Sometimes it's a little intimidating."

"As Drew reminds me all the time, he's the professional. We're all just amateurs. So no letting yourself get intimidated by any of us. Besides, last night I thought I had one of our mysteries solved, only to find out this morning that the answer I thought was not the correct answer." She pointed to the theater ahead. "We must be early or late; there's no line."

Sam glanced at her watch. "We're a few minutes late, but we should be able to get in still."

After they went inside and grabbed some popcorn, the ushers took them up to a box to watch the movie. The usher said as he opened the curtain to show off their seats, "Best seats in the house, but if you were a little later, you would have gotten turned away. We're almost completely full. We have two other seats in the box across from you, and then we're full."

As he said that, the curtain from across the theater opened and Darby and Marc walked into the box. They sat down, and then Darby saw them and waved.

"What a surprise," Sam said as they got seated. "Not."

"Marc Billings is beginning to get much more interesting," Sam said as the lights went down.

At intermission, Darby came and found them. "Isn't this amazing? I've never been in box seats before. You can see everything. So how did you guys score those?"

Rarity answered honestly. "We were late. How about you?"

Darby frowned at Rarity's answer. "According to Marc, he had to use his connections. Maybe I should go home."

"Stay and enjoy the movies. Maybe he did call in a favor for them to save the seats for you. Like I said, we were just late. I talked to his ex-wife this morning."

Darby looked like she'd been hit with a two-by-four. "Marc was married before?"

"Tyra McAdams. Her brother, Rufus, hates Marc, so be careful there." The lights flickered. "Seriously, Darby, if you feel safe, use this time to get more information about Marc. Where he grew up, what he used to do for a living, besides racing. Get what you can. But if you feel uncomfortable at any time, let one of us know and we'll get you home safely."

"He seems to be a really nice guy," Darby insisted.

"I hope he's the best," Sam said as she squeezed Darby's hand. "You deserve a nice guy."

Marc stood by the stairs, drinks in hand. When he found Darby in the crowd, he waved toward her. It was time to go back to the movie.

"Let me know if anything happens." Darby headed toward the stairs and the waiting Marc.

Rarity and Sam went the other way. Rarity looked at her friend. "Why do I feel like I've just sent the baby goat into the forest? I hope she's going to be okay."

"Darby will be fine." Sam waved across the theater when they got back to their seats. "She's one of us."

* * *

Besides the information from Tyra that morning and seeing Marc with Darby later, Rarity and Sam didn't get much from the four independent movies they saw that afternoon. As they sat at the Garnet, iced teas in hand and waiting for a late lunch, they talked about the films.

"They weren't my style, but then again, I'm not an indie movie type of girl." Sam shrugged. "I would rather watch an action movie with a dreamy hunk than one that's all about your feelings. I tried to rate them fairly, though. So they'll be doing screenings all week?"

"Except Wednesday," Rarity clarified. "Then they'll do awards on Saturday night. I like having the film festival here, it brings in lots of traffic for all the businesses. I'm going to try to get some things around the house done tomorrow. Archer's coming over and making waffles in the morning, then we'll probably go to the festival for the afternoon showings. Katie's running the bookstore on Monday."

"Sometimes I feel like you're listing off what's in your planner when I ask what's going on in your world." Sam laughed when Rarity jerked her head up right as the waitress dropped off their meals. "Don't worry,

I don't mind it. It's just your way of processing the world. You were like this in college too and when you worked for that corporation. You got especially focused when you went through cancer treatments. You always have to know what's five steps ahead of you at all times."

"It's who I am. I don't even question it anymore. This is me. I'm surprised it doesn't drive Archer crazy or out the door." Rarity drizzled some of the salad dressing on her Cobb salad. "Tell me about what's going on in your life. I feel like we haven't hung out together in ages."

When she got home, she cuddled with Killer and read her notes in her murder book. They were pretty sparse. Mason didn't seem to have many people in his life. He had his ex-girlfriend and an assistant. He and his ex-wife didn't seem to talk. What about relatives? He was older, so maybe not parents, but siblings? Hadn't Jonathon mentioned a brother?

She grabbed her laptop and went looking for an obituary. There was a short one, but it didn't list anyone in his life.

Maybe she should find Jane or Talia. One of them should know something about friends and relatives. It was a long shot, but right now, Mason looked like he was a loner. He'd been inappropriate with Darby, so maybe people stayed clear of him now.

Sometimes people in films took their power a little too freely. Maybe he had been targeted by someone he'd pushed into doing something she didn't want to do.

Maybe, sometimes, occasionally. All crutch words that told Rarity that she had no clue what was going on. All she could hope for was that the others in the sleuthing club had better luck with their assignment. Maybe they'd spark something when they all talked on Tuesday.

And there was the maybe and something again.

She was done with sleuthing for the day. She closed her laptop and curled up with Killer. This she could do without using the word maybe.

* * *

Monday morning, Archer was in the kitchen when Rarity came in from her swim. She kissed him and excused herself to get changed. When she returned, breakfast was on the table.

"Here you go, just like the doctor ordered." He handed her a cup of coffee. "How were the movies?"

"Okay, I guess. Darby and Marc were there. He was trying to impress her. He'd gotten box seats for them." She set down her coffee and settled into a chair. "How was hiking with Tyra McAdams?"

"Interesting. I called Drew last night and told him what she'd told me. Your stopping by asking about her ex-husband had her riled up. The marriage wasn't as calm as she told you. Yes, I was listening to the two of you talk before I came outside. He cheated. She caught him. He didn't want to lose her and tried to patch things up. But the damage had been done. She's still in love with the guy, but she can't forgive him."

"So he's starting over?" Rarity cut into her waffle. "I guess if Darby knows the whole story, then it's up to her if she decides to trust him. I don't see him as the stalker. Although someone else could have been upset about her dating him. Like Tyra."

"You think Tyra is stalking Darby, trying to get her to dump Marc?" He took a bite of his waffle and chewed thoughtfully. "The brother, Rufus, seems to be a little too involved in the relationship. Maybe it's him."

"Okay, now it just sounds dumb when you say it. All I know is the sleuthing club is going to take away my junior inspector decoder ring if I don't come up with something before the next meeting." Rarity poured more syrup on her waffle.

"Sometimes the things you know that aren't true are the stepping stones to the ones that are true." Archer waved a piece of bacon at her before taking a bite.

"Thank you, Mr. Buddha."

"I prefer Dr. Buddha, if you please." He leaned back, finishing off the bacon. "Do you want to go check out a new hike with me this morning? It's not too far away and we should be back before it gets too hot. I'd leave the squirt behind."

"See that, Killer?" Rarity made eye contact with the little dog, currently sitting between them as if wondering which one would be more likely to feed him something off the table. "He called you names. I think you should bite him. Especially since he said to leave you home."

"It's a pretty gnarly hike. I'd hate for him to get tired and fall off the edge or something. I don't know what you'd do without the little guy."

"I'd replace him within a day, then feel guilty about replacing him. I'm not sure I can live alone again. I need someone to talk to when no humans are around." She blinked and said, "Huh."

Archer watched as Rarity pulled out her phone and sent a text message. "Want to explain?"

"Just a hunch. I'm wondering if anyone was watching over Mason's pets while he was here. And if so, do they know Mason is dead now?"

"The guy might not have had any." Archer rinsed his plate. "So, the hike?"

"I'm going to say yes. I need to get out and move. Thanks for asking." She stood and gave him her plate as well. "I'll clean up the kitchen when we get back."

"I dirtied it, I'll get the dishwasher started." he kissed her on the cheek. "Go get ready and set up Killer for the day. We might stop for a late lunch on our way back." He winked at her. "If you're good."

"I'm always good," Rarity called back as she made her way to the bedroom to change. She was probably just overthinking this whole investigation. If she got out of her head, maybe she'd have some productive thoughts about the murder. Like who killed the guy, for one.

She didn't think Marc Billings was much of a suspect. He also was a little bit more of a sleaze, if his ex-wife's stories were true. Sometimes, people viewed their relationships in filters. Like who cheated first. Or misunderstanding an outside relationship. It wasn't her business who Darby dated, but since she didn't have relatives, Rarity felt an obligation to at least ask if Marc had told her about what happened with Tyra.

They were on third-date territory. The subject of their exes had to have come up in some format. She'd see how honest the guy really was when she talked to Darby.

It wasn't really butting in if there were good reasons, right?

CHAPTER 14

Tuesday morning, Rarity was in the store early, cleaning. It was a task she took upon herself every week. Sometimes, the Monday person did it. Mostly when Shirley was the Monday person. With Katie and Darby, they struggled to get the cleaning portions of the to-do list done, so Rarity just came in early on Tuesday. She'd brought Killer with her, but Archer had volunteered to take him home after he closed his shop for the day. At least he wouldn't be alone all day.

The bathrooms and the front shop area had all been done. Killer was curled on the front couch, so she'd just mopped around him. Even if he got up before the floors dried, his little paw prints wouldn't make much of a mess as he walked around, looking for her.

Now all she needed to do was the break room. Then she'd dry a path to the couch and hang out with Killer until the floors all dried.

As she swept under the counter, something came flying out. She frowned as she leaned over it. It was a syringe. It must have been from the EMTs working on Mason, but typically, they were better at cleaning up after themselves. Especially needles and syringes. She put it on the counter and finished up her cleaning tasks.

Promptly at ten, the front door opened slightly. There was a chain lock on the door from a prior owner of the building and Rarity had engaged it, hoping to keep people off the wet floors. "Hold on a second, I'll be right there."

She double-checked the floors with a sweep of her hand before setting the book she'd been reading down and disturbing a sleeping Killer. All dry. The back room might be the only one still a little wet.

She walked over and unhinged the chain and opened the door to Jonathon and Darby. "Come on in," she said, then warned them about the back room.

Jonathon set the laptop bag on what he considered "his" table and then set the coffee carrier he had in his hands on the register counter. "Coffee by request. Including a mint mocha for Darby, but really, dear, that's just really hot chocolate."

"It has a shot of espresso in it too, so don't be dogging on my choice of coffee. I've got lots of energy and burn all these calories off in minutes." Darby took the coffee then opened the door to the back room. She leaned down to touch. "It's still a little damp."

"It won't be for long." Rarity took her coffee and took a long sip. Sure, she'd had one or two at home before coming in, but there was just something about coffee you didn't have to make yourself. "Darby, I wanted to talk to you about Marc. Do you mind?"

"You're going to tell me about his ex-wife and how they broke up?" Darby guessed and then laughed at the look on Rarity's face. "Marc and Tyra are still friends. She told him about seeing you on Sunday morning and about telling Archer her sad story. She knew it would get back to you and that you'd feel responsible to tell me."

"Not quite responsible, but yes. If I know the guy you're dating has a history of cheating, I'm going to mention it." Rarity glanced between Darby and Jonathon. "Am I wrong?"

"I think I should stay out of this. Back in the day, when Edith and I were dating, we didn't talk about our prior relationships quite as freely as you all do now." Jonathon was setting up his laptop to get ready to write this morning.

"I'm not mad. In fact, I'm happy that you feel a need to protect me. I don't have many friends; most of them live here and will be at the book club meeting tonight. And I have no family. I'm glad you cared enough to warn me. Besides, Marc and I aren't serious, yet. He wants it to develop, but I'm not sure. He doesn't live here and he's on the road a lot with that commenter contract he just signed. I just want to be friends until we see if this is something more." Darby sipped her coffee.

"You're a smart cookie," Jonathon said as he pulled out his notebook and started making notes.

"I feel better that you know. It was like I was keeping something from you. And even if it hadn't been my place to blow the whistle on Marc, there's no way I was going to keep something like that from you. Even if it hurt our friendship." Rarity opened the register. "I think we're ready for customers. Can you put out the sidewalk sign?"

"Sure, I'll be right back." Darby headed to the front and then disappeared outside with the sign.

"I'm glad that's over," Rarity said aloud. She hadn't been sure if Jonathon was even listening until he responded.

"Friends tell each other the truth." Then he focused on his laptop again, and he was lost.

It was an hour later when Jonathon came back out of the back room, a coffee cup in his hand. "Are you giving Killer shots for something?"

Rarity, deep into her website updating, frowned as she tried to process what he'd said, especially after she'd just moved everything from one side of the page to another. "What? No. He's healthy. He just got his shots at his annual last month, why?"

"The syringe you use is the one that Edith uses on Romeo. She said she could give him his shots since she was a nurse before she retired. So why do you have a syringe?" Now Jonathon was watching her.

"I found it under the cabinet when I swept. I thought it was from the EMT visit for Mason. Are you telling me it's not?"

Jonathon shook his head. "These guys are anal about making sure all the sharps are accounted for. If they'd lost one, someone would have come and checked the area."

She stared at him, wondering if they were thinking the same thing. "We need to get this to Drew."

"Yes. And don't touch the needle end. If it was the one that injected the poison, it might still have some on it." He grabbed Darby's arm as she started to go into the back room.

"Hey." She turned to him. "What's the matter?"

He held up a hand. "Give me a second before you go in. Rarity, do you have a box we can put that in? Then I'll walk it over to the station. Order lunch and I'll pick it up on my way back."

"Sounds good. Hold on a second, Darby. We need to get something out of there before you can go inside." Rarity didn't want to mention the needle or Mason since Darby had been one of the last people, besides the killer, to see Mason alive that night. She handed her a menu from Carole's. "Pick out your lunch while you're waiting."

Rarity found a box under the cabinet behind the register. She handed it to Jonathon with some bubble wrap. "So hopefully it won't poke through the box."

He raised his eyebrows, then took the packing material and disappeared into the back room.

Rarity watched from the door as he used a glove to move the needle onto the bubble wrap, then into the box. He closed the box, put some tape on the top, then let out a long breath.

"There, it should be safe, but just in case, I'm putting it into a bag and carrying that. Not the box. I've got stuff I still want to do with my one and precious life. Like see Drew get married."

Rarity took the lunch order, and after adding her and Jonathon's order to the list, she called it in as Jonathon left the building. Now that she knew what it was, she was glad it was out of the store and safely on its way to the police station. Let them deal with the potential poisoning issue. She hung up the phone and then noticed that Darby hadn't left the spot where she'd been since Jonathon stopped her. "Lunch will be here soon."

"That's what killed Pike, right? That syringe and whatever was inside it? That's why you didn't want Jonathon touching it and why you kept me out of the room. I'm not that sensitive. I know Pike was poisoned. I didn't kill him."

"Oh, dear. I don't think you killed him. I just didn't want you upset. You've had a lot going on the last couple weeks."

"I'm an adult, Rarity. You need to treat me that way." Darby went off with a box of books to shelve.

Rarity wanted to apologize, but she wasn't sure which sin in Darby's eyes was the bigger one: trying to save her from Marc or not letting her go into the back room because of the syringe?

* * *

Darby was still upset with Rarity when book club started, but she hid it well—almost. Rarity saw the questioning looks the others gave Darby, then Rarity, whenever Darby spoke directly to her. Which wasn't often.

"Jonathon? Since you're hanging out at Drew's and keeping us from getting into trouble, do you want to run the meeting tonight?" Rarity held out the whiteboard pen. She'd specifically chosen purple to see if he'd change to his regular black or use the purple. It was the little things that made her smile. Like messing with Jonathon.

"I can do that," Jonathon said, then switched the pen out to a black on the tray under the board. He saw Rarity's smile and shook the pen at her. "Anyway, what have we found out since last week? Who wants to go first?"

Rarity raised her hand. "I'll go first since my answer is not much. I checked out Mason's social media along with Talia's, his ex-girlfriend, and there's not a lot there. They've been broken up for a while, according to Talia's posts. Mason's doesn't mention Talia since the breakup. And it looks like he hired a professional to make his posts. Comparing those to Marc Billings, his look almost like a machine did them. No humor, no emotion, no life." Rarity saw the look Darby gave her. "And the reason I looked at Marc's was for the second question we had last time, who was stalking Darby. Marc's social media is open and seems to be a lot like him. Nothing came out of any of the digging, except for one creepy comment on Marc's and that has now been explained."

"And…" Jonathon prompted her. When Rarity shrugged, unsure of what he was leading her toward, he added, "You found today…"

"Oh, yeah, we found what might be the murder weapon in the back room. I thought it was from the EMTs, but Jonathon thinks it might be veterinarian grade. Or bought from a vet store." She saw that everyone was

SLEUTHING WITH THE STARS   123

looking expectantly at her. "It was a syringe. Sorry, I thought I said that. Anyway, Jonathon took it to Drew for testing. And now that's all I know."

"I doubt that, but we'll go on. Who else has a report?" Jonathon looked around the room.

Holly raised her hand. "I've been looking into Talia. After she broke up with Mason, she started dating Bret Black. I talked to him one night at the Garnet. He was drinking hard at the bar when I went to walk Malia home from her shift. She was scared to be alone."

"I was not scared, I was cautious. That's not the same thing." Malia looked around the room. "There was a lot going on in town, and I thought a friend might not quibble about walking with me home."

"Okay, fine, she was cautious. Anyway, Bret's a mess. He's in love with Talia but the girl runs hot and cold. And right now, it's icy in Bret's world. He said anytime they were around Mason, Talia would be all over him. But now that Mason's dead, she won't even return Bret's calls. Weird, huh?" Holly stood to get another cookie.

Rarity thought it was really strange. "You don't think Talia was just using him to get Mason back, do you?"

"From the way he responded to Darby, I think Mason had a type. Talia. I wonder why they broke up in the first place." Holly pointed to the board. "We know when they broke up, but maybe the answer is in the why."

"And do any of these people have a pet?" Rarity asked, motioning for Jonathon to write down the question. "After what we found today, maybe someone's like Edith and likes to save money on vet bills by giving their own meds."

"There are other reasons that someone would be administering meds to pets than being cheap," Jonathon said, but he wrote down the question.

"Oh, is Romeo sick?" Rarity stared him down. Finally, he laughed.

"No, he's fine. Edith's just cheap." He looked around the room. "More reports or questions?"

There were a few that he wrote down; then he assigned out the questions to people. "We need more data points, people. We need to find out when these people arrived in Sedona. When and if they left, well, besides Mason. We have that information." Jonathon stared at the board.

"Let's each take one person and fill in all the blanks for Jonathon. Well, he'll have to make us a checklist of what to find out. Then we can bring them back and compare them. Maybe we'll find a hole that way." Shirley put her knitting away. "I'm choosing Talia. Holly should have this guy, Bret. The rest, you all can divvy up."

"I'll take anyone but Tyra. She already thinks I'm too nosy," Rarity said as Jonathon made a list of people they needed to talk to about either of the two mysteries. Then he assigned them out. Rarity had Jane Carey.

Before Jonathon could dismiss the group, Rarity raised her hand and asked, "Why this one? She was his assistant. She's really quiet and now she's looking for a new job."

Jonathon nodded. "See. You know so much about her already. This will be a piece of cake for you. I'll email everyone the question list. Hopefully you either have the information already or can get it using creative conversation techniques. You guys can do this. I have faith in you. Besides, we always close our cases."

"That's true, but we've never had Hollywood stars in the mix," Malia added with a grin. "Okay, maybe not A-listers, but everyone has to start somewhere, right? What if one of these actors is someone who might make it big soon? And we become friends and they invite us to the screening of their big movie and then an after-party, and we find the love of our life?"

"At an imaginary after-party for a movie screening that hasn't even been made yet." Holly stared at her friend. "Why not just fall in love with this imaginary actor you're becoming friends with instead. Then you can have the big house, the yacht, the Italian villa, and the fancy parties."

"I'm not asking for the moon here. Just a little help in the dating pool. I'd even be happy with a writer. I'd have lots of time to shop," Malia pointed out.

Jonathon chuckled. "Maybe lots of time, but the money thing might be an issue."

"He can be from a wealthy family." Malia glanced around the room. "Seriously, don't you guys ever think about your dream guy? How do you know what you want, then?"

"You kiss a lot of frogs." Holly glanced at her watch as she stood. "Sorry, I'm working tonight. Let me know if you need some help researching online. I need to do updates on all the city servers, so I'll be just hanging around waiting for software to load all week."

Jonathon held out a hand. "Hold up a minute, I'll give you a list of people and places to check out."

"Okay, while Jonathon's setting up Holly with some work, anything else we need to talk about? Is Malia right? Is the fact that Mason Pike was an actor and a director getting in our way here? What can we do about it if he is?" Rarity asked the group.

"We had that famous doctor once and we found out what happened. I think if we keep our heads on straight,"—Shirley aimed the comment at Malia—"we just need to treat them like they're normal people."

"With really big houses and fancy cars," Malia added.

"A big house doesn't mean you're not a killer," Darby said.

Rarity's lips twitched, but Malia said it before she could. "Right? Look at you. You have a huge house and you still could be a killer. Maybe you killed Mason when he tried to get to second base."

Shirley giggled. "I haven't heard that term since high school. Seriously, girls, there's no way Darby could be a killer."

"No? Why are you so sure?" Rarity wondered where her friend was going with this.

Shirley nodded to where Darby sat. "She cries at the end of romance novels. I've seen her do it when we're slow here at the shop and she gets some reading time."

"In my defense…" Darby held up a hand. "It was a really sweet ending and they'd both gone through so much to earn their happily ever after, they deserved a little emotion."

As they got ready to leave, Rarity wondered if the romance or even reading test would predict if someone was a murderer. Just have them read the most romantically satisfying book and see if they cried. If not, something must be wrong with them.

CHAPTER 15

Probably because she worked in the movie industry, Rarity started her research on Jane Carey on a job networking site, LinkedIn. Jane's account had a lot of connections, but she hadn't even updated that to show she was looking for a new job. Her résumé showed she'd worked for Mason as a personal assistant for close to twenty years. Rarity kept going down rabbit holes on the site with Jane, but it never seemed to amount to anything. On Google, she found a page that said she was an assistant to Mason, then went off on all the things Mason had done.

Jane was invisible in real life, looking like she faded into the background with mousy brown hair and dull eyes. She was almost invisible in the virtual world. Rarity wondered if she was married or had kids. Rarity needed to dig deeper into other sites, like Facebook and Instagram.

A shadow fell over the laptop and Rarity looked up to see Shirley watching her. "What?"

"You've been on your laptop for almost two hours; what are you working on?" Shirley emptied the box she'd been unpacking, then cut the tape so she could fold it down and put the cardboard in the back. "Are you working on Jonathon's assignment from last night?"

"Yeah. I guess I should wait for his questions. She has a LinkedIn account she hasn't updated, even though she's looking for a job."

"She's networking in person here. I saw her at the showings the other night. She flits from one group to another, like a bee collecting pollen but she's looking for referrals." Shirley leaned against the counter. "I'm sure she'll be at the theater tomorrow. You should go and try to talk with her."

"I guess that's an option. I could take her the tape for the movie since she never came to pick it up. I know she's trying to get herself set up again, but she told me the attorney is paying her to deal with Mason's effects. So she should deal with them, right?" Rarity was a little annoyed at the woman. It wasn't like she didn't have a thousand things to do. Now, she was going to have to go to the theater and see if she could track Jane down. Sure, it would be easy, Jonathon had said, but he'd lied. She frowned, looking at his empty seat. "Where is he, anyway?"

"He took the morning off. He's going to his critique group tonight since he's in town. The man is giddy about seeing these people twice in a month. If I was Edith, I'd be a little concerned."

"She has nothing to worry about," Jonathon said as he came in the door. "I'm a one-woman man. Well, besides all of you in my sleuthing club who like to tell me what to do. But Edith knows where she stands."

"See, you're backtracking already," Rarity said as she closed her laptop. "Anyone need lunch? I brought some soup from home."

"I ate before I got here, but thanks," Jonathon said as they turned to look at Shirley.

She blushed as she said, "I'll be taking my lunch off-site. I should be back by one."

Rarity studied her. Shirley had put on makeup and wore a dress this morning. Rarity had assumed it was because of her Mommy and Me class, but no. She had a lunch date. Three guesses on who it was with. "You look nice. I'll see you later."

"It's not what you think," Shirley started, but then a customer came in and headed straight to Rarity to ask about one of the books that a film introduction had mentioned.

By the time she'd finished with the customer, Shirley was gone, and Jonathon was deep into his writing. Rarity worked on the store's internal staffing and event calendar, then sent a copy of next month's calendar to the staff. There were some holes that needed filling, and she wasn't sure about events, but they'd let her know and then she'd send out a final one next week. Her team was good about stepping in. She wondered if Drew still wanted Darby to be with someone at all times. The harassment had stopped. Almost as soon as Mason had died, but it couldn't have been him since he and Darby had just met the day he was killed.

Rarity wondered if she was missing something there. But besides looking like Mason's ex-girlfriend, there weren't any connections between Darby and the now deceased filmmaker that she could see. She waited for Shirley to get back and then went into the back to heat up her soup. While that was in the microwave, she took Killer out the back door to the alley.

Memories of the night Mason was killed surrounded her as she waited for him to finish. It didn't take long, Killer didn't like the heat, even with his super-short hair. Her security system had been turned off that night, but since then, she hadn't had a problem with it. She went into the closet to make sure, but no, the system was up and running.

She took her soup out of the microwave then sat at the table with a book. Killer stayed with her, curled in his bed in the back room. He had three beds at the shop and two at home. If you didn't count the actual furniture he claimed as his own.

Rarity had to admit it, her dog was spoiled. She set her book down and texted Drew again about a possible pet for Mason.

When his text came back, it made her smile.

No need for concern. He had a pet tarantula with a pet sitter who came in once a day. The sitter has been in contact with Jane and has agreed to continue to watch it until its new owner can pick it up. Who leaves a spider in a will?

She texted back the first thing that came to her mind.

The rich are different.

With that off her mind—she'd had nightmares about a dog or cat starving as it waited for Mason to come home—she finished her soup, getting lost in the story she was reading.

"Rarity, can you come out and help? Shirley's getting slammed," Jonathon asked from the doorway.

Rarity nodded. "I'll be right there." She rinsed the bowl and tucked it back into her lunch bag, then set the bag by the book. She would take the book home tonight and finish it for a Staff Recommends review.

Shirley had three people with books in line to check out and several others standing and waiting to be helped. Rarity made eye contact with Shirley, then headed to the young lady that Shirley had nodded toward. "How can I help you?"

The store stayed busy until closing, and the walk-in traffic just died at 5:00 p.m. Jonathon headed out to get the sidewalk sign and bring it inside. Then he turned the sign in the window to "Closed." "Okay if I take off? I'm meeting the gang for dinner before our critique group starts."

"I'm fine and I know my way home, even if Archer's busy, so go, leave." Rarity smiled as he packed his laptop bag then headed out. Rarity followed and locked the door behind him.

Shirley was almost as quick to leave. "I've got a few things to do and it's Women's Wednesday at the church. I need some calm in my life."

"You deserve it. We were busier than I expected this afternoon," Rarity said as she started closing down the register.

"I blame the film festival. I swear, I sold more books with movie adaptations this week than I have all year. I wonder if one of the presenters talked about some of these in a session." Shirley had her purse and keys in hand. "Thanks for letting me take a longer than normal lunch."

"We were fine. And when you came back, you kind of paid for it with how busy we were then. Thanks for being such a team player."

Rarity finished up the closing tasks quickly. Even though Archer wasn't coming to walk her home since he had taken a group out for a hike today, he had promised to call when he got back. So tonight was just about snacks for dinner, trashy television, and Killer until Archer called.

She thought it was going to be perfect.

Rarity was already home when she realized Shirley hadn't told her where she'd gone or who she'd gone to lunch with. She'd assumed it had been Terrance, but he wasn't sitting on his front porch when Rarity arrived home. Which didn't mean that they *hadn't* gone to lunch together.

It was just a little disconcerting. And, she reminded herself when she unlocked the front door to her house, none of her business.

* * *

The next morning, she left Killer at the house since she was leaving the store early and meeting up with Archer at the theater. She'd put on a sundress and tucked a sweater into her tote. When she got to the store, Drew was standing outside the door with Jonathon, waiting.

"You're five minutes late according to your sign," Drew said as he took her keys and opened the door.

"I had to go back and make sure I'd filled Killer's water bowl. He's going to be alone for a while today. Do you want to go entertain him sometime today? I was going to ask Terrance, but I haven't heard from him." Rarity turned off the security system and took the keys back from Drew.

"I'm working today, but if I get a chance, I'll pop in. Don't worry, I still have my key." He smiled at her, a long, sweet, sexy smile.

"Stop saying it like that, especially with that smile. It makes people think we were together once upon your dreams." She turned to Jonathon. "He watched the house and Killer for me when Archer and I went to visit his mother and stepfather a few months ago."

"I wasn't thinking anything." Jonathon smiled, heading to his favorite spot. "Except I was hopeful when you first showed up. But then you fell in love with that Archer kid and no one else was even on the planet for you."

"So why are you here, besides to drop your father off at his writer day care?" Rarity set her stuff on a shelf under the counter.

"That might be a viable business concept," Drew said as he leaned against the counter. "Actually, I wanted to see if you'd heard anything more from Darby. Any more incidents? The chief's getting a little concerned about the overtime."

"Why are you asking me and not her?"

"Because she'd tell me what she thinks I'll want to hear, and you'll tell me the truth." Drew picked up a book and scanned the back. "Oh, the plate on the truck came back to a young man who's an assistant for one of the film crews. He said he hadn't moved the truck since they'd arrived in Sedona. But when we went to look at it, he said he thought it had been moved. He'd parked near the back of the hotel lot. Now it's parked in the front row. With the keys inside. And he's missing a leather glove. We're dusting the truck for prints."

"So anyone could have been driving. Darby told me that it's been quiet. I don't know if that's because you had a car there, or for other reasons, but I know she's getting tired of all the company. Darby's a private person, which is one reason I don't think she'll actually go through with this bed-and-breakfast idea with her friends. It would mean that she'd have people in her house twenty-four seven." She tapped her fingers on her lips. "Malia was with her last night. Let me give her a call."

She went to the back room to call Malia, who confirmed that Darby hadn't had an issue for a few days. "I'm staying tonight. Then Katie's here for the weekend. We need to assign people again starting Sunday. Unless Drew thinks it's done?"

"I'll ask him." Rarity came back into the shop after letting Malia know that she'd call her before Sunday. Then she told Drew and Jonathon what Malia had said. "Should we take off the police car and see if things change? And if not, give Darby back some privacy?"

"As long as you're convinced that she'd say something if it starts up again. I don't want to be playing armchair detective on this thing, if there is a thing." He set the book down. "I'll take this. I'm not feeling good about not knowing the why behind these things."

"Darby takes everything in stride," Rarity commented. "I'm worried too. Until we find out why someone was stalking her, and why they stopped, I'm not going to rest easy."

"Okay, so we're on the same page. Now, what do you know about Mason?" Drew asked as Rarity snuck a peek at Jonathon.

"Haven't you been keeping your son in the loop?"

He shrugged. "I'm gone, he's gone. We don't have time to talk like we used to."

"Dad, please don't tell me you guys have this all solved and are planning a takedown tonight?"

"Okay, I won't tell you," Jonathon said; then, as Drew's face turned beet red, Jonathon added, "Calm down. We don't know anything we haven't told you. Did the syringe get tested?"

Drew sat down at the table. "Fine, here's what we know. The tests on the syringe haven't come back yet. Mason's lawyer is stonewalling; he says the executor and the sole heir are out of town. As soon as they come back, he'll set up a meeting. I only knew about the pet spider because I had a friend who lives nearby and got me the phone number of the house sitter."

"I still think it's weird that he had a spider as a pet. *Revenge for the Attack of the Venus Spiders* could have been his next movie if he'd lived." Rarity needed a cup of coffee.

"Don't even joke about that. These movies have all been strange, right?" Drew said as the bell over the door announced a customer. "Anyway, I'm going to recommend that we take the detail off Darby. If anything happens that's even a little bit out of the ordinary, let me know and it's going back on. At least until this film festival is over. I still feel like there's a connection."

"And we're sure the Scotland guy is out of the picture?" Rarity asked, watching Drew's face as he answered.

Drew nodded. "I watched the interview with his local cops. He was embarrassed about how he acted. He said that he thought they had a connection. But he admitted he pushed. His new wife is trying to train him better. At least that's his story."

"I keep going back that it's attached to Talia. That the stalker thought Darby was her." Rarity pointed out her logic.

"That's possible, unless you get close. Then you can see the difference in age. But size, hair, looks, it all fits. Talia, Darby, Mason. Is it just a coincidence that they were all here in town at the same time?" Drew had pulled out his notebook from his pocket and was drawing circles on circles, forming Venn diagrams. "Anyway, I need to get to work. Let me know if things change."

Rarity handed Drew the book he'd been looking at. "Let me know how you like it, and I'll put it on the Staff Recommends list. We don't have many male reviewers."

"Thanks, but I can buy the book." He tried to hand it back to her, but Rarity shook her head.

"Sorry, I'm not taking it back." She stood and backed away from Drew's outstretched hand. "Tag, you're it."

"And you're a nut, thank you. I'll send you the review as soon as I'm done." He held it up as he exited the store, his version of a wave.

She kept going back to Darby. The Talia theory was strong. One, they looked alike, and two, Darby had stopped getting threats. So why would someone try to break into Darby's house? They must have followed her there. But why would Talia have a house in Sedona? She was only here for the film festival. She had a lovely California home that Rarity had seen on Facebook. So if this stalker was smart, they'd be looking for Talia in one of the upscale hotels.

Shirley had come in for her shift and was reviewing the children's shelves. The good thing about hiring smart people was that they took responsibility for their assigned areas. The Mommy and Me class kept Shirley looking for trends in picture books and elementary chapter books. Katie handled the middle school and high school or young adult book ordering. She needed to ask Darby what section she wanted to take over. She had such wide interests, like traveling, the Scotland section, and real estate.

Something was niggling at Rarity's brain as she thought about the Talia and Darby connection. The house.

She went to the local short-term rental site and searched for houses with a pool and eight bedrooms. She thought Darby's castle had at least eight. There were a lot of houses in Sedona that had pools, but eight bedrooms? That was different.

She came across three, including Darby's castle, but a note on the top said Currently Not Available.

Darby had rented the house out when she was in Scotland. That was why the stalker had thought it could be Talia.

One mystery down. Or one part of one mystery. She wrote the information down in her murder book and then went back to ordering books. She needed to restock before the next festival.

Now, she just needed to find out who had been stalking Talia and why.

CHAPTER 16

Archer was running late, again. He texted that he and his group were on their way back and he would meet her at the theater.

Save me a seat.

Rarity hadn't eaten since the soup she'd warmed up for lunch, so she headed to Carole's Diner for a quick dinner before the films started. Standing at the hostess stand, she saw Talia sitting scrolling on her phone. She took a chance and headed over to her table. "Are you expecting someone or like me, eating alone?"

"Just me. Bret went back to LA. He has an audition tomorrow, so he needed to go back early. He wasn't even supposed to be here, but then he showed up and surprised me. Come eat with me. I ordered a drink, but nothing else yet. Are you going to the showings tonight?"

"I am. I'm meeting my boyfriend there. He runs a hiking company and was late coming back from a hike. I thought I'd grab dinner first. I'd love to join you if you're sure."

Talia pointed to the chair. "I'd love to have someone to chat with. So, tell me about running a bookstore in a small tourist town. Is it even profitable?"

"Surprisingly, yes." Rarity told her about moving out of St. Louis after the cancer and starting over here in Sedona where her best friend lived. "It's been the best thing I've ever done. My prior relationship, well, he was all about him and his image. So when I didn't fit his idea of what a girlfriend—fiancée actually—should look like, he dumped me."

"What a butt. But men are like that. Especially if they're in the movie business. Mason and I were *the* power couple. At least I thought so. Together, we built our careers. Not to the top, but at least we made a good living in a high-priced area like Los Angeles. Then, he decided we were done." Talia snapped her fingers. "He made me what he called 'financially whole' again, introduced me to a real estate agent who had what I could afford with Mason's severance pay, I guess you'd call it. Then the next thing I knew, I was living alone and single again. At forty. I know, my website says thirty-five, but no one hires a woman after forty. It's rough out there."

"I'm beginning to feel grateful that I was in my early thirties when Kevin dumped me." Rarity gave her order to the waitress and then waited for Talia to order. "So now you have a new focus, a new man, and a new house. What's next on your horizon?"

"I like your thinking, girlfriend." Talia sipped her wine. "I love acting, but like I said, the jobs aren't there. I'm comfortable. I could live without another contract for years. But I want to do something more. Maybe find love again."

"So, Bret?" Rarity sipped her water.

Talia shrugged. "He's a nice man. He's just not Mason. Don't get me wrong, the man had his faults, but you can't help who you love, right? Anyway, I don't want to be the more financially stable person in the relationship. It's nice to be taken care of once in a while, am I right?"

"I don't know. I like where I am with my new guy. I have my own house, my own business, and I'm happy where I am. I've never been taken care of, I guess." Rarity leaned back as the waitress set a large Cobb salad in front of her. Talia had the lunch-sized version with the dressing on the side. Even with just eating a salad, Rarity thought she looked like a glutton, at least next to Talia. She decided to change the subject. "Is this your first time in Sedona?"

Talia dipped her fork into the salad dressing then took a bite of mostly lettuce. "No, I was here last year. Bret and I rented a lovely house here in town that looks like a castle. Thank goodness for home rentals, right? I hate trying to live out of a hotel, but I wasn't planning on coming, then the film got nominated and you have to attend these things."

Bingo. Talia had stayed in Darby's house before. So two check marks on Rarity's list. "Sounds like you're doing a lot of these festivals."

"It's the season. Anyway, Sedona's nice. It's a little outdoorsy for me, but I love the little courtyard at the hotel where I'm staying. I've been reading scripts all week there. When I go back next week, after I meet with Mason's attorney, I'm booked solid for auditions. My agent has been busy using these nominations to get me back in the doors."

"That's fun." Rarity took a piece of the bread that came with the salad and put some butter on it.

"You can have mine. I haven't eaten bread in decades." Talia smiled as she pushed the plate forward. "My dossier also doesn't list my correct weight on it. But I'm close. It's horrible to have to make a living from the way you look on camera. You're so lucky."

Rarity blinked. She wasn't sure what Talia was referring to, but she wasn't going to feel guilty about having a roll at dinner. Then she followed up on the sentence that had caught her attention. "Do you still have business interests with Mason?"

The wording made Talia frown for a minute. It was fast enough that later, Rarity would doubt that she'd even seen it. "Oh, a few business interests that will fall to me, and some personal ones as well. And of course, Oscar."

"Oscar? Do you have a son together?"

Talia's laugh came easy again. Whatever line Rarity had crossed before had been either forgotten or filed away. "Oh, honey. Oscar is Mason's pet spider. The poor dear is coming up on twenty. I'm sure Mason thought he'd be gone by now; he got him as a joke when we were together. The tenth anniversary of the movie's release. Now, I get to finish raising a spider."

Soon after, with most of her salad left untouched, Talia left to go get ready for tonight's events. Rarity stayed and finished her salad. All of it.

As she finished, she took out a small notebook and made notes on the highlights of their discussion. And more questions. Was Talia, Mason's heir? What did she get besides Oscar? And who knew about this? Besides the lawyer.

She paused as she thought about her dinner with Talia. She'd started to warm up to the woman, until Talia had started talking about finding a man to take care of her. Man, she'd hate Archer. He loved hiking. It would never make him rich financially, but he did what he loved. Just like she did. She decided that Talia's idea of being financially comfortable was way different than her own. Then there was the silent judgment about Rarity eating bread. That alone was enough to restrict the woman from Rarity's could-be-friends-with list.

One question answered, more added. The math on this investigation wasn't going in Rarity's favor.

* * *

Archer slipped into his seat about thirty minutes into the first film. He kissed her on the cheek as he got settled. "Did I miss much?"

Rarity smiled and shook her head. "The plot's a little thin. I'm sure you'll get caught up quick. Long drive?"

"I couldn't get the group to leave. Finally, I said I was heading up to the apartment to get ready and that Jack would see them out. They got the hint then. Anyway, they booked two more hikes next week. I'm loving this film bunch. They like to hike and they tip well. They said I wasn't missing out on the movies showing tonight anyway. Tomorrow night's films are the contenders. Tonight's were just filling the ballot."

"Shhhh," said a voice from behind him.

She squeezed his hand and tried to keep from giggling. The best thing about watching movies at home was that you could pause them and talk anytime you wanted to. Here, you had to be mindful of others in the theater.

When they started walking home, he helped her put on her sweater. "It's cooled down. The wind."

"It's fine. We can walk. Unless you drove to the theater."

He shook his head. "Nope. I parked the truck in your driveway. Then jogged into town."

"So you had film industry guys on the hike?" She wanted to hear if they'd said anything else. "Any talk about Mason?"

"Not much that was good. You've heard the expression not wanting to talk bad about the dead? These guys had no problem breaking that rule. They said the movie proved he was washed up and not connected with anything remotely modern. Apparently, this is the first movie he'd directed in years. They weren't very nice toward him, but they pay and tip well."

"I had the same feeling about Talia when we had dinner today. Just not very nice. Kind of judgy of other people. Snarky but trying to be funny about it."

"Wait, you had dinner with Talia? How did that happen? I didn't take you for the fangirl type." Archer looked over at Rarity as they walked.

"Then you know me well. Anyway, 'someone' stood me up, so when I went to Carole's to grab something to eat, she was sitting alone. I took a chance and asked if I could join her. She said yes, then started asking me about how I wound up here. She told me that she'd rented Darby's house last year when they came to the festival. So that's probably why the stalker thought she was there."

"She admitted to having a stalker?"

"No, I put that piece together. I actually think, and so does Drew, that Darby's stalker was really just looking for Talia." She waited for a response, but when he didn't say anything, she turned toward him. He was just looking around as they walked. "Thoughts?"

"Not really, but it makes more sense that it would be someone famous and not Darby. So why would someone stalk Talia?"

"That I don't know. Unless it was Bret. He knew about last year's rental. Maybe we've been looking at the contacts wrong." She thought about the incidents. "The break-in could have been him just trying to get in. The note, he missed Talia because he was there and she wasn't. The flowers. The only thing it doesn't explain is the black truck almost hitting Darby. Maybe that was just an accident."

"You should send this to Drew." He paused. "Or tell Jonathon. He's been at the bookstore during the day, right?"

"Yeah, I'll talk it over with him tomorrow. Do you have to get home early?" Rarity wanted to suggest hanging out, but she didn't want Archer to feel obligated to stay when he was tired. But he hadn't fallen asleep in the theater, which was a good thing.

"Nope, I'm opening the store at nine, then Jack takes over and I've got a morning hike to take out. These guys from today asked if I'd do a private hike for them. So more movies tomorrow night?"

"I'm not sure it's helping find Mason's killer, but if the guys say these are the good films, I'd like to see them." She nodded to the house. "Come in for a bit?"

"I was thinking you'd never ask," he said as he reached for her keys.

* * *

Friday morning, Rarity was at the bookstore before anyone else. Shirley was running the elementary-level book club on Saturday so she would come in a little later. Thursday had come and gone without anything happening. Something that Rarity used to take for granted, but not lately. She and Archer had gone to the theater and seen more films. She hadn't loved any of them. But that happened.

Today, Darby and Katie showed up together just a few minutes after Rarity opened the door.

"Guess who got flowers last night?" Katie asked, pointing to Darby.

Rarity looked up and smiled. "I hope the card was signed."

Darby came up to the counter where Rarity was doing the opening tasks. "Yes, it was Marc who sent them. And since he's out of town this weekend for the race, when he called to see if I got them, he asked me if I'd have dinner with him next Wednesday night. Well, he asked about Tuesday, but I told him I was busy."

"Which is great. Girls shouldn't be changing up their schedule just to fit the guy's plans," Katie pointed out.

"Drew called and said he thought the stalker incident was closed. That it was a miscommunication between Talia and Bret. Did you hear that?"

When Rarity nodded, Darby frowned. "Wait, you're not surprised at all. You knew about it. Did you tell Drew?"

"I talked to Drew last night. He wanted to let me know that he stopped by the house Wednesday and spent some time with Killer. He set him up a grooming appointment for next weekend." Rarity shook her head. "I know he was the one to bring Killer to me after Martha died, but Killer is my dog. Sometimes he forgets that."

"But then Killer has lots of people who care about him and his welfare. That can't be a bad thing, right? It takes a village." Katie paused for a second. "Maybe for Killer, it's even more important since he was so isolated with his first owner."

Rarity hadn't thought about it that way. Drew's pronouncement had seemed a little overstepping, but she let it go. Especially since she had needed to tell him what she figured out about Talia and Bret. He called this morning, saying he'd talked to both of them and Rarity was right. Bret had thought that Talia had rented the same house this year and had left the note. And sent her flowers because he thought she was mad at him.

Darby might not have even thought of a stalker except for her history with the guy in Scotland. She made assumptions. And through those filters, especially with the angst of Mason's murder, it had all added up to something more. Drew was still trying to find out who had borrowed the black truck, though.

And he'd told her that his father was running late. Again. He had taken Romeo to the vet because he seemed listless.

Rarity wondered what the difference between listless and lazy was, but she hadn't said anything.

Rarity made assignments for the day and then pulled Darby aside. "Hey, if you're staying on longer than fall, I'd like you to take on something or a project. Like the book clubs. Or an outreach program. Just think about it and let me know. And I need a list of the types of books you love so you can be our whatever expert."

"Like a Scotland guru?" Darby grinned as she glanced around the bookstore.

"Exactly, but think bigger. Maybe travel or romance or time travel? You make the decision." Rarity opened her email program. "I plan to get to inbox zero status before the end of the day."

"It's an impossible dream," Darby said.

Rarity smiled. "Yes, but a woman's dream should exceed her reach, or what is heaven for? Or something like that. Let's get to work. It's going to be a busy weekend with the film festival wrapping up."

As they worked, Rarity kept an eye on the door for Jonathon. When he finally arrived with his laptop and Romeo in tow, she walked over to talk to him. "Everything okay?"

"He's healthy as a horse. They ran every test known to dog after I told him I was concerned, but Romeo is just lazy. So we're going to take walks in the morning before I come in for bookstore duty, and when I'm home, we're walking before I sit down with coffee. It will do both of us good to be more active." Jonathon wiped at his eyes. "It's dusty out there."

"No, it's not," Rarity said as she gave him a hug. "I'm glad Romeo's okay. I was worried."

Jonathon chuffed. "You were worried. You weren't going to have to be the one to tell Edith. She loves this dog."

"Well, now she'll have him for a long time." Rarity went back to the register. "So did Drew tell you about closing out Darby's stalking case?"

"Yes, and that officer is hopping mad. He thought maybe he'd found a ring of thieves, preying on women who lived alone. He had a whole presentation made out for things for patrol officers to watch for. Which is still important, but the lack of a stalker kind of took the air out of his tires. It's hard when mankind turns out to be better than what you're expecting." Jonathon arranged his writing table, and Romeo had found a spot to sleep near him on the floor. All was right in the world again.

Sam came into the store as Rarity was closing up. "Hey, what's going on tonight?"

"Archer and I are heading to the film festival. Do you and Drew want to come?" She finished closing up the register and put the day's receipts in a bag that she tucked into the safe.

"Drew's working," Sam complained. She looked over at Jonathon, who was packing his laptop. "I suspect you're having a video chat date night with Edith?"

"I am, sorry, or I'd volunteer as tribute since Drew is unavailable." He stood and gave Sam a hug. "Thanks for asking about me, though."

As he and Romeo headed out to the front door, he called back, "Don't forget to set your security system."

Rarity waited for the door to close before turning to Sam. "And there it is. I thought for a moment that the ex-cop was going to realize that I'm a freaking adult with a brain."

"He hovers because he cares." Sam laughed as she put the leash on Killer. "So you don't mind me being a third wheel?"

"Not at all," Rarity said as she held up a finger. "Let me lock the back up and check the security system. We have time to change if you want."

"I'll have to see what's in your closet that I haven't borrowed yet." Sam grinned as she pulled a book off the shelf. "With Drew busy all the time, I've had more time to read. So that's one advantage."

Rarity checked the back door and its locks. She turned and thought she saw something behind her, but it was a leather jacket hanging up on the back of the door to the shop. How long had that been there? She took it off the hook and looked in the coat's pockets. A small notebook with a pen was in the left pocket, and a wallet in the right one. Archer didn't own a jacket like this and it was too small for Jonathon.

She opened the wallet and found Mason's driver's license. This was his coat. She needed to get this to Drew. It must have been missed in the rush to get him out of the back room before the movie ended. A picture fell out of the wallet. It was of him and Talia at a restaurant. The photographer had superimposed the words "Valentine's Day" and the year. This year.

Had Talia and Mason gotten back together? Or maybe tried and failed, again? She'd never said anything like this to Rarity during dinner.

She opened the notebook and found a to-do list for the quarter. Most of the items were about festivals and events. Some about developing a new screenplay. *Send a thank-you to Rarity at the Next Chapter.* And one that made her pause. *Move Talia home.* He'd inked a heart behind that task.

CHAPTER 17

"Well, you got to see Drew," Rarity said to Sam as they walked to the house. After finding the coat and its surprises, Sam had called Drew, who came to pick up the items.

Sam nodded but then added, "At first, he asked if I'd just give them to Jonathon. I had to explain to him that his father had just left. Sometimes I think making time to see me might just be too much for him to fit into his busy schedule."

"I'm sure that's not true. He does depend a lot on his dad at times. Frankly, Jonathon loves it. He wants to be back in the action, but I know he's torn between being here and being with Edith." Rarity paused, thinking about the father and son duo. "Maybe Drew's feeling the same push and pull between work and a personal life."

"Yeah, but Jonathon retired to be with Edith. And the kids, of course. Drew is a long way from retirement, and I'm not sure I want to be the little woman at home, waiting. Especially when he has such a dangerous job. An officer in Flagstaff was shot the other day. By a kid. Law enforcement is a hard job. He's edgy all the time. I think it's getting to him."

"Or he's thinking about something else." Rarity didn't think Drew acted edgy the other day when it was just him and his dad at the shop. But this afternoon, he had seemed a little jumpy when Sam was around. She hoped he wasn't rethinking his relationship, because before this discussion, Sam seemed happier than she'd ever been.

"I guess I'll let it be for now. I don't want to confront him in the middle of an investigation. He has enough on his mind. But did you see how he ran out of the bookstore as soon as he got the jacket? It's weird, right?" Sam paused since Killer was busy with a scent in a patch of rocks.

Rarity had noticed his abrupt departure. "I'm sure the case has him busy, not to mention all the film people starting to leave this weekend. If it's one of them, he needs to figure it out soon or they'll all be back in California. You know the mayor is always clamoring about unnecessary travel."

"Let's just have a good evening." Sam bumped her shoulder to Rarity's. "When are we meeting Archer?"

"I thought I would have heard from him by now." Rarity pulled out her phone and realized she'd missed a call and had a text message. "And there's the problem. The tour is running long. This group decided to do a second go at the hike to see if they could beat their time. So they're eating, then going back out. He won't be coming tonight."

"I bet he's heartbroken not to be there," Sam teased.

Rarity nodded. "He wasn't excited last night, but these guys said tonight's films are better. Anyway, the money will be good on this tour. He's trying to get a down payment saved to buy a house he can flip. With Drew's help. I guess you and I are going to be doing a lot of girls' nights once that happens."

"It could be worse. They could be at the bar playing pool or darts. I've dated one of those guys before and it's all about FOMOOAGT. Fear of missing out on a good time. We have to admit, we picked driven men to fall in love with." Sam laughed. "Maybe I just need to learn to swing a hammer or paint. We could paint this new house of theirs."

"Sounds fun after a long day of dealing with running our businesses." Rarity sighed then added, "The things we do for love."

They changed into cute dresses and flats, fed Killer and turned on the television for him, then headed back into town. Rarity thought they still had time to grab a bite to eat, so they stopped at the Garnet.

"Malia's working, so I'll seat you in her area," the bubbly hostess said as soon as they walked in. "I haven't seen you two here forever. Where are the guys?"

"Working." Sam put a hand on her forehead like she was about to faint. "So we're here to party like we're single."

"Sure, you are." The hostess giggled. "Anyway, I'll tell Malia you're here. White wine?"

"Perfect," they said in unison.

When Malia came out, she had a basket of chips, guacamole, and salsa she set on the table along with the glasses of wine. "Hey, Darby's throwing a I'm-not-being-stalked party on Sunday. You guys are in, right?"

"Sure, what do I need to bring?" Rarity pulled out her phone to put the event in her calendar.

"Nothing but you and a suit. She's having Garnet cater it. So, potato bar. And of course, adult beverages. If you're picky, you should bring your own." Malia stared at Sam.

"Hey, I'm not picky. I just like what I like." Sam grinned as she grabbed a chip. "I'm having the strip with baked potato and veggies. And a salad out first so I don't inhale all these chips."

"I'll have the same, but with chicken. And ranch instead of the vinaigrette Sam's having." Rarity pushed the menu away from her.

"I don't know why I even ask before putting the order in with you two. Did you see the salmon special? It's Friday."

"Oh, no, I'll have that instead." Rarity changed her order. "Thanks."

"I'll stay with the steak. Last time I went for blood work, my doc said I was anemic." She handed Malia the menu. "My annual's coming up and I'm feeling a little worn down again. I don't want him to think I didn't take his advice last year."

"I'm not sure changing your eating habits now will fix a year of not taking his advice," Rarity said, then saw the look Sam was giving her. "Fine, your body, your choice."

"I think that's a different motto, but whatever. I'll get these in and bring out the salads. I'm so excited about the party. Katie's invited guys from her classes. Maybe Mr. Right will show up and sweep me off my feet."

"I thought you were dating someone, Dane O'Conner. What happened to him?" Rarity found it hard to keep track of Malia and her friends.

"Dane broke up with me before he joined the army. He said it wasn't fair to ask me to wait or have a long-distance relationship. His loss, right?" She nodded to a man trying to get her attention. "We can chat about it on Sunday. I'll be right back."

Sam sipped her wine, avoiding eye contact.

"You knew about Malia and Dane breaking up. Why didn't I?"

Sam shrugged. "I don't know why, probably because I overheard the conversation. She and Holly were talking about it a couple of months ago at one of the book clubs. She didn't want to seem weak, so she asked me not to tell anyone. I assumed she'd tell you when she was ready."

Rarity felt hurt that Malia hadn't shared such a big change with her, but she decided to let it go. And, she thought, she needed to hang out with the girls more often. Between the bookstore and Archer, she'd been pretty busy and had turned down impromptu get-togethers. She needed to be better at saying yes.

When Sam touched her hand, she looked over at her. "It's not a bad thing to have a busy life. Just don't forget to make time for friends. It's a hard learned lesson, otherwise."

"Which is why you came to St. Louis to sit with me during chemo days." Rarity nodded. "I need to prioritize these types of nights more."

"Yes, you do. Besides, I only came to St. Louis because that rat Kevin was ghosting you even though you lived together. There was no way I was going to let you go through that time alone." Sam squeezed Rarity's hand. "Not on my watch. Now tell me about Darby being stalker-free. I missed that discussion."

When they got to the theater, many of the stars of the films were outside, signing autographs and talking to the small crowd. Rarity looked around at the dresses. "Maybe we should have upped our game here. Tomorrow we'll have to dig out the formal wear."

"That will be fun." Sam pulled out her lipstick and refreshed it. "Hopefully we'll both have dates tomorrow. Let's take a selfie in front of the festival sign."

They did, and as they wandered through the crowd, they heard excited chatter. Rarity joined a group of moms who attended the Mommy and Me class. "What's going on?"

"Rumor is that Bret Black was just cast as a lead in the next Marvel movie. And we get to see his latest movie tonight. I hear Talia Brooks is negotiating a new series with Netflix. This is all so exciting to think that we saw them back when." Cate grinned at Rarity. "Oh, there's Talia now. Excuse me, I need her autograph. Maybe I can sell it later and pay for Junior's college."

Sam stood next to Rarity as the rest of the crowd rushed to where Talia was holding court. She looked at Rarity. "You don't believe the rumors."

"No, because Talia said she was just starting to do auditions next week. Unless this has been in the works for a while. And if so, why would she be working on the auditions? Something smells bad."

"Oh, I hope it's not me," Terrance said from behind them. "I haven't used this cologne for a while. Maybe it turned to vinegar."

Shirley patted his arm. "Hush, I think you smell amazing. You girls look lost. Where are those handsome men of yours?"

"Working. At least that's the story. Can we sit with you guys? That way we don't have to swat the men away like flies?" Rarity asked Terrance.

His smile widened. "I get to go to the movies with three lovely women. My teenage self would be going out of his mind."

"Just remember you're outnumbered, so in any discussion, we win." Shirley nodded to the doors. "Shall we get some popcorn and get settled?"

As they walked to the door, Rarity and Talia locked gazes. Talia dropped hers first. But before that happened, Rarity saw the flash of fear. She had been lying about the Netflix series and she knew Rarity had caught the lie. Talia probably started the rumor herself. And if it proved to be untrue tomorrow? She could deny starting it and say she hoped that she would be considered in the future. The woman was an actress. She knew how to play a crowd.

Rarity just wondered what else she had lied about and to whom? Now that she'd found the notebook from Mason, she knew that he and Talia had been planning on getting back together. So why would Talia lie about that now? Wouldn't it give her sympathy points in the press?

Nothing about this Hollywood crowd seemed real. Including the plastic spider the killer had left on Mason's chest. But had the killer left it there? Or had Mason tried to leave them a clue?

Did this have something to do with Oscar?

Rarity was glad when the movie started and she could stop participating in the small talk. The darkened room gave her time to think about what she'd just discovered. Or thought she'd discovered. She took a small notebook and pen out of her purse and wrote down the idea. She didn't want to forget this. And maybe the sleuthing club could help her flesh it out.

Because there was something there. She just couldn't see it right now.

Once the films were over, Terrance tried to get them to ride with him. He would drop Shirley off, then Sam, and finally Rarity.

"We can be home before you even drop off Shirley." Rarity shook her head. "I rode the bus to school for too many years. I know how this works. I'll walk Sam to where we can see her house, then I'll head home. I'll be fine."

"But I'd rather…" Terrance started, but Shirley put a finger to his lips.

"Hush, the girls will be all right." She took his arm and tugged him toward the parking lot.

"Thank goodness for Shirley. Terrance wasn't going to give in. What is it about men that they all want to protect us, even when there is nothing to protect us from?" Sam asked, then went into a discussion about the second film they'd seen and the way the director had kept making jump cuts from one subject to another. Finally, she asked, "What movie was your favorite?"

"You're going to laugh, but it was the documentary about the prisoners making quilts for the foster kids. All those old men looked like they could be someone's grandfather, yet they're in a maximum-security prison for murder. And they were lovely."

"Why would I laugh? I loved that one too. I was sad when the one guy got kicked out for not following the rules. But I guess that's what happens when you go into one of those places. You have to follow the rules to the letter." Sam was quiet for a moment. "When my brother was going through all that, the police, they'd show up at his house and just trash it, looking for evidence. Sometimes, even when you're innocent, you can look guilty."

They walked in silence after that, then ran into Drew and Archer. "Hey, what are you two doing?"

"We came to find you since you're not sitting at home, pining for our company," Archer said as he kissed her. "Just kidding, how were the movies?"

"Interesting," Rarity said as they started walking again. "Come over to the house and we can sit with our feet in the pool. I want to run something by you."

"And by 'you,' you mean Drew?"

"No, I think we all could have input. Maybe I'm just overthinking it," Rarity said as she took her keys out of her purse.

Archer took them and then said, "I think overthinking is your specialty. That's why you see things other people miss."

"Like me. I'm not ashamed to admit that the sleuthing club has pointed me in the right direction many times. I just don't tell my captain that. If he asks, I was the one to figure out the killer's evil plan. All on my own," Drew said as he and Sam followed Archer and Rarity into the house. He picked up Killer and rubbed his neck. "Hey buddy. You know I'm brilliant. Right?"

"And modest," Sam added as she took off her shoes and headed out to the backyard. "Rarity, do you have any Truly's?"

"And some beer?" Drew asked.

"She has both. I did the grocery shopping this week while she was at the bookstore. That's the good thing about being a hiking tour guide, I have time to get things done during business hours." He glanced at Rarity. "Do you want me to break out the chips and salsa?"

"Only if you guys do. We had some for dinner. Malia's treat." Rarity slipped her bare feet into the pool, pulling up her dress so it didn't get soaked.

After everyone got settled, Rarity went over what had happened at the theater. How Talia must have planted false news or had someone plant it to get attention tonight. "I'm wondering if she did the same thing with Mason. Maybe told him what he wanted to hear?"

"Maybe. The only ones who can answer that are Talia and Mason. The notebook, though, gave me an opportunity to question her again. The problem is she was at a prefestival dinner with Bret Black at the time our boy had spider venom shot into his system." Drew sipped from the can Archer had given him. "Mason was supposed to be at the dinner, but he begged off when he and Shirley set up the signing and movie event at the bookstore. Talia has an alibi. As does Bret. Too many people have verified that they were there—from the beginning when Bret gave an award out to one of his friends, to the end when Talia accepted Mason's award since he was working."

"Maybe the dinner got out before the movie started." Rarity still thought Talia was her best suspect. Bret, maybe not, but Talia? She had lied about her relationship with Mason. Lied either to Rarity or to Mason himself. It looked like she was the gold digger that she'd been accused of being for so many years.

"Sorry, Talia was at the dinner. She didn't leave until after Mason had been taken out of your shop. Most of the potential suspects from the film industry community were at that same dinner. If he was killed by one of the people he worked with, it wasn't in production. Maybe administration or someone from the actual studios. I don't know, that feels like a stretch without a motivation."

"Let's put the shop talk away and talk about going somewhere in the fall. I'd love to chase leaves in New England." Sam leaned back, staring at the stars. "Maybe find a dark park so we can look for galaxies."

Rarity smiled at her friend. That was why she adored Sam. She always was looking for the next star.

CHAPTER 18

That night, Rarity dreamed of spiders. Big ones, little ones, spiders all over the bookstore; then when she tried to go out the back, she walked in on someone bending over Mason Pike. He looked at her and grinned. "One bite and I'll be as good as I used to be. Just hold on a second."

She started to scream as the spiders ran up Pike's legs and the figure crouched next to him now turned into a man-sized spider. Her heart was pounding as she tore herself from the dream.

She reached for the clock and saw it was almost five. In the dim light from the window, she saw Killer awake and staring at her. She pulled him close and rubbed his ears. "Did I scare you? I scared myself enough. Sorry, buddy."

She decided to get up and get ready for the day. Saturdays were busy in the bookstore, especially during book club weeks. She didn't have to deal with Shirley's kids, as she called the elementary school group, but she would be dealing with parents either dropping their kids off or buying books as they waited.

Some of the women met at the coffee shop after dropping the kids off to talk about all things family. At least that's what Rarity assumed they talked about. Amy was a high schooler now, so she'd be here next week for book club. Unless her social activities or dance competitions kept her away.

Rarity needed to find another middle schooler to take over Amy's book reviews. She'd ask Katie if there was a bookworm in the group who needed an assignment. Being part of the bookstore community had turned Amy from a shy reader to a social butterfly. She gained friends at the book club; then, with her work with the backpack project, her confidence had exploded.

And she needed that kind of kid energy for the upcoming school supply drive in late summer. Rarity wrote down her thoughts, adding to her to-do list as she ate breakfast and got ready for her day. As she did, she remembered the spider dream. Was she missing something that her subconscious was trying to remind her about?

At the bookstore, Shirley was getting ready for her club and Katie was manning the register. Rarity didn't have a lot to do so she wandered the nonfiction shelves, looking to see if they had a book on spiders and other desert creepy-crawlies. They didn't. She went back to the front and grabbed her laptop.

As Rarity scanned the offerings on the screen, Katie pointed to one of the books. "Oh, I don't think I wrote down that one. I sold the last copy last week over at the festival booth. We went through all the local attraction and nature books. It was a crazy weekend. Sorry I didn't mark it down." She pointed to several others that Rarity was considering ordering. "And those two as well. I don't think we ever stocked that last one, but it's supposed to be good. My roommate last year, Charity, her boyfriend Todd works at the reptile store in Flagstaff. They sell spiders, snakes, those big lizards, all the things I never wanted as a pet. I want something cuddly like Killer. Not something that could kill me. Anyway, he said they stock that book and sell tons."

"Oh, what's the store name?" Rarity put in an order for all the books.

Katie closed her eyes. "I know the answer to that question. Hold on a second. Duh, it's I Like Spiders and Snakes. Like that really old song?"

"I think the song is about someone who doesn't like those things," Shirley added. "So they sold books in a pet store?"

"Tons, according to Todd, but that might have been five or fifty in a week. He wasn't good at details. But he swore that one of the spiders' bite was an aphrodisiac. At least for men. Stupid, right?"

"I read that somewhere. That there were doctors who were prescribing for someone to buy a spider out of Brazil to cure that problem. As if the medical profession doesn't have enough quacks. I guess going back to witch doctors makes as much sense as some of these anticancer diets they sell on the internet." Shirley rolled her eyes and then smiled at the little girl who'd just walked up to the register with her mom. "What about you, dear? Do you like spiders and snakes?"

The girl's eyes widened. "No! That's not the program today, is it? My brother always looks for them in our backyard. He's an idiot."

"Now, don't call Allen an idiot, Vanna." Her mom nudged her to put the books on the counter. "Besides, you read the flyer, Miss Shirley's talking about books and movies. That should be fun."

"As long as it's not snakes or bugs. I hate both of them." Vanna pushed her books toward Shirley. "I got an A on my English test so Mom's letting me get an extra two books today."

As Vanna and Shirley discussed the books she'd chosen, Rarity pulled Katie aside. "Look, I need to run into Flagstaff to talk to someone at this store. Do you think Todd will be there?"

"I can check." She pulled out her phone and texted someone. "Charity says Todd's working today until two. You need to leave soon to make sure you don't miss him. If it gets slow, he'll volunteer to go home. He barely gets thirty hours."

"Can you guys handle the club and the store?" Rarity looked around. Most of the kids were gathered around the fireplace.

"If it gets crazy, we'll call Darby in," Katie said, bringing Shirley into the conversation since she was free. "Right, Shirley?"

"As long as you're back by four. I need to leave then to get ready for the event tonight," Shirley said.

"The event is at seven." Rarity reached for her open planner. "Or I thought so...."

Shirley nodded. "It's at seven. Terrance is taking me to Flagstaff to a steakhouse he likes before the closing ceremony."

"Oh, sorry. Yes, I'll be back by four."

"Where are you going?" Jonathon asked as he sat his laptop bag down on the counter.

Rarity had a choice. She could lie, but if she found something, she might need Jonathon's help. "To a pet store. Do you want to come along? Did you bring Romeo?"

"He stayed home. Drew's off today and said he'd take him for a walk later." Jonathon picked up his tote. "I can drive. My truck's out front."

"You don't have to go. I know you have writing you want to do." Rarity grabbed her tote. Now she was glad she'd left Killer at home. He hated book club Saturday.

"Sometimes you need a break from the writing to think about the plot. I won't say I have writer's block, because I don't believe in it, but I am a little stuck on this. Maybe I'll see something on the way that will refresh my hero's outlook." He held up his keys. "Ready?"

Rarity nodded, giving in. "Fine, but I'm buying you lunch and gas."

"That sounds like a bad combination, but then again, my thoughts run the gamut of a typical twelve-year-old boy at times." He followed her out, remotely unlocking his truck and then holding the door open for her when they reached it. "Here you go."

"I swear you're the last of the gentlemen." Rarity slipped in, then put on her seat belt as Jonathon closed the door, then came around and got in the driver's side.

"I hope not. I trained my son better. So where are we going?" he asked when he started the truck and pulled out of the parking lot.

"Let's see…565 South Pine in Flagstaff. It's a specialty pet store." Rarity had written the address down on a slip of paper after deciding to visit Todd.

"Are you getting another pet?"

"Are you kidding? Killer wouldn't stand for it. That Yorkie rules the house. He should have been named King Fluffy or something royal. It's his way or you hear about it. I've changed his food three times because he decided he didn't like it after I bought a month's supply." Rarity rubbed her face. "I bet Romeo eats everything you put in front of him."

"And a few things we didn't." Jonathon started telling stories about Romeo and how he stole the raw chicken on the counter that Edith was planning on putting in a marinade for the grill. She left the room to answer the doorbell for a delivery and when she came back, the chicken was gone. Jonathon told Romeo stories all the way into Flagstaff.

When they got there, he looked at the sign. "I loved that song. Mostly because I was the one who didn't like the creepy-crawlies. Edith doesn't mind them. She dealt with the frog and turtle phase, but then the next pet the kids asked for was warm blooded and fuzzy. Like they should be."

Rarity smiled, agreeing with Jonathon's definition of a pet. Then they went into the store. Classic rock played on the overhead speakers, and as they came inside, a young man dressed all in black greeted them.

"Welcome. What can I help you with today? I have to tell you up front, we're out of feeding mice. The next shipment is supposed to be here on Tuesday."

Rarity wanted to ask if she and Jonathon looked like snake owners, but then again, she didn't want to know. "Are you Todd?"

"Nope. I'm Jax. Todd's in the back with the spiders. Head to the left."

She followed Jax's directions and found a young man wearing round glasses and looking like the really tall elf from those Santa movies. He wasn't Bernard, what was his name? "Todd?"

"Hi, you must be Katie's friends. She said you might be coming by. Well, she actually told me to wait for you or she would hurt me." Todd looked at Rarity and then Jonathon. "I take it you're here for a Brazilian wandering spider. We aren't allowed to sell those anymore. I can get you a nice tarantula if you want. But it won't help, you know, down there."

Rarity blushed. She didn't have to see her face in the mirror to feel the heat on her skin. "No, we aren't, I mean, we aren't together. We just need some information about any venomous spider that could kill someone. How would that work?"

"Sorry, I get asked for the spiders that enhance your sex life a lot. Especially when there's an age gap. My bad. Anyway, depending on the spider, venom can kill in a second or leave the victim to die a long, painful death." He listed off several spiders to watch out for and what the effects would look like.

As he talked, Rarity could feel Jonathon's eyes on her. It was going to be a long, quiet ride home. Unless she explained to him what Todd had been talking about. She broke into Todd's monologue.

"So, where would someone get enough venom to kill a full-sized man almost instantaneously?"

"Dude, are you looking at murder or assisted suicide? Either way, there are laws against both. I can't help you kill someone. It just doesn't feel right." Todd held his hands out between them and took a step back, running into a cage.

"No, we're not killing anyone. Someone already died and we're trying to find out why," Rarity said, patting down the air in front of her with her hands. The last thing she wanted was for Todd to freak out and let these spiders loose on the floor.

"Oh, well, there are places that milk the venom out of spiders. They shock them. It's cruel and inhumane, in my opinion." He tapped the glass in front of a large wolf spider, according to the sign on the glass cage. "Isn't it, buddy?"

"How do you get this venom? Buying on the black market?" Jonathon stepped into the questioning.

"I, of course, have never done such a thing, but if you ask Jax, he can give you a card and an email address. Send this dude what you need, then he'll give you a price. When you pick up the venom, you pay the cash. Easy peasy. But don't tell Jax I told you. He doesn't think anyone knows about his connections."

Jonathon took Rarity's arm. "Thanks for the information, Todd."

As they walked toward the door, she paused at the empty cashier counter. "We need to talk to Jax."

"No, we need to get this information to Drew and he'll have someone come talk to Jax. Having one supplier doesn't mean he was the killer's supplier. Let's let law enforcement take this arm of the investigation from here. You did good finding this possible murder weapon. Take the win."

As they got into the truck, Jonathon started it, then moved to the next parking lot. They could still see the front door of the store. But, from the angle, Rarity didn't think Todd or Jax could see their truck unless they stepped outside to look. She turned to Jonathon. "Are you sure we shouldn't talk to Jax?"

"Positive. This is why I'm part of the group. To keep you all from crossing the line. One person is already dead. Let's let Flagstaff come over and chat with Jax about his side business." He turned the radio's volume down. "Let me call Drew, then we'll go grab lunch."

Once the call was made, they settled on a Mexican restaurant, and after ordering, Jonathon pulled out the small notebook he always carried. "You did good with this. What made you think of the spiders?"

"A really bad dream," Rarity said, sipping her frozen margarita. She wasn't driving, and being around all those spiders had given her nerves a twinge. She told Jonathon about the dream. "I've also heard something about people using the spider bite as, well, you know. So I got to thinking that if Mason and Talia had a spider as a pet, maybe he might think, why not. Especially since from his to-do list, they were back together and she was moving back in."

"So that's what Todd thought. That we were together and I needed some help in the bedroom." Jonathon sipped his coffee. "Honestly, if not for Edith, and your age, you'd be my type, Rarity. You're strong, independent to a fault, and intelligent. Archer is a lucky man."

"I think that at times, he doubts that statement." Rarity smiled. "Thank you, though. I should have thought that maybe Todd would get the wrong idea and I could've warned you."

"It's a bump to any older man's ego to have someone think you've caught a pretty young thing. Just don't tell Edith I said that." He smiled as they brought out the food. "They're always so fast here. I wanted to tell you what I found out about Talia Brooks."

"Anything useful?"

"Well, Drew told me about the Netflix thing, and you were right. A quick call to her agent asking if she was being considered wiped that off the board. The agent wasn't too happy that rumors were circulating since they were trying to get her a new role now. If producers thought she'd already accepted something, they wouldn't offer and probably wouldn't let her audition. He got off our call quickly, saying he needed to clean up this mess." Jonathon talked in the moments he wasn't devouring his enchiladas.

Rarity had a chicken taco salad that was so good, she wanted to eat the entire shell. "So she was just trying to get attention at the showing. She seems to like that a lot. Was Drew able to verify if she and Mason were getting back together?"

"Drew no, but I have a friend in the LAPD. His wife has a gossip blog. I guess they call her an influencer now. He told me over drinks one night that she makes more money from advertisers than he does after almost fifteen years at the department. But he has benefits, she doesn't. Match made in heaven. Anyway, she said there were some rumors going around about Mason and another girl. Someone who worked for him a few months ago. Then last month, Talia announced that they're back together and she's moving to his mini mansion in the valley. Daisy, that's the wife, she talked to Mason, and he confirmed the Talia thing, but told her that the other thing was bogus. False news."

"Or,"—Rarity was beginning to see between the lines—"Talia found out he was moving on and nixed it. Then came home."

"That was my take. And Daisy's. She said Talia's one of those who doesn't want something unless someone else has it."

As she finished her salad, she thought about what Jonathon had found out. Talia and Mason had been reuniting. Yet, when Rarity had talked to her that night at dinner, she'd mentioned Bret, and him going home for an audition. And that he'd only come because he needed to see her. Rarity needed to go back to her notes after she'd talked to Talia and see if she'd written down exactly what Talia had said. And if Bret was here the night that Mason died. Maybe he wasn't happy with Talia's new plans and had changed them?

CHAPTER 19

When Rarity got back to the bookstore, it was crowded. Some of the kids were still hanging out, waiting to be picked up by their parents. Katie was near the fireplace watching them. In addition, a line of customers curled through the bookshelves to buy books. Rarity hurried over and tucked her bag under the table. Jonathon had dropped her off and gone to check in with Drew to do more work on the Talia and Mason connection.

"What's going on?" Rarity asked Shirley as she bagged a book and handed it and the receipt to the customer.

"The film festival announced that they're doing a raffle tonight and tickets are given to anyone who brings a new book for the schools affected by the wildfires in California this year," Shirley said. "Did you know about this?"

"Not a clue," Rarity said, bagging the next customer's book.

"The announcement was in the paper this morning. If you win the grand prize, you get two thousand dollars, five nights in a hotel, and tickets to the movies for all five days. And a Hollywood tour of the town, the movie studios, and a day at Disneyland. My kids would kill to go to Disneyland. Each person gets a raffle ticket if they bring a new book. Two, if they bring five," the next customer excitedly told them. "I'm surprised they didn't warn you."

"Wow." Rarity looked at the line. Several of the people had five books in their hands. It was going to be a really good month, but she was going to have to do some serious restocking soon. "Hold on a second, I'll bring out the second register."

It took Rarity just a few minutes to get set up. "I can take credit cards." She held up her hand, and several people jumped over to start a new line.

Over an hour later, they were down to just a few people in line. Shirley glanced at her watch. "I hate to ask, but it's four."

"Go, get out of here. Katie and I can finish this up. The kids are all gone, right?" Rarity rolled her shoulders and saw Katie's nod. "Shirley, I'll see you at the closing ceremony. Oh, I feel like a jerk because I haven't thought about asking, but how's George? Everything okay?"

"He's doing fine. He's back at the home, but Kathy is with him. She's hanging out for another week, at least. I saw him this morning. He's sleeping a lot." Shirley closed her eyes. "Nope, I'm not going to cry. I'll go over tonight after the event and Kathy can head to my house to sleep. He's going to need to try."

"I'm sure he's trying," Rarity said. She wasn't sure exactly what to say at this point.

Shirley patted her arm. "Let's all think good thoughts."

As they were closing up the store, a woman ran into the store. "I'm glad I caught you."

"We'll be closing soon," Rarity lied since they already should have been closed, but she didn't want to be rude. And they weren't open tomorrow, so if the woman needed reading material for the weekend, it was her last shot. "Can I help you find something?"

"Oh, no. I'm Gretchen Wiler. I'm Sedona's connection with the film festival. I hear we threw you a curveball today. My assistant was supposed to contact you and tell you about the giveaway months ago when this was planned, but I guess she forgot. Anyway, I apologize if the run on books was overwhelming."

"On one hand, I should be thanking you. I'm going to have a good month and I probably need some roof work done. But yes, it was a little overwhelming. Nothing we couldn't handle, but I was short staffed without notice." Rarity tried not to sound like she was complaining. She knew she was going to be happy about the profit, but she also needed to do something nice for Katie and Shirley.

"Well, my sister-in-law called me after she'd left the bookstore and told me you were shocked about the giveaway and about the line. I really apologize. I know you like giving excellent service, and…" Gretchen paused as she noticed a flyer with the next book club date. "And you also had one of your book clubs this Saturday. This is why I told Angie to get in touch with you. Anyway, I apologize again. Are you coming tonight? I'd love to buy you and any member of your staff a drink at the event."

"We are coming." Rarity turned to Katie. "Are you staying at Darby's?"

"We're all coming together." Katie grinned as her phone buzzed. "The pizza's at the house if it's okay for me to leave."

"Go ahead. I'll see you at the event," Rarity said as she turned back to Gretchen. "We survived, so no worries. I'm sure the girls would love a free drink."

"Just have them use my name at the bar. I'll leave a tab open." Gretchen glanced at her phone. "I work most of the festivals here, but I am really, really glad this one is over. The Hollywood people are just divas. Complaints about lodging, food, the closing times of the restaurants. You name it, they complain. Friday's opening dinner was delayed for two hours. The kitchen was livid. And poor Mason Pike. That was horrible. His assistant, Jane? She's so upset."

"It was a shock," Rarity said in agreement. "So have you heard anything about his death? From the festival people?"

"Talia Brooks, have you met her? Anyway, she goes from grieving widow to hitting on anything male. I've had complaints from the theater staff that she was getting handsy." Gretchen rolled her eyes. "I swear, I'm about to quit this job. Or at least tell the mayor I'll do all the festivals except this one. Let them bring in a professional wrangler."

"I've met Talia. She can be a handful." Rarity tried to sound like she agreed with Gretchen. Maybe she'd tell her something she didn't know that would help with the investigation.

Gretchen snorted. "That's an understatement. Jane corrals her for me now and then. Although I don't know why. Jane told me that she and Mason were dating and when Talia found out, she swooped back into Mason's life. That's why you never date someone you work with. Breakups are murder and if you have to see the guy every day at your job? It's worse. Anyway, that woman is an angel, cleaning up Talia's messes. Anyway, I need to get home to get ready. One more night, right?"

"Exactly. Tomorrow you'll wake up and the festival will be all done." Rarity was thinking about the connections between Talia and Jane.

"Unless we have a freak snowstorm that traps everyone in town tonight. I know, a bit theatrical, but with this group? Who knows. Oh, and we have a breakfast tomorrow. The festival that won't die." Gretchen smiled as she turned to leave. Then she turned back. "It was great to meet you. Maybe in a week or so we can do lunch to get to know each other better and I'll have my brain back to normal."

"Sounds good. Just let me know." Rarity followed her to the door, then locked it before going back to finish her closing tasks. No one else was going to come rushing in to buy a book now.

Archer was meeting her at the house. Now all she had to do was walk home, feed Killer, and get ready. Rarity thought she was as excited for the film festival to be over as Gretchen was, but for different reasons.

When she got home, Killer wouldn't even look at her.

"Am I getting the silent treatment for leaving you home? Romeo stayed home today as well, so your friend wasn't at the bookstore." Rarity went over and scooped him up, then sat on the couch. She had a little bit of time before she needed to be ready. And Gretchen's appearance had given her more than just an apology for not warning her about the book drive. Talia had been a diva for her as well.

Was this entire thing about Talia? She wondered, who was Mason's heir? Had he changed the will to include his longtime live-in girlfriend? And if so, had he changed it again when they broke up? Was his death about money? He said that the spider movie had been a sleeper, but had continued to pay increasingly more in royalties as the years went by. And as bad as it was, it had started his career as a director.

She reached over and grabbed her laptop from the coffee table where she'd left it last night. Hopefully, it was still charged. Killer was still curled near her on the couch and she didn't want to disturb him.

It booted up and she typed in a question on how much Mason Pike was worth. She was shocked by the balance. Of course, some of this was speculation and Rarity had already seen how people just said what they thought would make them look good, but whoever had written the piece had done some research into what Mason was paid for his movies, as well as the advance for his book. And he'd been smart and put his extra money away, instead of buying a newer, bigger house. He'd been in the same house he'd bought with the *Attack of the Venus Spiders* movie money. He'd even addressed the issue in his book, and the author of the column had included this quote in the article:

> *Money comes and goes quickly, especially in this business. You might think the next paycheck is around the corner, but really, it's two, three, maybe even five years out. You need to plan for the future as if this is the only money you'll ever receive for your work.*
> *At least if you want to eat tomorrow.*

Rarity sat back. Apparently Mason was of the scarcity mindset. She'd heard too many people talk about manifesting abundance, and Mason had mentioned it during his talk that Friday, but he'd protected his butt first. Then he trusted the universe. And someone had killed him. Had it been about the money? And a better question was, who got his estate now?

According to the article, Mason was an only child, and his parents were both deceased. He'd never had children nor had he remarried after his divorce, so the answer could be anyone. Including Talia. She wasn't mentioned in this article at all.

Would Talia kill Mason for the money? He thought they were getting back together. So what about Bret? Was he Talia's not-so-secret boyfriend? Or was it just a front so people wouldn't guess she was going back to Mason?

This could be its own reality show. Instead of being up front, you had to figure out what everyone's relationship status really was. It was giving her a headache, and she'd never liked those shows anyway.

Killer was going to be mad, but it was time to get glammed up for tonight's events. Fireworks were scheduled after the awards presentation. Hopefully, the fireworks would stay in the air and not erupt before between the nominees.

Rarity had already picked out her dress for the evening. Short but with sparkles all over it. The fabric was soft and light, something that she would appreciate if the evening stayed warm. And she'd found dress-up walking shoes to go with the outfit. She wasn't one of the actresses, so she didn't feel the need to take out her heels for the night.

The way things were going, she probably could donate them and not miss the shoes at all. She'd worn heels every time Kevin had taken her to dinner. They'd gone to the fancy steakhouses and the fine dining restaurants. Anywhere Kevin could be seen and talk to others. It was all about the show back then. She was just a pretty appendage. Until she lost her hair and her face started showing the effects of working a full-time job and the cancer treatments. Until she was too tired to wear the heels. Then he'd shown his true colors.

Even when he'd tracked her down here in Sedona to apologize, Rarity wondered what the game was behind his sudden change of heart. Who did he need her to impress today?

Archer didn't worry about what she wore, unless he thought she would be chilly. Or the time he bought her new hiking boots because he thought her old ones were too heavy. He wanted to be with her for her. And after his step back when his father was in hospice, he'd been the perfect boyfriend.

Except they hadn't talked about the next step again. Was he waiting for her to ask? Or what? Maybe next weekend they could carve out some time to really talk about where they were going.

And as she stared at her image in the mirror, she realized she didn't have the brain cells to worry about the next step in her relationship right now. Maybe Archer was feeling the same way. She closed her eyes and took a long breath, letting it out slowly. Worry never got her anywhere. Besides, how did she even get on this mental track? She had a murder to help solve and a Hollywood-style party to attend.

She finished with the makeup and her hair updo. Then she took a look at herself in the full-length mirror. It would do.

Rarity's assessment was confirmed when she opened the door to Archer a few minutes later.

"Wow, you look amazing. Maybe I should go home and change into my suit. I thought black jeans and a button-down would work, but I look like your hayseed country boyfriend next to you." He kissed her on the cheek lightly, as if trying not to mess up her makeup.

"You look hot in anything, so don't worry about it." She grabbed her shawl and went over to check that the back door was locked. "Okay, Killer. We're going out for a bit, but we'll be home soon. I've turned a movie on for you."

"Did you check his water dish?" Archer went over and looked. "Sorry, yes, it's full. I guess I shouldn't question your pet mother responsibilities."

"It's nice having someone here to help out." Rarity stopped and smiled. "Sorry, I don't want to overstep."

He paused and leaned against the island. "It sounds like we need to have a talk about where we are and where we're going. Can we put it off until another day? Or do you want to skip this thing and sit out by the pool?"

"In your dreams. Yes, I think we should talk, but not tonight." She took his hand. "I feel like we're tiptoeing around each other. But you don't have to respond. We'll set a date and talk then."

"Sounds good," he said as he adjusted her shawl. "You look totally out of my league and I'm probably going to have to beat all the other guys off you with a baseball bat. Do you have one I can borrow?"

"Sorry, no, Drew keeps our league equipment." She kissed him, then wiped the lipstick off his cheek. "You're amazing."

"Let's get this thing over with. The Hollywood guys have an early hike with me tomorrow. I'd cancel but again, they tip like crazy. I'm just stacking the money right now. I don't know what pot I'm putting it in, but it's going to be full to the brim."

"Did you hear about the book donation drive? They posted it in the paper today and my store was a madhouse." Rarity talked as she gave Killer a rub and then headed to the door. "Oh, and I met Gretchen Wiler today. She said her assistant was supposed to warn me about the book drive. Of course, they could have gotten the books at any store, but with the Next Chapter being in town, we got the majority of the hit from the drive. I should thank her and give her a check for the drive as well."

As they walked into town, they talked about little things. The night, the moon, the stars, and the events of the day.

The only thing they didn't talk about was their future. But for tonight, Rarity thought as she breathed in the cooler air, that was just fine with her.

CHAPTER 20

That night's event was even more over the top than last Saturday's event. Outside, a large area of the theater's parking lot had been blocked off, with patio lights strung all around and crisscrossing in the middle. Small tables were scattered around the area, and a large table with boxes behind it was next to the entrance. Rarity saw that several boxes of books had already been collected and put into a rental truck at the side of the theater.

"Okay, so all this craziness is worth it, just because they're working on replacing the libraries in the burned-out areas." Rarity squeezed Archer's hand. "I love it when people get together to help out others. Especially when it comes to providing books."

"The small bribe for playing didn't hurt either. Even Jack was talking about the trip. He said he's never been to Disneyland." Archer shrugged. "What? It's just human nature to be thinking about what's in it for me."

"With the number of people who bought five or ten books today to get two chances at the prize, I guess I have to believe that your view of humanity isn't as jaded as I thought." She scanned the area for anyone she knew.

Talia was holding court in one corner. Other actresses had set up in different areas all around the lot. Rarity wondered why they bothered. The voting had ended at five with the end of the last movie. Gretchen and her helpers were probably still in a room finishing out the tallying of votes. But attention was attention, good or bad.

"White wine?" Archer asked and when Rarity nodded, he touched her arm. "Grab us a table and I'll be right back. Somehow, we got here first before any of the gang."

Rarity moved over to the side where she could watch the entrance for her friends as well as keep an eye on the crowd. Drew would have appreciated the spot since it was right against the brick wall of a dress shop in town. He liked having something at his back. She gathered several chairs around the table then took several pictures of the event on her phone. Including the book drive table. She might not be able to match the prize that the festival offered, but maybe she could do some sort of book drive for the Sedona kids. Dolly Parton had built an entire charity around getting books to kids under five. Maybe that could be her legacy too.

But on a little smaller scale. Dolly did everything big, especially her hair.

Since her phone was still out, she texted Shirley.

Remind me to get the gang together to brainstorm an event or drive for books for Sedona kids. Like my fund I have for the book clubs. But bigger.

Then she put her phone away. Unless they did pictures, she didn't need it.

Archer came back with two glasses of wine and Sam. "Look who I found."

Rarity patted the chair next to her. "Sit with me and we can gossip about everyone."

Sam laughed but did what she was told. "Just don't let me drink my fill of the wine tonight. They upped the quality for this event, but I still don't want the hangover I had last weekend. And I think I said a few things out of the vault. Like commenting on the mayor's girlfriend?"

"To your defense, that dress did make her look like a lady of the evening. How could you know that they'd been dating for a year and she was a local lawyer?" Rarity said, holding back the laugh. "Anyway, I'm sure she's forgotten all about it."

Just then, the mayor, Ken, and Alexia, his girlfriend, walked by the table. "Good evening, Rarity. I wanted to thank you for helping with the book drive. Gretchen said you were a trouper with the mix-up."

"I'm just glad with all the books we sold at last week's festival that we were able to still have a good selection. I was just thinking about what we could do for Sedona's kids. Keeping kids reading is my top priority." Rarity had stood, as had Sam and Archer, when the couple walked up to the table. "Maybe something in connection with the school supply/backpack drive we do each year. I'll reach out as soon as we iron out some details."

"My Women in Leadership group would love to partner with you on this. We're always looking for charity programs to support that match our agenda," Alexia said, glaring at Sam as she did. "Women should support women, don't you agree?"

"Definitely," Rarity said. "I'll make sure we connect on this. Maybe I can have the kids running the program this year stop by one of your meetings? They love getting involved in local government. This is really exciting. I love it when we work together as a community."

Alexia slipped Rarity her business card. "Call me. We'll do lunch."

Then Ken put a hand on her bare back. "We need to keep moving. Lots of people to meet, dear. Nice to see you all coming out to support one of our local events. Sedona Strong."

After they left and were out of earshot, Sam sighed. "I hate that catchphrase. It's like we went through a hurricane or a tragedy or something. Anyway, did you see the look she gave me? I don't think she's forgotten my comment last week. She did dress a little more appropriate tonight. Only her back and a bit of leg are showing in that dress. Last week, she showed everything, especially since her skirt was so short."

Drew, who had joined them at that point, pulled her back in a hug. He leaned close and fake whispered, "You know that Ken is technically my boss and can fire me for any reason, not just cause. And your voice carries."

Archer laughed and held up his glass. "To keeping your job."

"And that's why I love you," Rarity said. "You didn't say keeping our women in line."

"I would never"—Archer looked stricken, then winked and added—"say that within your earshot."

"Now boys, you're going to get the male species banned from this table," Jonathon said as he walked up with more wine. "I enjoy spending time with strong women. One of the reasons I married Edith."

"Speaking of Mom…" Drew sat next to Sam. "She and Joanna and her husband and Savannah are coming up next weekend, so I'm hosting a barbecue on Saturday night. I've told the chief I have to have the weekend off and he granted it."

"You have too much overtime this month," Jonathon pointed out. "Just saying you shouldn't be overly grateful. Greg has his reasons."

"Thanks, Dad. Now I feel really special." Drew rolled his eyes, then continued, "Anyway, I want you all to come too. You're my Sedona family. Sam's already committed to come, so Archer, can you convince Rarity?"

"As long as Killer's invited, I don't need much convincing. I've had to leave him alone a lot these past few days. He's about to move out and go live with Terrance." Rarity smiled at Archer. "Did you want to say no?"

"After that? How could I? Drew, mark Rarity, Killer, and me as attending. What should we bring?"

"I'm having it catered by the Garnet. Don't get excited, they're serving pulled pork sandwiches and lots of salads and some veggie thing for Malia. If she's still not eating meat." Drew leaned back and studied the crowd. "And there's the rest of our group now."

"I didn't know you were having it catered," Sam said.

Rarity saw the concern in her friend's eyes. "We'll bring desserts. And drinks."

"I really think we'll be fine," Drew started but then laughed. "Knock yourself out, but we're going to be swimming in food."

"Where am I bringing dessert?" Shirley asked as she greeted the group.

Before anyone could answer, Gretchen stood on the small stage and started the night with a small speech. She thanked all her helpers and, to Rarity's surprise, gave a nice shoutout to the Next Chapter and Rarity and her staff. Gretchen was a class act.

Then she introduced Ken, who talked about civic pride and unity. Then the chair for the festival stood and laid out the plan for the evening.

"First, we gather and get fortified with a few drinks for the awards ceremony. I can check that box off my list." She held up a clipboard and the crowd chuckled. "Now, we'll head into the theater for the awards and speeches. Then we'll come back here for fireworks and a few more drinks to console the losers and congratulate the winners. Hopefully, after all that, we'll disperse on time and the cops won't have to close this party down. Tomorrow morning, we're having a sunrise gratitude breakfast. Well, kind of sunrise, we start serving at nine. I hope you can all attend. We'll announce our book drive numbers and the lucky winner during breakfast. So let's go see what film won this thing."

She started to leave the stage, then stopped. "I forgot the most important thing. Starting next year, there will be a new award here at the Sedona Film Festival. The Mason Pike Memorial Award will go to the best independent science fiction/fantasy movie entered. We thank the Mason Pike estate for the award money as well as their sponsorship of a scholarship for a local Sedona high school graduate each year who will be majoring in film production and screenwriting. Thank you, Mason, for your commitment to the future of our industry. We miss you, my friend."

As they got ready to move into the theater, Rarity looked at Drew. "So whoever is in charge of Mason Pike's estate is moving quickly. Have you heard from the lawyer?"

"No, and believe me, he'll be getting a call from me as soon as I drop Sam off at the house. And a call every hour until he answers. Even if this was in the will, I should have gotten a call back on who is on the heirs list. And don't tell me that Pike had a scholarship set up for Sedona kids before he died. The festival, yes, I get that. But why Sedona kids? Someone made that decision in the last week or so." Drew was on his phone, texting as he talked. He glanced at Sam. "Sorry about cutting the night short, but I should go in. Do you want to come with me or…"

"I'll walk Sam home," Jonathon said, putting his hand on his son's shoulder. "You go do what you need to do."

"Now I know how Rarity feels," Sam said as she kissed Drew. "I can walk home all alone, I promise, but since Jonathon insists on being a gentleman, I accept his offer. Besides, I want to see the fireworks."

"I'm happy to help out." Jonathon smiled and then waved Drew away. "Go on. How can we talk about you if you're still here?"

"No snooping while I'm gone," Drew said, directing his comment to Rarity.

She shrugged. "Not promising anything. Especially if new information drops in my lap. I'm blessed that way."

Archer laughed. "Dude, she's right. Except I'd call it a curse, not a blessing. Anyway, she won't get far out of my sight. Go solve the case so we can put this behind us."

After Drew left, the group headed into the theater. Rarity and Shirley went to the restroom with Archer and Jonathon in charge of getting a second drink. Darby had texted that they'd saved seats in the theater for them.

As Rarity stood in line, she heard Mason Pike's name mentioned by someone closer to the door. Talia Brooks was talking to Jane Carey. Loudly.

She glanced at Shirley, who nodded. She'd heard the same thing. As people washed their hands and they moved up, their words got tenser in tone. Finally, they were close enough to actually hear the conversation.

"You just can't go making decisions like that without talking to me," Talia said. "You're an idiot."

"And you're a witch, but we deal with what we're given," Jane said as she turned around to leave. She saw Rarity in line and froze for a minute. Then she smiled and walked toward the door. When she got near Rarity, she smiled and said, "Actors, it's always all about them. Hope you're enjoying your evening."

And then she was gone. Rarity didn't see Talia leave, and when she came out, Shirley was waiting for her. "That was intense," Rarity said.

"Talia breezed past me just a few minutes ago. She was on her phone but I didn't hear much. Mostly something about Jane not being controllable."

"Maybe Jane just found and lost her new employer. I knew she was looking for a new placement, but I don't think I could work for Talia either." Rarity saw Archer waiting at the door to the main theater. "And there's our escort. He's a cutie."

"Of course you'd say that." Shirley paused before she added, "Terrance looks very distinguished in his suit, don't you think? No, don't answer that. My husband is sleeping less than a mile away and I'm looking at another man."

"You're married, not dead. And George might be a mile away physically, but mentally, he's eons away." Rarity saw the look on Shirley's face and knew she'd gone too far. She looked like she'd been slapped. "I'm sorry. I shouldn't even be mentioning this, but I worry about you. And if being around Terrance in any type of relationship including platonic friendship makes you happy, I'm glad. Kathy's worried too."

"Kathy wants me to sell the house and move closer to her. There's no way. I have a good life here. Good friends," she said as she took Rarity's arm. "And I'm not giving up that to become Kathy's babysitter. Although I'd spoil those kids rotten."

"You would. And it's better for all concerned for you to stay here," Rarity joked as she and Shirley walked toward Archer. Then she added, "Especially for me. I'd miss you too much."

They made their way down the aisle to their seats, and as she was looking around the theater, she saw Jane talking to someone Rarity didn't know. She was all smiles now, after her tiff with Talia. She told Archer about what she'd overheard. "It must be hard to work for someone and not like their significant other."

"Jack does okay," Archer responded, reading the program for the night.

"Well, that's fine, but maybe it's different for men," Rarity said, still watching Jane and the unknown man. She saw her give him her business card. Still looking for work. Then Archer's words hit her. "Wait, what did you say? Jack doesn't like me?"

He looked up from the program. "Just checking to see if you're listening. Jack thinks you're great. For an older lady."

"What is he, nineteen?" Rarity stared at Archer. "I'm not that much older than he is."

"He's twenty and he thinks anyone over twenty-five is old. He considered asking Holly out, but then he found out she was almost thirty and it was a deal-breaker," Archer said. "I don't think you're old at all."

"Thanks, I think. Anyway, Holly's too serious for Jack. She needs someone who already has his life together." She opened her small purse and pulled out a lip balm. "Oh, I forgot to transfer the movie into this bag. Of course, it wouldn't fit, but Jane's here and the movie isn't. I guess I'm going to the breakfast."

"I'm hiking," Archer reminded her.

She looked over to where she'd seen Jane, but no one was there. "I'll find her tomorrow."

Sam squeezed her arm. "I'll go with you. That hotel serves an amazing breakfast. What time do you want me to pick you up?"

"Nine? That way we can get there before all the croissants are gone." Rarity liked the plan. "Just don't let me forget Pike's movie so I can get one thing off my to-do list."

The theater lights went down and the music swelled. It was time for the awards.

Later that night, back in the parking lot, sitting around a different table, she leaned into Archer's shoulder as they waited for the fireworks to start. "Now I know why I don't watch those awards shows on television. They're really boring unless you have a horse in the race."

"You weren't rooting for Mason and Talia's movie?" Archer entwined his fingers in hers.

"Not even close. I liked that one documentary. And it won its category. The film that took the most awards was kind of boring, if you ask me." She looked around the table. Shirley and Terrance had excused themselves after the awards. Katie was sitting with Jared, whom she'd introduced to the group after they'd come back outside. Sam and Jonathon were sitting nearby, quietly talking. In contrast, Holly, Darby, and Malia were singing along with the song the DJ had started while they waited.

Her family was all here or had been at different times of the night. At least it was everyone she cared for, like family. Had Mason had anyone in his life he didn't pay to be there? Jane, of course, but she was his assistant. And Talia had apparently moved on, either after his death or before.

The music changed, and the lights around the lot went out. Then the first of the fireworks went off and the crowd let out its first, but not last, ohhh of the night.

CHAPTER 21

Sunday morning, Rarity checked her bag twice before leaving the house, making sure the envelope with Pike's first film was in the tote. If she didn't run into Jane Carey today, she'd mail it to Pike's lawyers on Monday. It felt like unfinished business and maybe a bit of bad luck to hold on to it.

Sam knocked on the door at eight forty-five. "We can park in the hotel lot for free today, so let's get going before the rest of town heads that way. A lot of people want that book donation prize."

"It would be fun if a family got it." Rarity checked the house and locked the back door before hurrying to join Sam. "Be good, Killer."

As they got into the still running car, Sam checked her eye makeup in the mirror. "I look like I didn't get any sleep at all. I was all tucked in by eleven. Jonathon walked me to my door, waited for me to unlock it and go in, then stood on the step until he heard the lock engage. I watched him through the sidelight."

"He takes his walking assignments seriously." Rarity smiled as she remembered all the times he'd walked her home in Archer's place. "It's kind of nice."

"Yeah, in a paternal way. I wonder if he and Edith have always been this way with their kids' friends. Treating them like family, I mean." Sam pulled out of the driveway and headed into town.

"Archer said once his grandmother died and his dad had his issues, the Andersons were like a second family. He was always over there since his mom was dealing with family things and working." She turned the music down. "You and I were that way. We were together so much the people in town called us the sisters."

"Jake hated you," Sam admitted.

"What? I liked him." Rarity turned to look at her. It was true she had liked Jake. Of all of Sam's high school loves, he was the most stable. He had plans for college and beyond and wasn't just out for a good night.

"He said you were always around. We didn't get time alone. In fact, I think that's why we broke up. He wanted me to commit to Northwestern in Chicago and get an apartment the first year. We were looking at University of Arizona."

"I didn't know that," Rarity admitted. "But Arizona was a lot warmer than Chicago. And I had a scholarship there. You didn't have to come along."

"And miss doing the college years together?" Sam flashed her a huge smile. "I wasn't ready then to settle down. I wanted to go with you and have adventures. Like the time we crashed the frat house party and were the only nonsorority chicks there?"

"Why would I join a sorority when I already had a best friend?" Rarity remembered the party. She'd been invited to pledge but Sam hadn't, so she'd turned them down. And never regretted it. "I'm too much of an introvert to live in a sorority house."

Sam pulled into the parking lot. She turned the engine off, not looking at Rarity when she said, "I knew you were invited to pledge. Stephanie Elliot told me you turned them down. You didn't have to say no just because I didn't get an invite."

Rarity didn't say anything until she got out of the car. Then she gave Sam a quick hug. "What fun would it have been without you?"

"None, of course." Sam's smile returned. "But did you regret it?"

"Not once." She hitched her tote onto her shoulder. "Let's get inside before we can't get a seat."

They walked into the grand hotel entrance and headed straight to the large ballroom where the breakfast was being held. She saw both Jane and Talia standing across the room. They seemed to be in an intense discussion. "I think Jane's a glutton for punishment. Go claim us a spot and I'll drop off this film case before I forget again."

"Okay, but give me your sweater so I can run to the buffet after claiming our seats." Sam was eyeing the food items on the table. "I hoped they'd have chocolate croissants. We come here on Sunday when Drew's folks are in town. Edith loves their Scotch eggs."

As Rarity made her way over to Jane, Miranda, the producer with the romance film, stopped her. "Hi, it's Rarity, isn't it? I just wanted to thank you for the help with the book drive. I hear Gretchen's assistant failed to even notify you. I'm so sorry but I wanted you to know how much this is going to help those libraries. My sister is still in high school and her library is completely gone, along with the main administration building. The fire left the classrooms and the gym untouched. Wildfires are so fickle. You never know what's going to stay standing. Of course, it helped that the two buildings that stayed were made of concrete blocks."

"Miranda, you're more than welcome. And if the festival wants to do another drive next year, just let me know. I'll keep in touch with Gretchen." Rarity took a business card out of her purse. "Here's my information, in case you hear something and want to give me a heads-up."

"Smart. If there are several people watching out for you, maybe one of us airheads will follow through. And I include myself in that description. I guess we're getting started. My movie didn't place, but it's been a fun festival anyway." Miranda headed to her chair as Gretchen walked up to the podium.

Rarity glanced over to where Jane and Talia had been talking, and both women were gone. She went back to fill her plate and sat next to Sam.

"Mission accomplished?" Sam asked.

Rarity sipped her coffee that had been filled in her absence. "No. I got sidetracked and by the time that was over, Jane had disappeared. It's like this darn thing wants to stay with me."

"Maybe it's holding the ghost of Mason and he's trying to help you solve the murder," Sam said with a giggle. "It could happen, you know."

"It's Sedona. Anything could happen here. We're the home of the vortex, right?"

* * *

Back at the house, Rarity fell into the couch, wondering if this was the one case that would never be solved. Darby's stalking incident had been easier to solve, mostly due to the mistaken identity factor. Bret Black had been stalking someone, just not Darby. And in his defense, he didn't see it as stalking, just trying to figure out what was happening in his on-again, off-again relationship with Talia.

Talia—she was involved in all of this. She and Jane seemed to always be at odds with each other. Had the ex-girlfriend been jealous of the control Jane had over Mason's life? If so, she'd seemed to move on quickly. From Bret, back to Mason, and now, back to Bret. He must feel like a yo-yo. She knew feeling sorry for his attachment to Talia was futile. You loved who you loved. But she seemed so opportunistic. Making up the Netflix contract, for one. And maybe she'd been using Mason too. Especially this new, rekindled relationship, which seemed like only she and Mason were privy to. Had Talia been messing with his head and not planning on moving back in? And why would Jane hold that against her? Or were they fighting over something else?

It occurred to Rarity that she'd never checked out the rest of Jane's social media posts. Grabbing her laptop, she opened it. At least she'd have something to report to the sleuthing club on Tuesday. When she found the right Jane Carey, Rarity sat straighter and kept scrolling. The page was a memorial to her old boss. Picture after picture, candid shots, not posed, pictures were plastered all over her Facebook feed. Including one with her and Mason's arm around her.

Had Jane been in love with Mason?

She texted Drew and asked if there were any fingerprints on the syringe she'd found in the back room.

One word came back. *Yes.*

Then her phone rang. "Hey, Drew."

"What do you think you know?" he asked, not wasting time with a greeting.

"I think Talia killed him, but I can't figure out why. Money? Who's the person behind the charitable donations to the festival and the Sedona scholarship? Do you know yet?"

"That I know. His lawyer had a certain allowance to make donations around the moviemaking industry. He thought it might go a long way in keeping Mason's name out of the mud here. He said he reached out to the stepbrother listed in the will, and he died last year. Two guesses on who the other heir is, and first guess doesn't count."

"It's Talia, right? Did Jane get anything? I know she's just an employee, but they were together for years. And she was in love with him."

"Why do you say that?" Drew's reaction to the statement was quick.

"Check out her Facebook page. She's got pictures of him all over. I didn't know you could attach that many pictures to one post." Rarity realized she was getting off track. "So whose fingerprint is it?"

"Unknown. We've asked for a release through a judge, but so far, they're stonewalling. I'll let you know if we make an arrest."

"Oh gee, thanks, Dad." Rarity tried to pull everything together that Drew had told her into a question. One he couldn't avoid answering. Or at least his lack of an answer would mean she was on the right path. "Oh, one question. This stuff was for his performance issues, right? Could he have delivered the shot himself? Especially if he thought he was getting lucky with Darby?"

"Interesting question," Drew acknowledged, "and really good thinking, but the answer is no. Apparently this provider from the snake shop said he sold Mason three shots the last week since he'd forgotten his supply at home. Then he shut up when we started talking about conspiracy to murder charges. The coroner said the blood report showed three times the amount of toxin than the syringe we found in the kid's car. Someone mixed all three shots in one syringe. The kid swears they were separate when he sold them. He also said he wasn't stupid, so there's that."

"Someone wanted to kill him with the venom."

Drew sighed. "Looks that way. And it had to be someone close enough who knew he was using it in the first place."

After talking to Drew, Rarity decided to go for a drive. She needed to think about Mason's death and his life before. Who would have wanted to kill him? Did he have someone else in his life who was close enough to know about Mason's habit and could have gotten close to him that night at the bookstore?

She bundled Killer up with his leash. "Want to go for a short drive? Maybe we'll even go to the pet store. You're almost out of dog treats."

Killer thought that was a great idea and ran to the door to wait for her.

As she drove out of the subdivision and around town, she started thinking about who Mason would tell about his situation.

Not a guy, definitely. Drew and Archer both had been uncomfortable with even the idea of using the spider venom in any way. Rarity smiled as she remembered the way Archer had covered his ears even, like a young boy.

So the killer had to be a woman. He said they had asked a judge to gather fingerprints, but he didn't say on who. Talia? Or Jane? Or someone else?

Jane obviously was in love with her boss. Especially after seeing her Facebook page. But had Mason ever seen her that way? She was Talia's and Darby's total opposite. Dark, straight hair compared to their red, curly hair and green eyes. Jane wasn't ugly, but she'd never be called beautiful. At least not in the California movie industry. He probably appreciated her quick wit and dedication, along with her intelligence, but for Mason, the attraction must not have been there.

Rarity found herself at the theater. The doors were open, and it looked like they were cleaning up after last night. She parked and put Killer on his leash; then she walked up to the still blocked-off parking lot. No one even looked at her as she wandered around the empty tables and chairs. A piece of paper, maybe a business card, was in the corner of the lot. She leaned down and picked it up. It was for the snake shop in Flagstaff. On the back was a name: Jax.

She stared at the card then looked around the area, trying to remember who was here last night. They'd sat over by the side, and in each corner, a different movie group had taken up shop. And in this corner, Talia had been holding court. If she remembered right. She texted Archer and asked if he remembered where Talia had been sitting.

Talia who?

Okay, so Archer wasn't going to be a help here. She texted a *never mind*, then sent the same question to Jonathon.

This time she hit pay dirt. He did remember.

She started to call him then saw someone heading her way. She put the phone away.

"Can I help you?" the man in a polo with the theater's logo asked.

"Oh, I thought I left my shawl here last night after the fireworks. You didn't find one, did you? It's pink with sparkles?" Rarity asked, hoping that someone else hadn't had the same shawl and had left it.

"No sorry. I'm going to have to ask you to leave. We're tearing down the area and I don't want you to get hurt." He held his hand out toward the entrance. "You can call the theater on Wednesday. Ask to talk to Cheri about your shawl. If it was here and someone turned it in, she'd know."

"Oh, thank you. I appreciate the help." She tugged on Killer's leash as he sat down to wait for her. They went back to the car where Rarity called Jonathon. "Hey, are you sure they were in that corner?"

"Southwest by the street, yep," he answered quickly. "Why? What did you find?"

"I'll bring it Tuesday night." She paused. "Look, I'm heading into Flagstaff. I'll chat with you Tuesday."

"Okay, I've already talked to Shirley and I'll be at the bookstore tomorrow with Romeo to write, if you want to stop by." Jonathon was giving her another option.

"I'm not sure what I'm doing Monday," she said. "Anyway, I better go. I don't want to be on my phone driving."

"You have a Bluetooth system, but whatever. Romeo wants out anyway." He paused then said, "Just be careful and call me on your way home."

"I'm not out sleuthing," Rarity said. Okay, so she was, but Jonathon didn't need to know that.

"Whatever you want to say. I raised two kids and was a police detective. Rarity, I can tell an omission as well as a lie."

"Okay, well, I'll call you on my way home." Rarity ended the call. She knew that Archer had a Find My Phone app on both their phones, just in case something happened. Besides, she wasn't actually going sleuthing, was she?

As she drove to Flagstaff, she decided to go talk to the guy at the spider store again. Maybe he remembered seeing Mason when he bought the toxin from Jax. And maybe, Mason had had a companion with him.

CHAPTER 22

"Jax doesn't work here anymore. The boss fired him when the cops told him what Jax was doing." The young man, Todd, who'd helped Rarity and Jonathon before, was standing in the front of the store, his arms crossed. "He wasn't doing anything wrong. He was providing a service to old guys."

"I'm sorry that Jax was fired." Rarity knew Todd probably thought it was her fault, and maybe it was, but she'd driven all this way to find out something and she wasn't going to be bullied. "Look, all I want to know is if you talked to Mason Pike when he was in the shop."

"Mason Pike? Yeah, I talked to him. That guy is a legend. Have you seen *Attack of the Venus Spiders*? He was in the store about a week before he died. Oh, wait, don't tell me the stuff Jax gave him was responsible. It's impossible. Now if it was from a Sydney funnel spider, that stuff is deadly. Jax just had the Brazilian wandering spiders at home. He bought up the supply once the owners discontinued selling them in the store." Todd looked confused. "Seriously, I don't know what the police are thinking, but one spider isn't the same as another. Besides, Mason has a pet tarantula. He knows spiders. Or he knew them. I've seen Oscar on the internet. Mason's always posing with it. Or he was. Every time he posted on social media, we'd get a rash of kids in here who wanted their own spider. Now I guess that will stop."

Rarity wasn't getting anywhere with Todd. "So was there anyone with Mason that day?"

"With him? Oh, like a date?"

Rarity smiled. "Yeah, like a date, or maybe just a friend."

Todd shook his head. "No, he came into the shop alone."

Rarity thanked him and left to head to the pet store. Killer needed a treat after being in a shop filled with snakes and spiders. He was shaking in her arms the whole time they were in there.

As she put him in his bed on the passenger seat, she kissed his head. "Don't worry about it. I'm not bringing home one of those pets for your companion. Maybe a kitten someday, though."

Rarity laughed at the look Killer gave her. People didn't think dogs were smart, but he definitely had understood what Rarity had said and he wasn't having any part of it.

"Okay, maybe not a kitten."

Rarity got into the car and started the engine. She looked over at Killer, but he had his back to her. He'd get over his mad when they got to the pet store. He loved going there.

She turned up the music. At least she'd tried to follow up on the lead. When she got home, she'd let Drew know what she found and where and then dust her hands of it. She had to admit that the sleuthing club had failed this time. Maybe it was the fact that all their suspects were out-of-towners. She didn't have a lot to go on. She'd been distracted with worrying about Darby.

As she pulled into the parking lot for the pet store, Killer barked and watched the building coming closer. "Sure, now you're happy again. Mommy's a failure and you're going crazy because you get to go pick out your treat."

At least she wasn't a failure to her dog. He thought she was amazing. As long as she didn't mention kittens. She sighed. When she got home, she'd pull out the murder book one more time. Maybe something would trigger her. And she could put away all the excuses she'd made as she drove away from the snake shop.

One more thought cheered her as she put Killer in a cart on top of his store blanket they kept in the car. She wasn't alone in this. Maybe one of the other club members had come up with something and with what she knew, they'd put the puzzle together.

All she knew was she wasn't giving up just now. Maybe she would have to on Tuesday, but that was Tuesday's problem. Today she needed to find the right treat that Killer might like for longer than a week or two. He was very picky.

* * *

Rarity's phone rang when she was coming into Sedona. She used the Bluetooth to answer. "Hello?"

"You said you would call when you were back in town." Jonathon said.

"Hi, Dad. Anyway, I just got back in town. Killer and I decided to have a late lunch at the Wildflower. They have a doggy menu too." Rarity had never been to the quaint restaurant near a stream, but she'd enjoyed her time there and her lunch. She always had a book in her tote, just in case.

Silence filled the car. Finally, Jonathon responded, "I guess I should take Romeo there before I head back to Tucson."

"Are you leaving soon?" Rarity tried to read between the lines. Darby was safe since her stalker had been Bret Black and he'd been looking for Talia. If Jonathon was planning on leaving, did that mean Drew had solved the case? She always knew it was a race between Drew and the sleuthers. He was the professional; she assumed he'd figure it out before they did at times. All questions she couldn't ask. But there was one she could. "Has there been a break in the case?"

"Drew's out confirming some interviews now. He thinks he's got a case, at least to force them to do fingerprints and a DNA sample." Jonathon paused. "Before you ask, he didn't tell me who. But he said he wants it done before they leave for California tomorrow."

"They?"

"Yep, not him or her so that doesn't narrow it a lot." He sighed loud enough that she could hear him. "I really thought we'd get there first. Maybe having Darby's mystery at the same time dulled us to the Pike case?"

"I was wondering the same thing," Rarity said, smiling as she turned on her street. "My trip turned into a dead end. Pike visited the snake shop but Todd said he was alone."

"Todd? The guy we talked to?"

"Yeah. He's the boyfriend of Katie's ex-roommate Charity. And he thinks we got Jax fired." She used the remote to open her garage. Then she stopped the car, not pulling into the driveway. "Hey Jonathon? Can you call and ask Drew to head my way? I've got a problem."

A line of tarantulas stood guard in front of Rarity's garage door. She didn't realize they were fake until Drew and Archer pulled up at the house and Drew carefully walked to the garage and then picked up one and held it out.

"Plastic," Drew called out, but then he stopped. He walked backward to the truck, keeping an eye on the garage. "Rarity, close the garage door. We need animal control out here."

Archer had walked over to her car and stood by the door on the driver's side. "Just do it," he said. "I'll go over and see what we're dealing with."

He waited for her to close the door, then joined Drew in his truck. Rarity saw him listening in on Drew's call to the animal control department; then the men talked. Rarity's phone rang. It was Archer.

"What is it?"

"The spiders are plastic, but there's a live snake in your garage. Two, Drew thinks."

Archer paused and she watched as Drew leaned closer to the phone, which must have been on speaker. "Sorry, I wasn't going to take the time to be certain. And you have a window open in the garage. I don't think the glass is broken but the screen is off. Whose feathers did you rustle today?"

Rarity went through her day, from seeing Jane and Talia fight that morning, to finding the card at the theater, to her conversation with Todd. As she talked, Killer kept looking at her, then at the house he could see from where they were parked on the street.

"Well, that gives me some places to start. How would you and Killer like to stay with Sam for a few days?" Now Drew had Archer's phone. "Or Archer?"

"You're worried." It wasn't a question. Rarity could hear the fear in his voice.

He nodded. They were still in the truck and watching the garage, no doubt, for escaping snakes. "I am worried. Here's animal control and a cop. It's going to be a while. Go to Sam's. Please."

Archer took the phone from Drew. "What's your pleasure? My tiny apartment above the shop or Sam's guest room with a fenced-in backyard for our boy? I'm fine either way."

"I'll go to Sam's." Rarity started her engine. "She has clothes that will fit me. Call me when you catch them."

"The spiders or the snakes?" Archer teased.

"Shut up. I love you." Rarity smiled and put her fingers to the glass window as she drove past Drew's truck.

"I love you too."

Sam had already been alerted to Rarity's arrival. When Rarity pulled in the driveway and got out with a confused Killer, Sam came out of her house and greeted Rarity with open arms. "I can't believe someone did that to you. Did you scream when you saw the spiders? I would have. I hate the things."

Rarity didn't have a chance to answer before she was swept up into the house, shown the guest bedroom, and handed some yoga pants and a large T-shirt with a pair of thick socks.

"Get comfy. We'll have fun. Like a sleepover, but we have booze. And anything we want to eat. Thank goodness for delivery." Sam stopped her chatter when the doorbell rang. "Maybe someone already sent over delivery. When did you eat?"

Again without waiting for an answer, she left the room. Rarity thought about sinking into the soft bed and putting a pillow over her eyes, but she thought she might dream of spiders and snakes. So instead, she and Killer followed Sam out to the living room.

Jonathon was there with Romeo and his laptop bag. "I'm here until one of the guys gets free. I'm assuming it will be Archer, but you never know."

"Come in. I'm sure we would have been fine, but I'm not killing the messenger," Rarity said, smiling as Romeo came up to her to sniff her hand. "This is crazy."

"Maybe, but I brought my murder book. Do you want to go over what you found? Maybe there's a connection somewhere." Jonathon looked over at a recliner. "Okay to claim that?"

"Of course, I'll go get my book too," Sam said as she went down the hallway. "There are drinks in the fridge or I can make coffee?"

"I'll take some water," Jonathon said as he snapped his fingers and pointed. Romeo went over by the chair and lay down. Killer laid next to him. He set his bag down. "Let's get something to drink before we start."

Rarity showed him to the kitchen, and by the time Sam came back with her murder book, they were back in the living room, sitting and talking about the dogs.

She sat next to Rarity. "Tell me what happened. I have a feeling something happened after breakfast this morning."

"First, you tell Jonathon about breakfast. I might have missed something you saw." Rarity nodded to Sam.

"Okay, well, it seemed like everyone was still there, which I thought was weird. If the festival ended on Saturday night, why would you go to a Sunday brunch?" Sam looked at Jonathon and Rarity for an answer.

"Free food? Maybe their planes weren't leaving for a while. They drank too much on Saturday night?" Rarity listed off the reasons she could think of.

"Okay, fair points. I guess it's just me who likes to get home after two weeks of being away. I'll be honest, a weekend away and I'm ready to go home. I guess I'm just a homebody." Sam went on to tell Jonathon about getting there, then about getting them a place to sit, and how Talia had come up to say goodbye.

"Wait, you didn't tell me that." Rarity stared at her friend.

"You were going to find Jane and then Miranda stopped you. You were talking to her when Talia came over to the table. She said it had been a pleasure meeting everyone in town and how much she loved your little shop. She said she'd wanted to visit my crystal shop but had run out of time. I didn't think she even knew who I was."

"I was just about to say, I didn't remember seeing her at the shop, but she came in to see Darby because everyone was saying her double worked there," Rarity added. "I still need to get Jane that movie. I don't want to have to ship it to her."

"We'll go over to the hotel tomorrow morning, first thing," Sam promised. "And we can go to breakfast afterward. Maybe we should go shopping and get out of Sedona for the day."

Jonathon waved his hand in front of Sam's face. "Before we start planning the mani/pedi appointments, can we finish adding to the murder book?"

"Oh, yeah, sorry." Sam finished telling Jonathon about the breakfast at the hotel with the festival people.

Then Rarity started over with the morning, telling her side, adding a few things to Sam's narrative. After she was done, she added, "You know, I've never realized this is why our group works so well with solving mysteries—we all see something different. I was focused on getting the movie back to Jane and how I failed at that task again."

"And I was focused on the food and seeing who was around us. Call me starstruck, but this was really fun. And some of the actors are already listed as up-and-comers, so I get to say I met them back when they were nobodies." Sam paused. "Okay, maybe that doesn't help in this situation, but some days it does."

"I think there's something there," Rarity said but then shook her head. "I just can't put my finger on it."

"Well, let's finish updating the book with your spider and snake attack. There is no doubt that it's a warning to stay out of the investigation. It's like an old movie threat." Jonathon picked up his pen again. "Let's go over what you did after breakfast."

"Wait, I remember one more thing." Sam's face brightened. "Talia asked about your book clubs. Or she commented on them. She said how wonderful it was that you had things for all ages, including adults. So we talked for a minute about the Survivors' Book Club and why you started it. She said it should be a movie. I told her that we sometimes turn into a sleuthing club, and she said it really should be a movie. Then her phone buzzed and she left me."

"Talia knows that I'm running a book club that investigates local murders?" Rarity met Jonathon's gaze. "Let's finish this and talk about Talia as a suspect. I wonder where she was this afternoon."

As they finished updating the book, Rarity groaned. "We're going to miss Darby's party."

"I've already called her to let her know. Don't worry, there are plenty of people there already. Darby has a crew. And Holly said she'd keep an eye out for any issues. Marc is out of town this weekend, remember." Sam nodded to the television. "Let's find a movie the boys would hate."

Jonathon set his murder book into his tote bag. "Don't worry about me. I'm just here for the entertainment."

Rarity smiled and made a mental note to apologize to Darby. Although she thought that the current group in the room would have been the oldest people there. Maybe it was better that she wasn't going.

Later, when Drew and Archer stopped by Sam's for dinner, Drew told them that the department was working on verifying Talia's whereabouts as well as Jax's.

Rarity stopped chopping lettuce for the salad. "Wait, why Jax?"

"If he thought you got him fired, this would be perfect payback. At least in a twenty-year-old's mind. Anyway, can you still stay with Sam tonight? I'll feel better after I talk to a few people."

"Sure. We have fun plans for the morning, and as soon as the two of you get out of here, we're heading to the bar to look for someone to dance with." Rarity finished chopping the lettuce and put it in the salad bowl.

Everyone was looking at her.

"What? Too much?" Rarity grabbed a tomato and started chopping. "I know, I know, I'll stay at Sam's tonight, but tomorrow we are going to grab breakfast right after I drop the movie off with Jane at the hotel. I already texted her and told her I'd be there at eight. Which is good because she's leaving town at ten."

"I think you're more worried about returning the movie than she is about getting it," Sam complained as she pulled the enchiladas from the oven and set them on top of the stove.

"I don't like things undone. I know, it's probably my control factor from when I was in cancer treatments, but if I say something is happening, I try to follow through. Unless my house is under attack from spiders, snakes, or other crawly creatures." Rarity took the tongs and tossed the salad. "There, my part is done. And Drew? We might even go shopping in Flagstaff tomorrow, so tell Jonathon not to wait up for us."

He laughed as he grabbed the dishes and put them on the table while Archer followed with silverware. "He can be a worrywart when it comes to people he cares about. Get used to it. He and Mom have claimed the two of you as family. I don't think that will ever change."

Drew went over to the stove, picking up the casserole dish with pot holders. "Rarity, would you put something down on the table for this? And one more thing, be sure to call me when you get back in town so I don't send out officers to look for the two of you."

"You wouldn't dare," Sam challenged him as she put a trivet on the table before Rarity could get to it.

He set the dish on the metal stand and then kissed her. "Try me."

CHAPTER 23

The next morning, Rarity was up early and had made coffee and put the dishes away from the dishwasher from last night's dinner. She was about to make some cookies or something when Sam came in from her bedroom, still dressed in a short pj's outfit. "You're too loud in the morning."

"We need to get to the hotel by eight." She poured her friend a cup of coffee. "Besides, I slept in this morning. Usually, I'm up at five on a weekday."

"This isn't a weekday for you, it's part of your weekend and mine," Sam reminded her.

Rarity sat at the table next to her. "I know, but I keep running all the things I know about Talia in my head. I know she's the one who killed Mason. It all fits. He thought they were getting back together. When Drew talks to the lawyer, I bet she's his heir. Bret thought he and Talia were an item. He even went looking for her when she came to Sedona without him."

"I think that's called circumstantial evidence." Sam sipped her coffee. "Besides, she was at that dinner."

"Which started two hours late, according to Gretchen. Okay, then add in the spider. She had to know about the shots. They were together for years," Rarity pointed out. "And I found the card with Jax's name on it where she was hanging out on Saturday. And they shared ownership of Oscar. Although why anyone would want a pet spider is beyond me."

Sam just shrugged, apparently not convinced.

Rarity's phone rang. The caller ID said it was Katie. "Hey, what's going on?"

"You need to hear this," Katie said. Then Rarity heard a voice speaking in the background, "Tell her."

"Katie?"

"No, ma'am, this is Todd. From the spider store? Well, I told Charity about what I'd told you and I realized maybe I forgot something. So she told me to tell Katie. And anyway, here we are. Mason Pike came into the store alone, but I saw Talia Brooks in the car, waiting. I guess she didn't want to come in. A lot of women don't like visiting the store."

"You're sure it was Talia?" Now Rarity had one more piece to her puzzle.

"Definitely. She was hot in the alien spider movie, but man, she's a lot older now. Still hot but not scorching like she was. Well, she was dressed in shorts and a tank rather than the one-piece she wore in the movie. That showed everything."

Rarity heard "Dude!" in the background.

Todd chuckled and continued. "Anyway, she was there with Mason. I thought you meant came into the store, but I guess I should have told you the whole story. I'm sorry. Here's Katie."

Rarity waited for Katie to speak.

"They came over this morning, Todd and Charity. He had told her about seeing Mason and Talia but only telling you about Mason. So she dragged him over so I could call you," Katie explained. "I'm sorry."

"No worries. This is perfect. It puts Talia in the picture again. Anyway, I'll see you Thursday? Or are you working today?"

"Thursday. Shirley has the store today." Katie paused and added, "But I will be at the book club on Tuesday night."

After she got off the phone, Rarity held up the paper where she'd been taking notes. "This proves Talia knew about the shots."

"Or she thought he was there to get spider food or get a new spider or something." Sam shook her head. "I still think it's thin."

"Okay, I'll take it to the sleuthers. Maybe someone else has something else that will solidify this so we can give it to Drew." Rarity finished her coffee and put her cup in the sink. "I really don't want to let Drew win this one."

Sam laughed as she followed her out of the kitchen. "You know it's not a competition, right?"

As Rarity dressed in some of Sam's clothes, she thought that her friend was dead wrong on that point. Rarity wanted the sleuthers to win.

* * *

At the hotel, Sam stayed in the lobby when Rarity went upstairs to room 321. She had the envelope with the movie in hand. She walked down the hallway, dodging a maid's cart, hearing the vacuum in the room she was cleaning. When she got to the room, she thought she heard voices inside.

She realized the door had been left open, using the security guard bar as a doorstop. She went to knock but then heard Talia's voice. The two of them were fighting. Again.

What in the world was going on?

"I didn't kill him so you could give away all the money. What were you thinking setting up not only an allotment for this crappy festival but the local students? That's coming out of your share," Talia told Jane.

Rarity called Drew on her phone and turned down her volume so they wouldn't hear him answer. Hopefully he could hear them.

"Watch your tone. Right now, it's all my share. And who are you going to complain to? I didn't kill him. I was just in the will. And if you say anything different, I'll say you're crazy. That you were jealous of my relationship with Mason. That he loved me enough to put me in the will, even if I didn't look like you," Jane said, or at least Rarity assumed it was Jane.

"You're lucky we did this now. If we'd waited and he'd gotten that local girl interested in his sorry butt, she'd have the money and that lovely house of hers." Talia paused a moment and Rarity froze. It sounded like

Talia was walking to the door, but then Rarity heard water running and realized that she must have gone into the bathroom.

Jane spoke. "I wish I would have hit her that day in the truck. Anyway, sponsoring the festival was a goodwill gesture. No one's even questioned us, not seriously. Later today, we'll be back home. I'm keeping the house, by the way. If there's anything in it you want, let me know because I'm going to trash his stuff and refurnish as soon as the estate settles. Then I'll give you your half and Oscar."

"You can have the stupid spider. I want the painting in the living room, though." Talia started listing off the items in the house that she was claiming.

Rarity saw the housekeeper coming out of another room and watching her. She put the phone to her ear and walked back to the stairs, not waiting for the elevator. When she was clear, she turned the volume back up.

"Two questions, did you get all that?" Rarity asked as she hurried down the stairs.

"Yes, and I have a squad car that should be there now. I'll bring both of them in for questioning. You'll have to testify to verify my account for the judge if it goes to trial, but I'm thinking that they're going to turn on each other. Especially if there's a deal on the table. What's the second question?"

"You already answered it. I'm collecting Sam and we're going to Carole's for breakfast. Let me know if you need us."

Drew barked out a laugh. "I think you've done enough. I take it you still have her film?"

"I'll leave it at the front desk for Jane. She'll probably not pick it up, but that won't be my problem anymore." She paused. "I knew Talia was involved, but I never guessed Jane. I felt bad for her."

"Sometimes emotions clog our reason," Drew said. "I've got to go. Get out of there as fast as possible."

Rarity caught Sam's gaze and pointed to the front desk. By the time Sam caught up to her, Rarity had left the envelope for Jane in room 321 with the clerk. "We need to leave, now."

As they pulled the car out of the parking lot, she saw the police cars come into the lot. They didn't have their lights or sirens on. Sam stared at the cars then looked at Rarity. "Where to?"

"Breakfast at Carole's. I'll tell you what happened over waffles."

* * *

Rarity had to repeat the story at the sleuthing club meeting the next day and after she did, she held up a book. "Here's next week's book. I've already called Deb and Ginny and let them know that we're back to being a book club."

"Well, I guess there's nothing else to do but celebrate. Our Darby isn't being stalked and the killer, or killers in this case, are in custody." Shirley had her knitting out and was working on a blanket. "Who tried to run over Darby, by the way?"

"According to Talia, that was all Jane. She hated that Mason was interested in a relationship with someone who looked like Talia." Rarity shrugged as she watched Darby turn red. "She had found the keys to the truck and took advantage of the kid's stupidity."

"Drew matched both women's fingerprints on the syringe, so we have actual physical evidence. And Jane's fingerprints were in the truck. Jax and Todd have confirmed that Talia was with Mason when he bought his supply for the visit. And Jax, after promising to shut down his side business, has been rehired at the store. He was staying at his mom's."

"Jane must have come in the front door when we were all in the back. I bet Mason was expecting her, that's why the door was unlocked," Rarity said, looking at Jonathon for confirmation. "He must have asked her to come and bring his supply. After he found Darby. The man was a letch."

"I hear the police confiscated all of Jax's venom supply and had his spiders put down," Malia said. "Isn't that just stepping on them?"

"I wouldn't want to put one of those spiders down on the floor. What if you missed?" Holly shivered. "Rarity? Is your garage clear?"

"Yes. And that fun gift wasn't from Jax, it was Talia who did it, trying to keep me and the club from investigating Mason's death." Rarity turned to Jonathon, who had more of the story.

"Drew found a receipt for the fake spiders from the craft shop, and she had an assistant buy the snakes. When the assistant found out about her arrest, he came in and gave Drew the receipt. She'd told him that they were needed for a promotional event around the movie. The studio is rereleasing it to honor Mason." Jonathon shook his head. "Remind me not to visit Sedona during the film festival next year."

"What doesn't kill us gives Jonathon something to write about," Darby teased. "Besides, you were having fun trying to solve the mystery. And thank goodness Jane hadn't come to get the movie sooner. Rarity wouldn't have been in the right place at the wrong time."

"We see through a glass, darkly," Shirley added, then looked around the confused faces. "What? It just means we don't know why things happen until the end."

At the end of the night, Rarity stopped Jonathon from leaving. "I guess you're heading back to Tucson? Edith has some books on order. Do you want them tonight? Or will you stop by tomorrow before you leave?"

"No, remember Edith's coming up with Joanna, Manuel, and Savannah, of course, for the weekend. Drew's having his party on Saturday. I can take them tonight, so she doesn't forget to stop by." Jonathon reached for the books.

As everyone headed out, she heard the door open again. Archer was there to walk her home. And he'd brought Killer with him. "Dinner's ready at home. Are you ready to leave?"

Rarity nodded. "Let me check the back door and turn on the security system. Then I'll be ready."

She went through the back room, turning off lights and checking the back door lock as she looked out the window. It was a full moon, and she could see a large plastic spider had been set on the top of the retaining wall behind her store. Was it a thank-you from Mason? Or just a leftover from their book signing and outdoor movie night?

Either way, she wasn't going out to gather the spider. She'd do it tomorrow. If it was still there.

"Rarity?" Archer called out.

She stepped away from the back door and headed to the security closet. "I'll be right out." Silently, she added, *Everything's fine. It's back to normal here*. But she wasn't sure her new bookstore had ever been normal. But that was okay, because it held family. And friends. And community. And what else could she want?

Maybe justice. And today, that had been achieved.

It had to be enough.

CHAPTER 24

Drew's backyard sparkled with lights all over the yard and fairy lights in the trees. The food station was set up on one side of the deck. Shirley had brought three or four different desserts that had been added to the food table. Two large galvanized tubs had been filled with ice along with soft and alcoholic drinks. Yacht rock was playing from a stand where a DJ sat, near a dance floor that Drew had rented. Chairs and tables were scattered all over the yard for seating.

He'd done a great job.

Rarity wondered if it was Jonathon and Edith's anniversary. Savannah was toddling around the yard, one hand on Romeo's back and the other waving as she chattered in her own language. She'd been dressed in a pink tutu dress and looked like the resident house fairy for the evening.

Archer brought her a beer, and they sat down at the table watching the gathering. She moved her chair closer and rubbed his arm. "Drew did good. Is this an anniversary party? Maybe for Joanna and Manuel?"

"No, they were married in October. And before you ask, Edith and Jonathon were married in June. And that's all I'm going to say. I've been sworn to secrecy."

She sat up and stared at him. "Okay, now I really want to know. What is stronger? An oath to a friend, or honesty to a girlfriend?"

"A best friend since we were kids. Blood brothers. We even pricked our fingers." He held up a finger then took her hand again. "Anyway, it looks like you're going to find out now. Drew's making an announcement."

She turned and watched as Drew walked to the DJ stand, swooping Savannah up in his arms. After planting a kiss on her head, he gave her back to his sister. He took the microphone from the DJ, who kept a soft song running in the back. Ed Sheeran, if Rarity remembered correctly.

"Friends, family, thank you for joining me tonight. And don't worry, this isn't the start of karaoke. I needed a minute with someone special. Sam? Would you come up here?"

"I don't know. Do I need a beer first?" Sam called out as she made her way up to where Drew stood.

"Maybe," he admitted as he kissed her lightly. "Anyway, I have a question to ask you, and I needed witnesses in case you forget your answer."

He fell to one knee, pulling out a ring box from his pocket as he went down. Then he flipped it open. "Sam? I adore you. I want to spend the rest of my life with you. I want to have babies and choose a dog with you. Hopefully, it will be larger than Killer but smarter than Romeo. Anyway, I'm rambling. Sam, will you marry me?"

Rarity watched as Sam froze. Everyone in the backyard seemed to be holding their breath for the answer. Even Romeo and Killer were watching the couple.

Then Sam looked into Drew's eyes and smiled. "Yes. A thousand times yes."

He slipped the ring on her finger, then swung her around the dance floor. When he finished, he picked up the microphone he'd sat down and said, "If you missed that, folks, she said yes."

Everyone clapped and hooted their happiness. Archer pulled Rarity close. "This is why I've been avoiding discussing our future with you for the last couple of weeks. Drew needed to finish this out. I'm so glad she said yes."

"She had to. She's in love as well. She's just a little quieter when the stakes are high, like this." She kissed Archer. "Let's go congratulate the happy couple."

As they did and everyone talked about the upcoming wedding, Rarity saw Shirley standing on the deck, watching. She grabbed a glass of champagne for both of them and walked over to her friend. As she handed her a glass, Rarity asked, "Are you okay?"

"Of course, I am. It's a lovely evening for those two, and long overdue. He's a true romantic." She wiped her eyes with a napkin. "I was just thinking about when George asked me to marry him. He wasn't as confident as Drew, nor as romantic. So he asked me when we were at the drive-in movie. *The Graduate* was playing. Dustin Hoffman was looking at that half-naked woman and George blurted out the question. I thought he was kidding. Now, he doesn't even remember the movie. Not our engagement, our lives, our kids, not even the boring Saturday nights when we were too broke to do anything but pop popcorn and watch a movie on television. Dementia's cruel to take all that from him. And me. I don't have anyone to talk about those times with anymore."

Rarity took her hand. "You have me. Anytime you want."

Terrance came up to them and took Shirley's glass away and sae it on a table. "You're not having fun. This is a party for these kids, and you're lost in the past. Come dance with me. One dance, maybe two, no commitments."

Shirley smiled and nodded. "And then I have this guy trying to make me smile all the time."

They moved toward the dance floor, and Rarity watched. No one knew the future. Sam was marrying a cop. A dangerous profession, but Jonathon and Edith had made it to retirement. Their daughter was married with a child running around the yard. Everyone was in a different part of their lives. Young, old, midlife, they all meshed into her found family.

Rarity wondered if this moment was what Madame Zelda's cards were talking about. The death of a friendship, the start of a true relationship for Sam and Drew. Her friendship with Sam would change too. Not stop, but change. Drew would be her person now. But Rarity would be there for Sam at every step. Just like Sam had always been there for Rarity.

Rarity didn't know what she'd do without any of them. She hoped she didn't ever have to find out.

Tonight, unlike the rest of the world, was perfect. Usually you had to settle for good. Or maybe even boring. But tonight, the stars aligned and it was a perfect evening.

And for that, she was thankful. Nights like this armed her for fighting for more. A fight she could win.

RECIPE

Chicken Tortilla Soup

I love this soup, even with the black beans. I'm not generally a fan of beans. My husband, the Cowboy, even likes the soup. Not something that happens a lot. Best thing is how easy it is to make.

Serve with a salad or a sandwich for a full meal.

Enjoy,

Lynn

Chicken Tortilla Soup

In a large soup pot (I like using my enameled cast-iron Dutch oven for soups), over medium heat, cook the following until tender in a little butter:

- 1 large onion, diced
- 4 medium carrots, diced
- 3 ribs celery, diced
- 1 medium zucchini, diced (I used frozen zucchini from last year's garden)
- 1 red bell pepper, diced
- 2 cloves of garlic, minced
- Salt and pepper

Then add to your soup pot the following:

- 1 can (15 oz.) black beans, drained and rinsed (if you don't, your soup will be gray)
- 1 can (15 oz.) corn, drained
- 1 can (15 oz.) diced tomatoes
- 1 can (6 oz.) green chilies
- 1 tsp. chili powder (or more to taste)

- 2 (32 oz.) boxes of chicken broth

Cook for ten minutes; then add two chicken breasts.

Cook for another twenty minutes; pull the chicken breast out and shred with a fork. Return to the soup and add salt and pepper to taste.

Fill individual serving bowls with ½ cup of tortilla chips, crushed into big hunks, and ½ cup shredded cheddar cheese.

Serve with sour cream or sliced avocado.

This soup freezes well.

ACKNOWLEDGMENTS

When I'm doing book events, I tell a story about how I found cozy mysteries. I try to skip over the part where I say I had breast cancer, but it's a part of who I am, and how I write. It's part of my story. Anyway, I was reading a lot during treatment, mysteries mostly. So as I went to a weekend clinic to get a shot to build up my immunity after a chemo treatment, I was reading while I waited. The nurse asked me what I was reading, and I explained that I didn't know what these mysteries were called, but I loved them. They were complicated enough that I could distract myself, but then pick them up again when I had reading time.

"You like cozy mysteries," she explained, then proceeded to bring me a bag full of books the next day when I came for my shot. She was a fan of the genre.

Through that fan, I became friends with Susan McBride (the Helen Evans Investigates books) and Laura Bradford (the Friend for Hire Mysteries). Both lived in St. Louis at the time and became my touchstone for all things cozy.

So thank you to cozy readers, like my nurse, who introduced me to the genre. Thank you to my publisher, Kensington, who saw promise in my Tourist Trap series, including my new editors, Michaela Hamilton and Cassidy Smith. And my agent, who helps me keep the business side of this writing life clean.

Are you over the moon for Lynn Cahoon?
Turn the page to enjoy the first chapter of *Confessions of an Amateur Sleuth*, a
Bainbridge Island Mystery coming soon from Kensington Publishing Corp.

CHAPTER 1

Interviewing is a conversation, not an interrogation. Especially when you don't wear a badge.

Something was missing. Okay, a lot of things were missing. Meg Gates stared at the local authors' shelf as she stood at the front door of Island Books, her mother's bookstore. She'd made the display eye-catching, but the shelves were almost empty. Three weeks ago, her mom had promised she'd get Meg the list of books she'd been curating since she'd opened the shop. Right now, only L. C. Aster's books inhabited the bookcase. Of course, Lilly Aster, Meg's other boss, had been writing for years, so she had a lot of books to showcase.

Meg wanted to highlight other local authors as well. She typed out a text to her mom since her phone calls had gone unanswered that morning.

As she clicked Send, the bell over the door alerted her to a customer. "Welcome to Island Books, may I help you?"

"Where's Mom?" Stephen "Junior" Gates beelined directly to the counter. "She usually works Tuesday mornings."

"Good morning to you." Meg rolled her eyes as she addressed her brother. Junior dressed like an accountant. Even on days off, he wore a polo shirt and chino shorts. He still worked for their dad at his accounting firm and the job fit his personality. Junior liked his life orderly.

"Why aren't you at work?"

"I take off the second Tuesday of every month to take Mom to Seattle for lunch. I called her when I got on the ferry this morning. But she hasn't answered." Junior tried to peek around Meg. "I guess she must have gotten my message since you're here to cover her. Is she in the back?"

"One, it's not the second Tuesday, it's the first. And no, she's not here." Meg leaned back on the stool. "Funny, I haven't been able to reach her by phone this morning either. She emailed me on Monday with my hours for the week. She didn't explain, but I'm working the day shift on Tuesday, and then on Thursday I have the entire day from open to close. She said I could close when it got slow Thursday night. Maybe she has appointments this week."

Junior seemed to analyze the information as he read the back of a memoir of an English prime minister that a customer had left unpurchased on the register counter. "But that doesn't explain her not picking up her phone. And why would she have appointments on two different days? You don't think she's sick, do you?"

"I saw her Sunday at church. She seemed fine." Meg thought about how her mom had looked that day. She'd eaten her entire lunch at the restaurant and even ordered dessert. Something Mom never did. "She looked great. She even had a tan."

"So you think it's just a checkup?" Junior set the book down. "I wish she'd called me back so I wouldn't have wasted a ferry ticket."

"You were already heading here when you—" Meg started but then stopped. Explaining to Junior that the world didn't run on his schedule was a waste of breath. She watched as he pulled his phone out and started texting someone. "So why did you come this week and not next week anyway?"

Junior's face turned red.

"Junior?" Now Meg was curious. Her older brother had always been the steady one. Meanwhile, Meg had been a three-time loser—she failed to finish college, then the tech startup she'd joined went bankrupt, and, of course, her wedding was canceled due to her fiancé's lack of understanding of the definition of faithful. Meg had returned to Bainbridge Island to live in an apartment over her aunt's garage and work at her mom's bookstore.

Junior, on the other hand, had finished his degree and gone to work for their father in Bellevue at his accounting firm. She loved her family, but she hated that she was always seen as the needy one.

He kept his gaze on his phone. "I've got plans next week."

"Plans. At work?" Meg noticed he'd turned even redder. When he didn't answer, she asked again, "What plans?"

"I'm going to a conference in San Francisco if you must know." He looked up and met her gaze. "Are you happy? Or do you need the rest of my schedule?"

"Why are you blushing about a conference?" Meg searched his face for clues. "Unless you're going with a woman. Don't tell me you're dating someone at Dad's firm. Please don't let it be your secretary."

Now Junior's face turned scarlet. "We don't have secretaries anymore. We have assistants. Besides, I'm not Dad. Anne works in corporate accounts. She's an accountant. We've only been dating for a few weeks. We'll be staying in separate rooms. Now are you happy?"

Meg felt bad about bringing up their father. His new wife, Elaine, had been his secretary, but they both claimed that the relationship had changed from work friends to something romantic only after the divorce. Meg wanted to believe him, but he'd been the first of her parents to start dating. Mom still hadn't gone out with anyone. At least as far as Meg knew.

She realized Junior was watching her. "I'm sorry. I shouldn't have brought Dad into the conversation. So, Anne, huh? She's an accountant and what else? Is she from Seattle? What does she look like? Is she nice?"

The door to the shop opened and with the bell's announcement, Dalton Hamilton walked into the shop. "Hey Junior, are you ready?"

"What's going on?" Meg looked from Junior to Dalton. The two men had been friends since middle school.

"Mom's not here so I checked in with Dalton to see if he had time for lunch." He picked up the memoir again. "Put this on my account. Tell Mom I'll call her later. When you see her."

Watson, Meg's tan cocker spaniel, had roused himself from his morning nap and started circling Dalton for attention. Dalton leaned down and gave the excited pup head rubs. Then he looked up at Meg. "Do you need me to take him out before we leave?"

"Would you?" Meg glanced at her watch. "He's been asleep for almost three hours now. I'm sure he needs a walk."

"Sure. And do you want me to bring you something back from the restaurant for lunch?" Dalton walked over and grabbed Watson's leash from behind the counter.

Junior groaned as he perched on the edge of the couch. "You've been spending too much time here with my sister. Her dog loves you and you know where everything is."

"Maybe you've just been spending too little time here," Dalton countered and then headed to the door. "I'll bring him back in a few and you can answer my lunch question."

"No lunch," Meg said as a group of tourists came into the bookstore. "I'm going to a writers' meeting this evening over at the Island Diner. I brought a lunch."

"I'll come with you," Junior declared as he followed Dalton out the door. "Just tell Mom I was here."

"When I see her," Meg muttered, then she smiled at a woman walking toward her. "What can I help you with?"

When Dalton brought back Watson, she had a line of customers at the register. He tucked the leash back under the counter as the dog headed to his water dish to refill. "Junior's waiting for me at Island Diner. Do you need me to stay?"

She handed a credit card receipt and a bag to the customer she'd been helping. "No, I'm good, but thanks for taking him out."

"My pleasure," Dalton responded as he made his way out of the shop.

The next customer watched Dalton leave, then handed Meg her card after she'd rung up the book purchase. "Your boyfriend's cute and thoughtful. You need to keep that one."

Meg smiled as she ran the card. She turned the screen toward the customer for her signature. "Dalton's not my boyfriend."

"Oh?" The woman turned and looked out the window where Dalton had disappeared seconds before. "Does he know that?"

Mom hadn't called back by the time Meg needed to close the shop. She could get dinner at the meeting, but she couldn't take Watson inside the restaurant. She needed to take him home and feed him. And turn on his favorite movie.

Yes, her dog was spoiled. But he was also good company and kept Meg from talking to herself. She'd found him on a rescue website one day and had gone down to the shelter the same day to adopt him. She did one thing right—take care of her dog.

By the time she got back into town, the meeting had started. She grabbed a waitress and gave her order, then sat down at the back of the banquet room to wait for food while she listened to the presenter.

A man leaned over and held out his hand. "Hi, I'm Lee Anderson. I'm a freelance food writer."

Meg leaned closer so she could lower her voice. "Meg Gates. I guess I'm a nonfiction crime writer. I'm working on my first book. Who's talking today?"

"That's Crissy Lorde. She writes cozy mysteries and she's talking about her experience self-publishing versus the more traditional route." He held up his notebook to show Meg. The page was empty except for the date that Lee had written on the right corner. "I'd share my notes, but so far, I've got nothing. She's just talking about her own journey in writing. But she promised ten comparisons between the two options sometime tonight. The way she's going, we might be here until midnight by the time she hits number ten."

Meg suppressed a giggle. The speakers at the writers' group ranged from people who were just there to sell their book, to professional writers like L. C. Aster who'd come to talk to the group about her thrillers last month. Meg was Lilly's author assistant and had recently told her boss that she was trying to write a nonfiction book about solving mysteries. Lilly had suggested that Meg join the local writing group to meet other writers and learn about the industry.

Writing a book was harder than Meg had imagined. Sometimes she felt like she had control of the nonfiction book about how to become your own Nancy Drew. Sometimes she thought the book was controlling her. The good part of the process was that it gave her an inside look at what authors like Lilly went through when creating the product. The bad part was she felt like an imposter a lot of the time. Lilly's advice? One page at a time. Don't look back until it's done, then you can see if it works or not.

Meg was beginning to think the "or not" advice was what eventually would happen. But she was going to finish it, mostly because she was tired of changing lanes when things got hard. She would finish this book. Whether or not it sold was out of her hands. But she could help it along. Like by attending and learning from the local writers. Which is why she was here tonight.

This presenter might not have been worth the time to attend the meeting, but as her mother always said, "You get what you get and you don't throw a fit." Besides, Meg could probably find at least one tidbit in the talk to get her excited about writing.

Apparently, Lee Anderson hadn't had the same upbringing. He pulled out his phone and started scrolling through his emails. He looked over at Meg when her food was delivered. "Wake me when she's done."

Meg had finished eating when the speaker finished her presentation. Crissy *had* listed out ten comparisons, and Meg had written them down, wondering if her amateur investigation book would be appropriate for self-publishing. She wanted the book in bookstores. And that meant an agent and a publisher.

Lilly had read the first chapter of Meg's guidebook and told her it was promising, so at least one person thought she might be on the right track. Besides, she wasn't going to worry until she finished the book. She took notes on marketing ideas and wrote down any editors who seemed to be accepting queries in her area. But she was mostly there for the hour of sprint writing and the happy hour afterward. She'd already met several nonfiction writers and they'd been friendly. She just hadn't made any new friends. Yet.

The group transitioned into a quick write-in. Thirty minutes of uninterrupted writing. Meg opened her laptop and got busy.

Lee found her again during the happy hour. "Did you get any words?"

"Four hundred new words and a chapter read and tweaked. I swear, every time I look at a page, I find a typo or something I want to say differently. Does the editing ever stop?" Meg sipped her wine as she scanned the group. Crissy was still holding court over by the bar talking about how she published.

"That's why I write for newspapers. I have a deadline so once it's out of my hands, I'm done. I can't play with it forever. So many people go over the first three chapters of a project and never move on. I'd love to write a book someday. Maybe like Anthony Bourdain, an exposé on the state of restaurants in the Pacific Northwest." Lee shrugged and looked around the room. "Someday, I guess."

"I don't know about Someday," Meg said.

Lee turned toward her, a frown narrowing his eyes. "What?"

"There's Monday, Tuesday, Wednesday…" She tapped her fingers as she listed off the days of the week. "And it all ends with Sunday and starts over. But Someday? I've never heard of it."

"Okay, fine. You got me. I need to just shut up and do it. Like in the Nike ads." He grinned and finished his beer. "I've got to catch the ferry, but I like you, Gates. Why don't you come with me to dinner tomorrow night? I'm reviewing a local restaurant. But we can't let them know that's why I'm there. You can be my cover. No one ever expects a food critic to have a sidekick. And we can talk more about writing nonfiction. I've got a few contacts you might want to interview. And my paper will buy your dinner."

"Sounds good." Meg glanced at her watch. She had a new project from Lilly she needed to start tonight. Especially since now, she wouldn't be home tomorrow night. "I'll meet you at the restaurant. Which one and what time?"

He opened his phone. "My reservation is for eight at the Local Crab. Do you know it?"

"Yeah, I've met the chef before. Maybe I'm not a good sidekick for this one." Meg hoped Lee didn't have a reputation for trashing restaurants.

"Don't be silly. You're perfect. I'm just a friend from Seattle. He'll never suspect anything, and I can get a clear reading on the meal without them trying to impress me." He snapped a picture of her as she was taking a drink. He laughed at her widened eyes. "I like to remember where I meet people. That way I don't forget their names. Although you seem pretty unforgettable."

Meg shook her head. "No sweet-talking your writing partner. This is just about writing. I'm not looking for a relationship."

"Good, because I'm not either. I just got out of a long-term relationship a few months ago and my head is still not clear from her games. So we're just friends, right?" He scanned the room as he talked.

"Exactly." Meg finished her wine and set her glass on the counter. "I've got to run. Watson is probably waiting for me."

"Oh, so there's a boyfriend?" Lee called after her.

She shrugged and headed out the door. If Lee was looking for something more, Watson would keep him from misinterpreting her agreeing to go to dinner. She liked Lee, as a possible friend. Besides, one of the rules of investigating was to find out more about others, not give out all your personal information. It was a skill she was still working on.

Meg didn't want to be an open book. Especially when she was working on an investigation, she needed to learn to be more invisible. It said so in her book.

As she left the Island Diner, a small blonde waved at her. Meg waved but didn't go back inside.

She'd practice her casual interviewing skills on Lee tomorrow night. Maybe she'd find out more about the food critic. And he could be her second writing friend. Lilly Aster was her first. Even if the famous author didn't know they were friends.

Meg was playing the long game.

She was almost home when she realized who had waved at her. Irene Olsen. The cruise salesperson who she'd been avoiding since she'd had coffee with her months ago.

The woman was relentless. As Meg hurried up the stairs, her phone buzzed with what was probably the first of many messages she'd get from Irene.

This day wasn't turning out to be one of Meg's favorites.

Want more Lynn Cahoon?
Turn the page to enjoy a preview of *Merry Murder Season*, a Tourist Trap
Mystery now available from Kensington Publishing Corp.

CHAPTER 1

As I watched the angry faces gathered around the tables in Coffee, Books, and More, my coffee shop and bookstore, I regretted signing a new ten-year contract to host and sponsor the business-to-business meetings here. Usually, the meetings went smoothly. Darla Taylor, owner of South Cove Winery, ran the meetings with an iron fist. Since it was the holidays, you would think that everyone would be in a festive mood. But there was no peace on earth, goodwill to men—I mean, personkind—feeling today.

No, Mayor Baylor had showed up to press the flesh because there was an election coming soon. The mayor typically only showed up around election time. He and his wife, Tina, didn't care about helping to run the huge Christmas craft bazaar scheduled in a few weeks or hiring enough elves for Santa's Village. The local power couple just wanted the votes to keep the smarmy Mayor Baylor in office. And the mayor had news for the group.

I'd broken the news last year that the mayor's office had planned to close Main Street for the holiday season, but, like all things that we don't want to deal with, people had already forgotten the warning. So, no one had petitioned the city council to rethink their idea.

No one except for one business that didn't even attend the monthly business-to-business meetings. Chip's Bar had asked for an exemption for motorcycles to use the street during the closure. With Diamond Lille's owner, Lille Stanley, voicing her support, the council's decision to grant the exception had been made back in August.

On Thanksgiving morning, only two days away, the barriers would go up, and cars and trucks would be banned from nine a.m. to midnight. Then the street would reopen to vehicles, allowing businesses to restock. Most of the businesses, like mine, had an alley behind our shops for deliveries anyway.

Darla banged the gavel on the lectern. "Folks, you knew this was coming. If it doesn't work, I'm sure the mayor and city council will be glad to discuss next year's plan."

Josh Thomas stood. "No one told us that there could be exceptions. My delivery truck needs to be loaded and unloaded in front of the store. What am I supposed to do? Unload in the dark?"

"There are streetlights…" Mayor Baylor interrupted what we all knew would be a long tirade from Josh. He was notorious for them, even when he was wrong. I thought this time, the antique dealer might just have a point. Instead of Josh continuing, another voice interrupted the mayor.

"And why are motorcycles allowed on the street? Those things are death traps. And they're so loud. If you're allowing motorcycles, you should just reverse the entire thing," Matty Leaven pointed out. She owned a jewelry store in town. Since she'd joined our business council, she always seemed to take Josh's side in discussions. "Maybe there needs to be new blood in City Hall. People who stand for the little guy."

Josh looked at Matty like she'd just won a Nobel Prize for standing with him. He wasn't used to someone agreeing with his ideas. Mandy, his wife, who came into my shop a lot for coffee, often laughed about Josh's infatuation with the jewelry designer. I thought he was playing with fire.

"Hold up, folks. This isn't about the upcoming election. We are a bipartisan group and our mandate doesn't allow electioneering during the meeting." Darla met my gaze and rolled her eyes. "Anyway, if we could get back on the subject, Main Street is closing. Any further comments can go to the mayor's office or any member of our city council. Their names and email addresses are on the city website. We'll talk more about the holiday festival next meeting, but Jill wanted to bring up our annual charity event. This year, we're partnering with Chip's Bar for a dart tournament to be held in the community center. The entry fee will be cash and a new toy, which will be donated to the California Central Coast Family Project for kids that won't be on Santa's delivery route this year. Jill, do you want to give us the details?"

I stood up, my list of talking points at the ready. None of them dealt with the closed road or the motorcycle exemption. I introduced myself, even though most of the people knew me. "Thanks, Darla. I'm Jill Gardner, I mean, Jill King. I own the coffee shop/bookstore you're sitting in and I'm your council liaison for the next ten years. Wow, that sounds like a long time. Anyway, I wanted to let you know that the dart tournament is also being sponsored by Coffee, Books, and More and is the brainchild of Chris Aquilla and Carrie Jones. It was at Carrie's suggestion that we started the book club last year."

I could see people starting to put their notes away. I was talking too much and needed to get to the point, quickly. Chris was digging in her bag, trying not to make eye contact with me for fear I'd ask her a question.

"Anyway, the fundraiser for CCCFP is this Friday night, sponsored by Chip's. The entry fee is ten dollars, and the bar is kicking in the money for the players' winnings so every dollar from entries goes to the charity. They're also kicking in fifty percent of that night's profits." I handed out flyers. "Please have these available for people to take. I believe Chris and Carrie have already stopped by your businesses to give you a stash, but just in case you've already handed those out, here's more. Both Greg and I are playing, and I hope to see the rest of you there as well."

"It's Thanksgiving weekend. We might have family at the house," a woman on my right side mumbled. She probably didn't think I'd heard, but I had.

"Bring them along! We have family in town as well. The more, the merrier." I pasted a smile on my face, hoping it didn't look as fake as it felt. Greg didn't want to go. He worried that the presence of law enforcement might dampen the celebratory mood. He also didn't want to go out when his family would be in town. I was hoping they'd tag along at least for the charity part of the night. The charity event hadn't been my idea, but I was supporting it like it had been. Besides, it was for the kids.

"Matt and I are coming too, but if you already have plans that night"—Darla looked pointedly at Marvin and Tina Baylor—"just drop a donation check off with Amy Newman-Cole at City Hall or before you leave here. We don't want any child to go without a Merry Christmas."

Josh glowered at Darla but didn't object. I knew that Mandy had already committed to coming on Friday night, so he couldn't say anything against the event. But I could tell he wanted to.

Darla ended the meeting and everyone scattered before Mayor Baylor could corner them. Tina had reached the exit first, blocking it and handing out *Baylor for Mayor* buttons as people left. I noticed that Matty Leaven snuck out while Tina was handing a button to another person. The girl was smart, that was for sure.

After everyone was gone, I moved tables back in order with the help of my barista on deck, Deek Kerr. He seemed quiet, distracted, and not his usual chatty self. Deek was a writer, so it wasn't unusual for him to be in his own world. I took his rag away when he'd cleaned the same spot for the last few minutes. "What's got you all up in your head? Plotting another book?"

He glanced toward the door. Everyone had left the coffee shop, and it was just the two of us. "I'm not thinking about a book. What do you think about Matty Leaven?"

"I don't know her very well. She seems to think like Josh a lot, though." I wiped the last table and went to the sink to rinse the rag. "Why?"

"I can't figure out her aura. It changes colors based on what she's saying. I don't think she agrees with Josh. I think she likes stirring up trouble." He poured himself a cup of coffee after following me to the coffee bar. "I'm probably just overanalyzing the situation."

"I don't like her at all," Tilly North, my newest barista, chimed in as she filled the treat display case. "She's nice to your face, then I overhear her saying mean things about people, like Josh and Mandy. She says awful things about Josh all the time to her friends while they're getting coffee. She's one of those people who thinks baristas or whoever is serving her are completely invisible. I worked with people like that when I was at the hospital. They think you can't hear them when they're talking right outside your room."

Tilly had been in a car accident and suffered a brain injury. She'd lost many of her long-term memories, like the fact that she and Toby Killian, another one of my baristas and one of Greg's deputies, had dated in high school. When she'd come to work for me, she'd been dating someone new. Now, that relationship was over, but Tilly had stayed in the area. She was a great addition to the bookstore team. And usually very perceptive about people.

"I'll watch her more carefully." I hoped that Josh wouldn't figure out that Matty was messing with him. He had enough self-esteem issues. He didn't need to know that Matty didn't like him. I poured myself a fresh cup of coffee. I had back-of-the-house tasks to do, namely accounting and scheduling, since Evie was in the city visiting her cousin, Sasha, and her daughter this week for the Thanksgiving holiday.

Toby had also dated Sasha. The boy sure did get around. It was a small town. We had connections all over the place.

"Just be careful around her, Jill." Deek was staring out the window again. "I have a feeling. And it's not good."

Now I was worried. Deek Kerr liked everyone. He could read auras, or at least he thought he could. Sometimes he told me things that, when I looked them up, didn't match the aura lore published on the internet. But when you're talking about magic and seeing things that aren't there, maybe the internet didn't have all the information. Deek was a good guy and he saw people clearly, which made him an excellent barista and bookseller.

I decided to change the subject. "Are you coming to Thanksgiving at the house? I haven't heard from either of you."

"Mom's out of town, so I thought I'd just hang at the house." Deek moved back behind the coffee bar. "I'll grab the boxes of books that need to be shelved."

"Deek Kerr, you stay right there." I didn't use my boss voice often but this was going to be one of those times. When he froze and turned to me, I continued. "There is no way you're not coming for dinner now that I know your mom's not going to be home. So what are you bringing?"

"Jill, it's your first family dinner since you've been married. You don't need strays hanging around." He blushed as he glanced over at Tilly, who now had her hands on her hips.

"Oh, so you don't think I should go, either?" she challenged him. "I don't appreciate being called a stray."

"I didn't say that." Deek stumbled over his words. Finally, he let his shoulders drop. "Look, I don't want you to invite me because I'm some loser who doesn't have family for Thanksgiving. Mom's just not into those traditions, so she's going on a cruise. I'm used to this."

"Which is why you're coming. My family isn't just those people who are related to Greg or me. You should know that by now. I won't have you sitting around the apartment eating ramen while we're having a turkey dinner. Besides, I think Harrold is bringing Lille, so I'll need some of my people to watch my back."

Lille Stanley, the owner of Diamond Lille's, was one of my Uncle Harrold's favorite people. Lille liked Greg and my Aunt Jackie too. She just hated me. Thanksgiving dinner should be fun. Not.

I'd say Lille would have Jim to chat with since he used to hate me too, but since he started dating Beth, he'd been more open to my presence. Besides, since Greg and I were married now, Greg's first wife Sherry was out of the picture.

"She hates you? How can anyone hate you?" Tilly's eyes widened. She was such a nice young woman, she didn't understand the concept. "Well, I'll be there to watch your back. I don't have the money to visit my folks now that they've moved to Tennessee. I don't want to be in the house all by myself. I love the holidays. Mom left me all the old Christmas decorations, so I've been working on getting the house looking like Santa's workshop for weeks."

"My mom never decorated," Deek admitted. "I hated the holidays growing up because we were always the one family who didn't have a tree or lights on the house."

"Well, Greg is going to get everyone to help string lights outside the house and we'll be decorating the tree after dinner. It's one of the King family traditions." I was looking forward to celebrating Thanksgiving this year. "Aunt Jackie and Harrold are leaving for a cruise on Friday. So you won't see her for two weeks if you don't come."

Deek stared at me. "I thought you wanted me to come."

"Stop it." I started laughing. "You love Aunt Jackie. I know you do."

"Did I tell you she updated my author questionnaire last week for people who want to schedule book events here? She thinks we should charge an event fee if they don't hit a certain amount of sales." Deek threw a clean towel over his shoulder as he talked.

I groaned. Aunt Jackie had been harping on that for a while. And she hated the Cove Connection book club. She thought that members should be required to buy the book from the store to participate. I didn't care where they bought or borrowed the book from, I just wanted people to be reading more. Besides, we worked closely with our local library on author events. "I'll talk to her. Just file away the changed copy and don't make any drastic movements. We're doing fine financially on author events overall. Some are just more popular than others. Everyone needs a shot in the arm every once in a while."

"Thanks. I'd rather not tell my newly published authors I don't think they're big enough to bother with." Deek nodded to the back door. "Am I excused? Those books aren't going to shelve themselves."

"Are you coming to Thanksgiving?" I stared him down.

He blinked first. "I'll bring focaccia bread. I've been working on my recipe."

Tilly watched him head to the back room. "He reads, he's cute, and he bakes? How on earth is he still single?"

From the look in Tilly's eyes, Deek might not be that way for long.

* * *

Greg came into the shop just before my shift ended at eleven. "Do you have time for lunch at Diamond Lille's?"

"I'd love to." I nodded to Deek. "You have the helm, good sir."

Deek laughed and pointed at Tilly. "This one thinks she's in charge. If I didn't know better, I would think I was still working with your aunt. Tilly loves the checklists."

Tilly playfully slapped his arm. "There's nothing wrong with a little organization now and then. With the sieve of my brain, writing things down is the only way I know I'll remember to do something. Oh, I forgot to tell you, I'm going to bring pumpkin cheesecake if that's okay."

I was a little thrown by the change of subject, but Tilly's mind just worked like that. And anything she thought came out of her mouth. Mostly. "Sounds great. I'll see you both on Thursday. Call if you need anything."

As Greg and I started down the street toward Diamond Lille's, he glanced back at the bookstore. "Are both of them coming to Thanksgiving?"

"Yes. Judith is going out of town. Toby, of course, will be there and Evie's already gone to see Sasha." I ticked off my staff members on my fingers as I listed them. "Anyone from City Hall?"

"Your friends Amy and Justin are heading to see his folks. Esmeralda is going to New Orleans to be with her family. And the rest of them are otherwise committed. I'd hoped that Tim and Dona might come and bring the baby, but they're going to her parents' place in Sacramento." He nodded to the antique store. "Josh and Mandy are going to her family's farm. He's not looking forward to it."

"He hates being around people." I knew there was more to the story, but at least Josh was trying to forgive Mandy's family for a few things that had happened before they were married.

"I should tell you that Jim and Beth are fighting. Mom called this morning to warn me." He checked the road, then we jaywalked across the street to the restaurant. It was good being married to the head detective, although jaywalking was about all Greg did to skirt the law. He was a rule follower.

ABOUT THE AUTHOR

Lynn Cahoon is an Anthony-nominated, award-winning, *New York Times* and *USA Today* best-selling author of cozy mysteries including the Kitchen Witch Mysteries, the Cat Latimer Mysteries, the Tourist Trap Mysteries, the Farm-to-Fork Mysteries, the Survivors' Book Club Mysteries, and the Bainbridge Island Mysteries. She is a member of Sisters in Crime, Mystery Writers of America, and International Thriller Writers, and her books have sold more than a million copies. Originally from Idaho, she grew up living the small-town life she now loves to feature in her novels. She now lives with her husband and three fur babies in a small historic town in eastern Tennessee and can be found online at LynnCahoon.com.

Kensington Publishing Corp.
oyce Kaplan
00 Third Avenue, 26th Floor
JS-NY, 10022
JS
aplan@kensingtonbooks.com
12-407-1515

he authorized representative in the EU for product safety and compliance is

ucomply OÜ
Marko Novkovic
ärnu mnt 139b-14
CZ, 11317
E
ttps://www.eucompliancepartner.com
ello@eucompliancepartner.com
372 536 865 02

BN: 9781516112067
elease ID: 155048300

www.ingramcontent.com/pod-product-compliance
Lightning Source LLC
Chambersburg PA
CBHW032143020726
47496CB00003B/698